T0146446

AL LACY'S

Hannah of Fort Bridger Series

Under the Distant Sky — Al & JoAnna Lacy

Consider the Lilies — JoAnna Lacy

No Place for Fear

Pillow of Stone — Al & JoAnna Lacy

Perfect Gift

Touch of Compassion — Al & JoAnna Lacy

TOUCH OF COMPASSION

BOOK SIX

AL AND JOANNA LACY

Multnomah®Publishers *Sisters, Oregon*

TOUCH OF COMPASSION
© 1999 by ALJO Productions, Inc.
published by Multnomah Publishers, Inc.
Cover illustration by Frank Ordaz
Design by Left Coast Design
International Standard Book Number: 9781590528983
Scripture quotations are from *The Holy Bible,* King James Version (KJV)
Multnomah is a trademark of Multnomah Publishers, Inc.,
and is registered in the U.S. Patent and Trademark Office.
The colophon is a trademark of Multnomah Publishers, Inc.

For information:
Multnomah Publishers, Inc., Post Office Box 1720, Sisters, Oregon 97759

Library of Congress Cataloging-in-Publication Data
Lacy, Al.
  Touch of compassion / by Al and JoAnna Lacy.
    p.cm.—(Hannah of Fort Bridger; bk. 6)
  ISBN 1-57673-422-6
    1. Indians of North America—Wyoming—Fiction. 2. Crow Indians—
  Fiction. I. Title. II. Lacy, JoAnna.
PS3562.A256T68 1999
813'.54 21—dc21   99-040168

146651086
04 05 06 07 08 09— 10 9 8 7 6 5 4 3 2 1

*This book is affectionately dedicated to our special friend
Wendy Colon.*

*Her prayers, encouragement, and numerous acts of kindness
over the years have greatly blessed and enriched our lives.*

*We love you and yours, Wendy,
and we treasure your fellowship in the Lord and
your loyal friendship.
God bless you!*

Al and JoAnna
PHILIPPIANS 1:3

PROLOGUE

W ithin three years after the American Civil War ended in 1865, peace had forced many Americans to the distant "Wild" West. Many had lost families or property or both during the war and wanted to get away. A great number of these were ex-soldiers who had developed a liking for the military; their only chance at that time to continue a military career was to enlist for Indian fighting on the frontier.

Because Indians west of the Missouri River were making life miserable for the white invaders, forts were being established rapidly and needed manpower.

There were also many other people wanting to go west in spite of the threat of hostile Indians. These were men and women who wanted to farm the rich land, set up cattle ranches, and establish towns, shops, and businesses the towns' populace would require. There was indeed an opportunity to build a new life in the West, but the adventurers would soon find the Indians formidable foes who would not be easily conquered. They were more than willing to die, if need be, to defend their homeland from the white invaders.

The earliest white men to traverse the West were the trappers, fur traders, explorers, and mountain men such as Jim Bridger, Jedediah Smith, Meriwether Lewis, William Clark, David Jackson, and William Sublette. Though these men came face to face with the Indians, none of them were ever harmed by them, because they were not claiming land as their own, and when they killed game, it was for food.

The trouble began when the white men started building fences and laying claim to land; and when they killed buffalo by the thousands, taking the hides but leaving the meat to rot. This infuriated the Indians, and they went on the warpath.

To the Indians, the white men were mysterious. They could not understand their insatiable hunger for land. In the minds of the red men, the earth and all its creatures belonged to all, the free gift of the "Great Spirit," or the "Sky Father," as some termed their deity. That a white man should build a fence around a parcel of land and claim it for himself was repugnant to them.

In the wars that inevitably followed, the white man always had better weapons, but the Indian courageously fought for what was his. There was genuine manhood and womanhood in the red race. For decades the Indian fought heroically and spectacularly for the possession of his hunting ground, but in the end it was futile. He was outnumbered.

Today, as citizens of the United States, we need to look back on the period of our forefathers' conquest of the West with honesty and face the fact that their dealings with the Indians were shameful. Our ancestors made solemn agreements with the Indians which they did not keep. The United States Senate had a habit of never getting around to fulfilling the treaties the military leaders and peace commissions signed with the Indians.

During the Indian wars in the West, many of the military commanders regarded the Indians as less than human, and worthy only of extermination. Many of the white settlers felt the same way. When the Indians fought back in the only way they knew how, they were labeled "savages." Weren't they simply protecting what was theirs, just as we would do today if some foreign power tried to take our fifty states and our freedom from us?

As a result of the attitude held by many military leaders toward the red people, some horror stories come down from historical records. Defenseless Indian men, women, and children were murdered in places such as Sand Creek, Camp Grant, and Wounded Knee. There were times when Indian warriors were fed strychnine when they thought they were being given good food by the kind white men. Whole villages of Indian people were put out naked in the subzero cold of Montana winters, and the U.S. government confined thousands of Indians in concentration camps they called "reservations."

In the Colorado–Wyoming–Montana area, seven tribes fought the invasion of the white men: Sioux, Cheyenne, Blackfoot, Shoshoni, Ute, Kiowa, and Arapaho. An eighth tribe—the Crow—were divided into thirteen clans, and most of the clans tried every possible way to live peacefully with the white invaders.

The Crow befriended the white men, and many of their warriors served the U.S. army as scouts. The mortal enemies of the Crow were the Blackfoot and the Shoshoni; thus the Crow were glad to aid the white man's army against them. However, even the friendly Crow were hated and distrusted by many white people, simply because they were Indians.

Living in Fort Bridger, Wyoming, our heroine in this series—Hannah Cooper—finds herself in the middle of the strife between white man and red man. As a Christian, Hannah has compassion on anyone who has genuine need, and she will fill that need if it is within her power to do so, even in the face of opposition.

But whoso hath this world's good,
and seeth his brother have need,
and shutteth up his bowels of compassion from him,
how dwelleth the love of God in him?

1 JOHN 3:17

CHAPTER ONE

The wintry wind buffeted the old barn, sending flakes of snow through cracks in the walls. Dale Roberts finished milking the second of his two Holstein cows and placed the full bucket on a shelf next to another bucket, then swung the stanchions open at the feed trough so the cows would be free to move about the barn when they had devoured the hay and barley. On the other side of the stanchions was another feed trough where the horses were munching on their meal.

Dale shuddered as the wind whistled through the barn and seemed to swirl about him. "Okay, Bossie…Bessie…you girls finish up your supper. I've got to go in and get mine."

Dale tightened the wool scarf at his neck and pulled the collar of his heavy sheepskin coat up to his ears. He tugged his hat snugly on his head, picked up the buckets of milk from the shelf, and headed for the barn's side door. When he opened it, the wind snatched the door from his hand and slammed it against the snowbank piled against the barn.

He struggled briefly to get the door closed and latched again, then took up the bucket handles and bent his head against the wind. The force of it caused him to stagger as he made his way to a wooden post with a rope tied to it at thigh level. Dale couldn't even see the outbuildings, much less the house even though it was only eighty yards away. It felt as if he were drowning in an ocean of white.

He pressed his right thigh against the taut rope and started forward, bumping other posts as he went. Wind-driven sleet stung his face and clung to his eyelashes. The Wyoming wind felt like a knife piercing through him.

It was a slow journey, but finally he reached the root cellar. He could now see the privy and the tool shed, which stood adjacent to each other some twenty yards from the back of the house. He paused to catch his breath, then pressed on, keeping his leg against the rope. When he felt his leg bump the last post, he was near the back of the house. The wind had sculpted the snow into fine-edged shapes at the back porch. He made his way carefully up the snow-packed steps and felt some tension leave his body when the door opened and he saw his wife's face.

He hurried inside, and Merilee swiftly closed the door against the snow blowing in behind him. He carried the buckets to a table at the back of the kitchen where a milk strainer sat on a twenty-gallon metal container.

Merilee rubbed her arms and shivered as she watched her husband pour the milk through the strainer. When both buckets were empty, Merilee rinsed them at the cupboard where a bucket of water stood beside a wash bowl.

Dale sniffed at the pleasant aroma in the kitchen as he took off his coat and hat and hung them on a peg by the door. "Mm-mm! Smells good, honey!"

Merilee laughed. "I'm glad it does. It's the third night this week you've had canned beans and smoked beef."

"That's all right. The children and I love anything you cook."

"Well, if things don't change pretty soon, we'll be out of meat," she said, swishing water around in a bucket. "The canned chicken is getting low, and so is the smoked beef."

Dale unwrapped the scarf from his neck and hung it next to his coat. "As soon as this blizzard blows out of here, I'll go after venison. The deer are out there somewhere. I'll find them."

It had snowed heavily for several days and made it impossible to get a supply wagon into Fort Bridger. The Roberts's crop last summer was not as good as usual, and their store of dried fruit and canned vegetables was a little on the lean side. It was mid-December, 1870, and so far it had been one of the hardest winters ever in southwestern Wyoming, with day upon endless day of blowing and drifting snow.

Dale and Merilee heard the sound of pattering feet, and the three Roberts children appeared in the kitchen.

"Should I set the table now, Mama?" asked six-year-old Barbie.

Merilee smiled at her little girl. "Mm-hmm. And the boys can help you."

"I'd rather do it myself. I'll just have to go around behind them and do it right if they help."

Davey, who was nine, poked her lightly with his elbow. "Boys aren't supposed to do stuff like that anyway."

"I know. But since we've had this big ol' snowstorm, you and Benny have gotten off easy. You haven't had to do any chores."

"We would if Papa would let us," eleven-year-old Benny said. "But he don't want us out in that blizzard any farther than the outhouse."

"And me and Benny *did* sweep the house for Mama yesterday while you were playin' with your dolls," Davey said.

"Okay, kids, that's enough," Dale said. "You boys get your hands washed while Barbie sets the table. Mama will be ready for us to eat in a few minutes."

Moments later, the Roberts family sat at the table and joined hands. Dale led in prayer, thanking the Lord for the food they had and asking Him to change the weather so he could go deer hunting and bring back some venison.

While they ate, Dale couldn't help noticing the solemn mood around the table. The Robertses were down to one sow and one boar, and only one rooster and four hens. The hens produced barely enough eggs for the family.

"I believe the Lord is going to give us good weather real soon so I can get out there and find deer and maybe some rabbits," Dale said. "Christmas is only five days away, and we're going to have venison for Christmas dinner!"

Merilee smiled. "That's right!"

"Hey, how about we play some games after supper?" Dale said.

Smiles appeared on the three young faces.

"And before that," Merilee said, "how about we have some snow ice cream?"

"Oh, boy!" Benny said. "I'll go out and get the snow. Sure don't have to go far to get it!"

"I'll help you," Davey said.

After the meal, Merilee and Barbie began cleaning up the table while the boys bundled up and went outside with a small pail.

Merilee had been carefully hoarding a small jar of maple syrup. She poured some of it onto the "ice cream" and passed around the bowls. As they ate, the children chattered happily about the games they would play after supper.

Dale and Merilee exchanged glances over the children's heads and read the other's unspoken words of thanks.

The Roberts family played games until the children began to yawn. As soon as they were ready for bed, Merilee tucked each child in, all warm and toasty under a mountain of blankets. They presented sleepy, smiling faces to their mother for good night kisses and were asleep before Merilee had left the room.

When Merilee entered the parlor, Dale was sitting in his chair in front of the fireplace. She started past him for her own chair, and he reached out and gently grasped her wrist, pulling her into his lap to nuzzle her soft neck. "Thank you for being such a wonderful mother," he said in a whisper.

She leaned back to look into his eyes. "And thank you for being such a wonderful father." She dipped her head to kiss his lips.

Dale pulled her close again and said, "It really gets to me when I see those precious faces so pinched and afraid. They're trying to be brave, but I know even though we had a happy time tonight, they're still fearful we'll run out of food."

"God knows our needs, Dale, and He has promised in His Word to supply. I don't know how or from where, but I know His promises are true. We've got to trust Him and do our best to teach our little ones to trust Him, too."

Dale nodded. "You're right. What do you say we talk to Him right now?"

Merilee remained snuggled on her husband's lap as they bowed their heads and gave the burden to their heavenly Father.

The wind continued to howl and beat the house with snow as Dale and Merilee climbed the stairs, looked in on their sleeping children, then made their way to their own room.

Dale came awake with a start and sat bolt upright. He sat very still in the darkness. *What was that noise? Surely there's no one about in this kind of weath—*

Suddenly he realized it was not a noise that had awakened him, it was the lack of noise. The battering, howling wind had stopped!

He glanced at Merilee, who was still asleep, and carefully turned back the covers. He slipped from the warm bed and made his way to the window. Outside was a broad space of whiteness stretching away in every direction. The night sky was brilliantly illuminated by twinkling stars. There were a few broken clouds to the west, but there wasn't even a breeze. Snow lay in deep mounds and drifts against the house and outbuildings, but all was still.

With a whispered prayer of thanksgiving on his lips, Dale climbed back in bed and pulled the quilts up under his chin. He was shivering from the cold, and Merilee stirred in her sleep.

She made a tiny moan and rubbed her face. "Honey," she said groggily, "you awake?"

"Mm-hmm."

"Something wrong?"

"No, darling. Something's right. Very right."

"Hmm?"

"Listen."

"Listen to wha—" Merilee sat up. "The wind! There's no wind!"

"And no snow falling. I just looked out the window. The sky is clearing up. I saw stars and a piece of the moon."

"Oh, praise the Lord!"

"You get back to sleep. I'll be getting up in a little while so I can go after some venison. The boys can feed the animals in the morning. Tell Benny to go ahead and milk the cows. No way to tell when I might be back."

"All right. Do you want me to fix breakfast before you go?"

"No need. I'll grab something I can eat while I'm in the saddle."

Merilee let a peaceful sleep overtake her. A tiny smile was on her lips as she snuggled close to her husband. *Thank You, heavenly Father,* was her last thought before she was asleep once more.

Dale Roberts crouched in the three-foot depth of snow near the edge of a dark forest where he had hunted deer before. He studied the trees and prayed for deer to come out into the open. A few stars still twinkled in the dawn sky. No breeze had come up since the storm blew out during the middle of the night.

Dale shifted the rifle from one gloved hand to the other and worked his arms against the cold. It had to be at least ten below zero.

Soon the rising sun sent bright beams across the rolling, snow-laden terrain. Dale glanced toward the southwest to see the sunlight touching the jagged peaks of the Uintah Mountains. He marveled at the beauty of it then looked back toward the forest.

His eye caught movement amongst the deep shadows. He squinted and quietly worked the lever of his rifle, jacking a cartridge into the chamber. "Please, Lord," he whispered, "venison for my family."

Hardly had he spoken when a huge buck moved up to the edge of the timber and paused to sniff the air. He had a set of antlers as large as any Dale had ever seen. "Come on out in the light, boy," he murmured, "so I can get a good shot. It wouldn't hurt if you came a little closer."

He glanced back at a snow-covered rise behind him then forward again. His horse was tethered just beyond the rise and out of sight. He hoped the horse wouldn't make a sound and frighten the buck back into the forest. He watched the stately animal, whose head was held high.

Seconds passed. It seemed the big buck was going to camp where he stood.

"All right," whispered Dale, raising the rifle, "if you're not coming any closer, this distance will have to do."

A split second before Dale squeezed the trigger, he heard two rifle shots, almost as one, from inside the forest. His own rifle cracked, and the buck's knees buckled where he stood.

Dale rose to his feet, smoke lifting from the muzzle of his

rifle. He trudged through the deep snow toward the buck, looking into the forest to see who the other hunters were.

His heart leaped in his breast when he saw a band of Indians coming through the dense trees, rifles in hand. The Indians paused when they saw him, then moved out of the deep shadows.

Dale heaved a sigh of relief and thanked the Lord in his heart when he saw that it was Chief Two Moons coming toward him while the other braves gathered around the dead buck.

Two Moons smiled and raised his hand in a signal of friendship. Dale did the same.

"Dale Roberts!" said the chief as they drew up to face each other. "You hunt deer as Crow do."

"Yes, Chief. I'm sure you've found game as hard to find as I have this winter."

"Is true. Plenty scarce. Game seem to hide from Crow."

"From us, too."

Chief Two Moons looked back over his shoulder, eyeing his braves, then said, "We shoot deer at same time."

"Looks like we did."

"Dale Roberts have wife and children to feed. Him take deer home."

"That wouldn't be right, Chief. Your men shot him, too."

"But we not hunting game right now. We see deer, we shoot. We plan take him back to village before Two Moons see you. But deer yours."

"What do you mean you're not hunting game right now?"

"We on more important hunt. Dale Roberts get much food from Hannah Cooper. Know Hannah Cooper."

"Yes, of course. With the blizzards we've been having, I haven't been able to get into town to buy anything."

Two Moons nodded. "Dale Roberts know Hannah Cooper's children. Crow hunt Patty Ruth Cooper."

"What? Hunt Patty Ruth? You mean she's lost somewhere?"

"Not lost. Stolen. Someone steal Patty Ruth Cooper. Hannah Cooper much worried."

"You're telling me that someone kidnapped her?"

Two Moons nodded. "Crow help hunt for Patty Ruth Cooper. Army hunt. People of town hunt. Two Moons and braves looking in forest when see buck deer. Decide shoot deer, send one brave back to village with it. But Dale Roberts take deer home to family. Crow must keep hunting for Patty Ruth Cooper."

"By rights I should at least dress it out and give you half of it."

"No," said Two Moons, shaking his head. "Crow find more deer after Patty Ruth Cooper found."

Dale's thoughts were on little Patty Ruth as he swung into his saddle and headed for home, dragging the dead buck behind. The child had such bright eyes and a loving spirit about her. Why would anyone want to kidnap her? He prayed for Patty Ruth and the whole Cooper family.

The sun was midway in the eastern sky when Dale finally topped the last hill and looked down on his farm. He could see a cavalry unit at his front porch, sitting their horses. One of the men spotted him and pointed. Others turned around in their saddles to look. Moments later, when Dale drew up, he noticed that two of the horses in the unit were without riders.

"Good morning, Mr. Roberts," Sergeant Barry Wilkins said. "How far did you have to go to get that deer?"

"A few miles. Does this visit have to do with Patty Ruth Cooper's abduction?"

"So you know about it?"

"I ran into Two Moons and his braves this morning, just after sunrise. The chief told me about Patty Ruth."

Wilkins nodded. "Captain Fordham and Lieutenant Carlin are inside talking to your wife about it, sir."

Dale noted the men's hunched shoulders and their breath

billowing on the cold air. "You men look like you're freezing to death," he said. "You're welcome to come inside."

"Thank you," Wilkins said. "But we're fine."

Dale stepped inside and the two officers standing in the parlor with Merilee greeted him.

Dale nodded. "I know you're here about Patty Ruth Cooper's abduction, but let me say one thing to my wife."

"Certainly," Fordham said.

"Honey, wait'll you see what I've got outside!"

Merilee's eyes brightened. "You got a deer?"

"A big ol' buck! We're going to have venison for Christmas dinner!"

"Oh, praise the Lord!" she said, clapping her hands together.

Dale turned back to the officers. "I met up with Two Moons and his search party earlier this morning. The chief told me about Patty Ruth. He didn't give me any details. All he said was that the child had been 'stolen.' When did it happen?"

"Last Friday," the captain said. "The weather's been a problem, but we were able to search on Saturday and again on Monday. We're mighty glad for this break in the weather."

"Does anyone know how it happened?"

"Patty Ruth was playing in the front yard of Julianna LeCroix's house," Dobie Carlin said. "Hannah was in the house with Julianna, and when it was time for Patty Ruth to come in, they couldn't find her. She had vanished."

"Just like that?"

"Just like that. Deputy Bower investigated the scene immediately, and some of our army personnel helped him. They could tell Patty Ruth had not wandered off. A search was made in every house and building in town. With the help of the Crow and the townspeople, we're searching in a wide radius around Fort Bridger—every house, barn, and outbuilding on every farm and ranch. We were just asking Mrs. Roberts for permission to search the house and all of your buildings."

Merilee glanced at Dale. "I gave permission," she said.

"Of course," Dale said. "Where are the children?"

"Upstairs…doing their school lessons."

"Gentlemen, you go right ahead and search."

Thirty minutes later, when every part of the house, barn, and outbuildings had been searched, Captain John Fordham stood in the parlor once again and said, "If you should see anything that looks suspicious—anything you think might be linked to Patty Ruth's abduction—please get word to Colonel Bateman or Deputy Bower as quickly as you can."

"Sure will," Dale said. "Could I ask you something?"

"Of course."

"You've mentioned Deputy Bower in this, but what about Marshal Mangum? Why isn't he heading up the search?"

"You haven't heard then…"

"Apparently not. Heard what?"

"Marshal Mangum was shot in the back by an outlaw a few days ago. Dr. O'Brien removed the slug. He says the marshal will be fine, but he's awfully weak. So he turned the search over to his deputy."

"Well, I'm glad he's going to be all right," Dale said. "And it's great of Chief Two Moons to join in the search. I didn't mention it before, but when I shot that buck this morning, the Crow shot it at the same time. I offered to let the chief take the deer, but he wouldn't. He said he wanted my family to have it."

"God bless him," Merilee said.

"Sounds just like him," Fordham said. "I was there in town when the chief and some of his braves came in. It really touched Hannah when Two Moons told her he and his braves would help search for Patty Ruth. She told him there were no words to express how much it meant to her. Two Moons thumped his chest and told her he understood the language of the heart."

Merilee's eyes grew misty. "I wish all the Indians were as kind to the whites as Two Moons and his people are."

Fordham nodded. "And I might add that if other Indians saw more kindness from white folk, maybe they wouldn't be so hostile."

CHAPTER TWO

A t Fort Steele, more than a hundred miles east of Fort Bridger, Colonel Loren Barlow, the fort's commandant, was working on some papers at his desk when there was a knock at the door.

"Yes, Corporal?" he called.

Barlow's office adjutant, Corporal Lester Watson, stuck his head in. "Major Roby and Captain Merritt are here with their report, sir."

"Good! Send them in."

Tom Roby was a short, stout man of fifty. Douglas Merritt was his physical opposite—a tall and slender man of forty.

"So, what's the verdict, Major Roby?" Colonel Barlow said when they were seated.

"We're in pretty good shape, sir. We calculate that we have enough antelope, deer, elk, and buffalo meat hanging frozen in the meat shed to take us through February. I'm glad you had us out hunting in November before this run of bad weather."

"It could be, sir," said Captain Merritt, "that we're now past the most severe weather. Maybe it won't be so bad before we get to spring."

Barlow shook his head. "I have to say that so far this is the worst winter to hit these parts in a long time. At least, that's what the locals say. And I think it would be a mistake to believe the worst is over. If we get another sunny day tomorrow, I'll have three units out hunting for more game. We need to make sure we'll be all right till spring. I hate to send men out in this subzero cold, but there's really no choice."

"I don't think we've had a day since mid-November with the temperature above ten degrees," Roby said.

Barlow toyed with his handlebar mustache. "Well, it's going to make us appreciate the warm weather when it finally gets here. I'll remind the men of this when it's good and hot next—"

A knock at the door broke off the Colonel's words. "Yes, Corporal?"

Watson opened the door and took a half-step inside. "Colonel, Sergeant Rafferty needs to talk to you. I wouldn't have interrupted, except he needs to see you right now."

"All right. Send him in."

Rafferty moved in as soon as Watson stood back to give him room. He quickly saluted, then said, "Colonel, sir, we have Chief Big Wolf at the gate under a white flag. He's got a half-dozen warriors with him. He's asking to see you."

Barlow frowned. "Big Wolf has a lot of gall coming here."

"I should say so, sir," Roby said. "He's proven himself nothing but an enemy."

"A bloody and vicious one to boot," Merritt said. "I doubt he wants to talk peace."

Barlow chuckled. "Yeah, I doubt it too. Sergeant, I'm not going to stand out there in that cold air and powwow with the old boy. Bring him in here."

"Yes, sir. I'll be right back with him, sir."

"Oh, and Sergeant…"

"Yes, sir?"

"Send Lieutenant Galton in here. He's the only one in the fort who can speak Cheyenne."

"Yes, sir."

While they waited for Big Wolf, Barlow, Roby, and Merritt

discussed the hunting units that would go after more game. Merritt also filled the colonel in on other types of supplies on hand, and Barlow was satisfied they were in good shape for at least another two months. Even if they had more heavy snows or blizzards, there should be sufficient breaks in between to allow their wagons to go to Cheyenne City for supplies.

Corporal Watson brought Lieutenant Steve Galton in before Rafferty was back with Big Wolf.

After saluting, Galton said, "Colonel, what do you suppose Big Wolf wants?"

"I haven't the slightest idea. But he's sure got a lot of nerve, I'll say that for him."

"I'd like to lock him and those savages with him in the guard house and keep them there for about forty years."

There was another knock at the door, and Galton opened it. He blinked when he saw the grim-faced Chief Big Wolf behind Corporal Watson, accompanied by two of his equally grim-faced warriors.

"Sir," Watson said, "the chief insisted that two of his braves come with him."

Barlow's face flushed with anger. He rose to his feet and said, "He doesn't set the rules here. I do! Send the other ones back outside. I'm only seeing Big Wolf!"

Galton spoke a few soft words to the chief. Barlow had only a partial view of Big Wolf's face, but he could tell it didn't sit well with him. However, when Big Wolf replied, there was a tone of resignation in his voice. He entered the office alone, and Lieutenant Galton closed the door behind him.

Big Wolf wore fur-lined knee-high buckskin boots and was wrapped in a heavy buffalo robe. He wore his full headdress. His arms were folded across his chest.

Roby and Merritt started to get up, but the colonel motioned for them to stay seated as he rounded the desk. When he stood face-to-face with Big Wolf, he said to Galton,

"All right, Lieutenant. Let's see what this is about. Ask him what he wants."

Galton spoke in Cheyenne, and Big Wolf replied as he held Barlow's gaze with his deep, dark eyes.

"He says the people of his village are on the verge of starving, sir. Game has been scarce, and they have had to consume more of their food stores for winter than they should have by this time. The supply is dwindling fast."

Barlow pulled his gaze from Big Wolf, looked at Galton, and said, "So what does he want from us?"

Galton interpreted the question to Big Wolf, who came back with a long answer. When the chief was finished, he took his eyes from Galton and set them on Barlow to read his reaction as the lieutenant said, "Chief Big Wolf says, sir, that his scouts have told him supply trains come in from Cheyenne City from time to time since the bad weather first came. And several moons…ah, several days ago some of his warriors saw the soldiers dressing out game they had shot. He knows we have meat stored somewhere here in the fort."

"So?"

"Well, sir, he wants to know if you will share some of the fort's food and meat with his people."

"Lieutenant, you tell this savage so he'll understand it clearly, we are not sharing one morsel with our avowed enemies."

As Galton translated the colonel's words into Cheyenne, the chief's face darkened. His jaw bunched in anger as he spoke a long string of sharp-edged words.

"He's ruffled by what you said, sir," Galton explained.

"Do tell," said the colonel without changing expression. "What did he say?"

"He said the white men have come as invaders to the land that has been occupied by the Indians for many centuries. They not only have taken land that did not belong to them and called it their own, but they have killed game the Indians would have had for meat. Because the white man's army has much food coming in wagons from the East and he knows Fort Steele has much meat in store, he had hoped we would share it with the people of his village so they would not starve."

"You tell him that the Cheyenne have waged war against white men who have simply come to the West to start a new life. We weren't looking for trouble, but they gave it to us anyway. And for that I will share no meat and no food with them. Tell him he can leave."

As the lieutenant gave Big Wolf the message, the chief's countenance fell. The look on his dark features was a mixture of despair and fury as he wheeled toward the door and waited for Steve Galton to open it. Without looking back, Big Wolf stomped through the outer office and out into the frigid air. The two warriors were waiting for him. He spoke a few words to them, and together they walked toward the gate, their backs ramrod straight.

Colonel Barlow stood in the outer office with the other men. When the three Cheyenne passed from view, he said, "That'll teach him the U.S. Army won't take his bloody attacks on white people lightly. He started this war, but we'll finish it."

It was just before dawn on Wednesday morning, December 21. Corporals Wendell Dixon and Chuck Yarrow moved about on the platform of the gate tower at Fort Steele, beating their arms against their sides and stamping their feet. Everything was white—the roofs of the fort's buildings, the road, and the fields and hills in every direction. Snow clung to the trees, filling the notches in the denuded branches and the crevices of winter-dead bark.

"Whoo!" Dixon said, "I think it must be thirty below!"

"I wouldn't doubt it," said Yarrow, tucking his carbine

under his right arm and tightening the wool-lined glove on each hand. "I'll sure be glad when summer comes."

"The sun will be up in a little while," Dixon said, "but the way it's been for the past few weeks, it won't give off any heat."

There was a split-second hissing sound before both men were struck with arrows. Yarrow clutched at the shaft buried in his throat. He staggered to the railing and peeled over the side. Dixon stumbled backward from the arrow in his chest. He fell to the platform floor, let out a groan, and went limp.

Seconds later, flaming arrows arched over the stockade walls on every side of the fort, striking several buildings. More fiery missiles buried themselves on the outside of the stockade walls and gate. Flames began spreading and licking their way upward.

A soldier in the barracks was the first to awaken with the smell of smoke in his nostrils. Soon every man in the barracks was groggily putting on his clothes. The first ones dressed dashed out to alert the rest of the fort.

An hour later, all the fires had been extinguished and the damage assessed. The stockade walls had suffered the most damage.

Colonel Barlow called all the officers to his office. He stood before them, his face blazing with fury, and said, "There's no doubt in my mind that Big Wolf is responsible for this. It's his way of retaliating for my refusal to share our food with him. Well, when spring comes, the fighting men of Fort Steele will show that savage what real retaliation is!"

The days passed with no more falling snow, but brutal winds blew across the prairies and mountains of Wyoming, and temperatures stayed below zero even in the daytime.

It was late morning on the day before Christmas. Merilee Roberts was in the kitchen, preparing to put a cake in the oven, when she heard Davey call from the parlor, "Mama, Papa's back!"

"And he's got a real big Christmas tree!" Barbie said.

Merilee wiped her hands on a dish towel and rushed to the front door, pulling it open just as Dale stepped onto the porch, dragging a six-foot blue spruce.

Barbie jumped up and down, clapping her hands. "Oh, Papa! Can we decorate it right now?"

"No, honey," Merilee said. "Don't you remember? We trim the Christmas tree after supper on Christmas Eve."

"Oh, yeah, Mama. I forgot."

Dale stood the tree in a corner and braced it against the walls, then said, "I could use some help from you boys. Got some supplies in the wagon."

Benny and Davey rushed to get their coats.

"Honey," Merilee said, "what did you find out about Patty Ruth when you were at Cooper's store?"

Dale shook his head. "They haven't found a trace of her."

Tears filled Merilee's eyes. "Oh, poor Hannah! What a sad and lonely Christmas. This is her first Christmas since her husband died, and now Patty Ruth is missing. Hannah's heart must be aching."

"Only the Lord Himself can see them through it," Dale said. "All we can do is keep praying for them."

Merilee nodded and wiped tears from her cheeks.

The boys had their coats on and were pulling on their stocking caps.

"Is there a big load, Papa?" Benny asked.

"Not like usual. The blizzards have kept the supply wagons in Cheyenne City."

"Can't blame them for not wanting to risk their lives and the lives of their animals," Merilee said. "So Hannah's shelves are getting low?"

"Yes. She's asking everyone to cut back on their purchases

so there'll be something for all. That's why I wasn't able to get everything you had on the list. And some things I took less of than usual."

Merilee sighed. "Certainly the weather will let up soon so they can get some supply wagon trains through."

"I hope so. Well, boys, let's unload the wagon."

Dale and the boys carried in the groceries and supplies, and Merilee carefully put away the cherished items.

After a small lunch, the children grew more and more excited about trimming the tree that evening. They seemed almost unable to contain themselves, and Dale looked on with a smile when Merilee bundled the children up and sent them outside to play.

When she called the children in after about a half-hour, their faces were red from the cold, but they were happy. As the afternoon moved on, Merilee had to smile to herself as she listened to their exuberant chatter and laughter. They still had as much energy as ever, it seemed.

While happy sounds filled the house, a cloud drifted across Merilee's thoughts. Alone in the kitchen, she whispered, "Thank You, dear heavenly Father, that I still have my husband...and thank You that all three of my children are safe and happy. Please take care of little Patty Ruth and bring her back safely to her mother and her sister and brothers. Comfort Hannah and those precious children. Please strengthen them. Give them peace and let them feel Your loving presence."

Hannah Cooper closed the store early and watched as her three older children trimmed the Christmas tree that stood in a corner of the parlor in their apartment above the store. When it was finished, Hannah left her overstuffed chair, gathered Chris, Mary Beth, and B.J. close to her, and admired their work. The tree was beautifully decorated with strings of popcorn, glass ornaments, and candles, which they would light later in the evening.

Mary Beth insisted that her mother, who was now enter-ing her seventh month of pregnancy, sit by the fire and rest while she cooked supper. When the food was almost ready, Mary Beth called the boys to come and set the table.

While Hannah's oldest daughter was dishing up the food, Hannah stared into the flickering flames. It was wonderful to hear the three voices in the kitchen, but her heart yearned to hear the little voice that was missing. If Patty Ruth were here, she would be bossing her brothers in Mary Beth's place.

And another voice was missing.

Oh, Sol. When you were taken last summer, I thought a lot about what Christmas would be like this year without you. You always made Christmas so special. You got as excited as the children. Remember how I had to be the calming element to keep you and the children from getting too wild? But it was so wonderful. I often just sat and smiled to myself as I watched my happy family.

Hannah rose from her chair in response to Mary Beth's call to come to the table. Chris led in prayer and choked up when he prayed for Patty Ruth's safe return.

Though no one had much appetite, they slowly ate the delicious meal Mary Beth had prepared. They ate in silence, each one eyeing the empty chair with the little black-and-white dog sitting beside it. Big Enough Cooper, better known as Biggie, missed the little redhead who often slipped him goodies under the table. Every time he heard the door of the apartment open, he would run to see if Patty Ruth had come home.

The meal was almost over when they heard footsteps on the wooden staircase outside, followed by a knock on the door. Chris answered the door and saw the cold, reddened faces of Colonel Ross Bateman and Deputy Jack Bower.

Chris invited the men inside. As he closed the door behind them, Hannah and the other two children appeared. Both men removed their hats.

"Good evening, gentlemen," Hannah said, giving them a smile. "Nothing today, I assume."

They shook their heads.

"Well, I appreciate the effort. I'll never be able to thank all of you properly."

"We'll get our thanks when that little redhead is back in this apartment," Jack said.

Ross cleared his throat and told Hannah they had called the search off until Monday. He and Jack decided that the men should be able to spend Christmas with their families. Hannah told them she understood.

There were more footsteps on the outside staircase. Chris rushed to the door and opened it before the knock came. It was Chief Two Moons, who had come to tell Hannah that he and his braves would continue to look for Patty Ruth all the next day.

"Thank you, Chief," Hannah said softly. "Please hear the language of the heart and know how very much my children and I appreciate your help."

A smile tugged at the corners of Two Moons's lips. "Language of the heart is heard." As he turned toward the door, he said, "Will bring Patty Ruth Cooper home tomorrow…if we find her."

"Nothing could make me happier," Hannah said.

When Two Moons was gone, Colonel Bateman said, "I wish all Indians were like him and his people."

Hannah nodded.

"Before we go," Jack said, "I have one bit of good news for you, Hannah."

"I could sure use it."

"I stopped by Julianna's house as soon as we rode in. Heidi's there, helping her cook dinner for this evening."

"And you'll be eating there, of course."

"Of course! Anyway, my boss will be eating there, too." A

wide smile spread over his face. "When I left the house, Lance and Heidi were holding hands and looking starry-eyed at each other."

Hannah grinned at the news. "That's wonderful! Those two were made for each other. The Lord just had to save your boss first. It probably won't be too long till we hear that Lance has proposed and Heidi has accepted."

"I'm sure you're right about that. Well, Colonel, we'd better be going."

Later, after the kitchen had been cleaned up from supper, Hannah asked Chris and Mary Beth to light the candles on the tree. Soon they were all admiring the beauty of the decorations and the brightly lit tree. They began talking of Jacob Kates, the little Jewish man who ran the store for Hannah, saying how much he was missing because he didn't know Jesus Christ, the true Messiah.

Chris talked about the Crow Indians and his desire to see them saved, especially his friend Broken Wing. Conversation dwindled, and as the logs in the fireplace crackled and popped, they sat in silence, each with his or her own thoughts.

Soon the clock on the mantel chimed twelve times.

"Well, it's Christmas," B.J. said.

"Merry Christmas, children." Hannah saw the strange look on their faces and said, "We all feel sad about our little one, but we must remember that we have each other. Let's get to bed now."

They all rose to their feet, though no one expected to sleep. Again they heard footsteps on the staircase.

Hannah frowned. "Who could be coming to our door at this time of night?"

"Only one way to find out," said Chris, heading for the door just as a knock was heard. He opened it, and the lantern light from within the apartment showed the face of a stranger.

Hannah took a couple of steps toward him. "Yes, sir?"

The man removed his hat, ran his gaze over the faces of the Cooper family, and said, "Mrs. Cooper…children…my name is Matthew McDermott."

Hannah took another step. "Mr. McDermott, I don't believe we know you."

The children looked on curiously.

"No, but you know this person I have with me."

A little redheaded girl with long braids, clad in a red coat and stocking cap, stepped into the light flowing onto the landing.

Time seemed to stop as the four Coopers stared speechlessly at this vision.

Finally, Patty Ruth said, "I love you, Mama."

And then everyone flew into action as they tearfully embraced the little girl.

For the rest of the story of Patty Ruth's abduction and return, see Hannah of Fort Bridger 5, *The Perfect Gift*.

CHAPTER THREE

On the Tuesday night after Christmas, Hannah Cooper kissed her children good night and thanked the Lord again that Patty Ruth had been in His protection every minute she was away.

When Hannah went into her own room, the same feeling passed over her that she had experienced all day. Something was amiss. She hadn't really let her mind think about what might be wrong. It was just a feeling scratching at the back of her mind.

She blew out the lantern and tucked herself into bed. Maybe it was just that she was so tired with the extra weight she was carrying, coupled with the stress she had borne with Patty Ruth's kidnapping.

She lay on her back and took several deep breaths, trying her best to relax. And then it came to her. The baby wasn't moving! She suddenly realized that the movements had been getting less frequent and less intense over the last couple of days.

As Hannah lay there, her hands resting on the mound beneath her heart, she tried to convince herself that possibly this baby was larger than the other four and there wasn't as much room for him to move around. *Him,* she thought. *Yes...him.* She wouldn't tell the children yet, but she had a solid feeling this was a boy.

A larger boy? Or was it twins?

Now wouldn't that be something! she thought, pondering the possibility for a few minutes.

"Sol," she whispered, "I miss you so much. Something may be wrong with the baby. I need you here to hold me and tell me everything is all right."

Tears surfaced, and Hannah wept for several minutes. When she was able to stop crying, she spent time talking to her Lord. Just as sleep was about to claim her, she felt a small tentative kick. Gently patting her tummy, she fell asleep.

After sleeping for some time, Hannah awakened and lay quietly, waiting for the wee one to move. She felt a mild fluttering, but nothing vigorous like it had been for months. "Maybe you're just as tired as I am, little guy," she whispered, "and moving is simply too much of an effort."

As the first pale light made its way into Hannah's bedroom, she gingerly sat up on the edge of the bed, groping with her feet for the soft slippers Chris had given her for Christmas. Then she put on her robe and made her way to the window. It was snowing again, but there was just a slight breeze.

"I know it's only the end of December," she whispered, shaking her head, "but I'm already looking forward to spring! I've never experienced such a harsh, cold winter." Hannah drew in a deep breath and let it out. "Okay, young lady. Enough of this. It's a new day, snow or no snow. And you have a mountain of tasks ahead of you. The first is a hot, nourishing breakfast for your troops. That is, if you can beat Mary Beth to the kitchen. Second task is to get to the doctor's office."

Edie O'Brien walked into the outer office of the clinic, glanced at the calendar, and sighed. "Wednesday, December twenty-eighth already. Where has this year gone?"

She went to the front door, unlocked it, and peered

through the window at the falling snow. Her eye caught sight of Hannah and Chris Cooper coming across the deep-rutted street. Chris had a good grip on his mother's arm as they slipped and slid some, having to stop and wait a couple of times for a wagon or buggy to pass.

Hannah was bundled in her warm wool cloak with the rabbit-fur-lined hood pulled close over her head and tied snugly under her chin.

Edie had the door open by the time the slow-moving pair made it across the street. She bustled them inside, fussing over Hannah as she untied the string under her chin. "Hannah, dear," she chided, "you shouldn't be out in this weather. You know you could've sent Chris over here, and Doc would've come to the apartment."

A sheepish look captured Hannah's face. "I know. Guess I would have if I'd known getting across the street was going to be so hard."

Edie hugged her, then held her at arm's length. "You didn't have an appointment. Is something wrong?"

Doc appeared at the rear door of the office. "Hello, Hannah...Chris. I hope everything's all right."

"Well, I'm not sure. I'd like you to tell me."

"This have to do with your pregnancy?"

"Yes. The baby has barely moved the past few days. I'm concerned. He or she was very active up until then. And I distinctly remember that my other four were very active in my seventh month."

"Let's get you in the examining room," Doc said as he took her arm. "Come, Edie."

Chris sat down in the office to wait and began to silently pray that everything would be all right.

Thirty minutes had passed when Doc came out with Edie and Hannah behind him. Chris jumped to his feet and looked anxiously first at the doctor and then at his mother.

Doc managed a smile. "I don't think there's anything to worry about. I'm sure the baby is less active than usual because of the strain your mother has been under. I'll keep a close watch on her, but I'm sure the baby will become active again soon. Now young lady, if you have any more problems, you send Chris to get me. If Chris is in school, send Jacob. I don't want you trying to plod your way through all that snow on the street."

Hannah saluted as a soldier would an officer. "Yes, sir, General O'Brien!"

"Hey, Mama!" Chris said. "You do a pretty good salute."

"I ought to, honey. I was married to an army officer." Hannah then looked at both O'Briens. "We're sure looking forward to having you over for Patty Ruth's birthday."

"And we're looking forward to being there," Edie said.

"We wouldn't miss it for anything," Doc said.

"Do Grandpa and Grandma seem all right to you?" Hannah asked as Chris helped her across the snow-packed street.

"I was gonna ask you the same thing," Chris said. "They seem…well, like maybe they're unhappy about something. Usually they smile all the time."

"We need to pray extra hard for them."

When Hannah and Chris entered the store, Jacob Kates was at the counter talking to Dale and Merilee Roberts.

"Hannah!" Merilee cried, rushing to her. "Are you all right? Jacob told us you've been having some problems with the baby."

"I'm fine. Dr. O'Brien says the baby's decrease in activity is due to the strain I went through when Patty Ruth was missing."

"Well, praise the Lord it's no more serious than that. And you have sweet Patty Ruth back!"

"Amen!" Dale said. "We were so thankful when Jacob told

us she was brought home on Christmas Eve."

"God had His hand on her all the time," Hannah said. "My heart goes out to Emily McDermott. Poor thing. She simply couldn't cope with her own little girl's death." Hannah glanced at the goods the McDermotts had placed on the counter. "Did Jacob have everything you need?"

"Almost," Merilee said. "We thought that since it's snowing again, we'd better come in and pick up what we could. I sure hope this weather lets up so the supply wagons can get through."

"It's going to get serious if it doesn't happen soon," Hannah said. "All my customers have been so good about taking the bare necessities so everybody can have some."

The Robertses paid their bill and left. Other customers were coming in, and Jacob went to help them find the things they needed.

Mary Beth, B.J., and Patty Ruth rushed to greet their mother and Chris when they entered the apartment.

"What did Grandpa say, Mama?" Mary Beth asked.

Chris and B.J. helped Hannah out of her cloak while she explained what the doctor had said.

Patty Ruth's big blue eyes were dancing as she said, "Mama, I was thinkin'…"

"That's different," B.J. said. "Our little sister has been thinkin'!"

Hannah gave him the look that meant he was to carry his insult no further.

Patty Ruth went on. "What I was thinkin', Mama, was that nex' year when I have my birthday, I'll be seven, an' my baby sister will be almos' a year old!"

"You mean baby brother," B.J. said. "Mama's gonna have a boy."

"She ain't neither!" Patty Ruth snapped.

"Yes, she is," Chris said. "This family needs another boy."

"Oh?" said Mary Beth, putting her hands on her hips. "And why is that?"

"Simple. B.J. and I are already outnumbered. Mama's a girl, so with you and Patty Ruth, there's three girls and only two boys. So when Mama has our baby brother, there'll be three boys to match the three girls. That's only fair, isn't it?"

Patty Ruth frowned and cocked her head. "You ain't thinkin', Chris. Since—"

"Aren't thinking, honey," Hannah said.

"That's right, Mama. He aren't thinkin'. Since the girls do more work around here, we need another one to help."

"Aw, come on," B.J. said. "You girls don't pull weeds around here in the summer. And you don't sweep and shovel the snow off the stairs and the front porch of the store in winter."

"Yeah, but how about the housework?" Mary Beth said. "We—"

"That's for girls to do because it's housework," Chris said. "You've heard of housewives, but you've never heard of house-husbands!"

"Yeah," Patty Ruth said. "So Mama's gonna have a girl!"

"You're gonna have a boy, aren't you, Mama?" B.J. said.

"B.J.," Hannah said, "the baby is what the Lord has made him or her. We must agree that the main thing is that he or she be born normal and healthy."

"That's right," Mary Beth said. "Just so the baby is normal and healthy. That's what really matters."

The other three agreed, but Hannah saw in B.J.'s eyes that he was about to say something else, and she gave him the look again.

When Friday, December 30, broke over Fort Bridger, Patty Ruth awakened before anyone else. She left her bed, crossed the room to Mary Beth's bed, and pinched her nose. "Hey, Mary Beth! It's my birthday!"

The older girl moaned and opened her eyes, trying to focus on her little sister. "What?"

Patty Ruth jumped on the bed, making it bounce as much as she could. "I said it's my birthday! I'm not a little ol' five-year-ol' kid no more! I'm grown up! I'm six!"

Mary Beth rubbed her eyes and sat up. She hugged Patty Ruth and said, "No, you're not, sweetie. You're still five."

"No! It's my birthday. December 30! I'm six!"

"You won't be six years old till noon."

"Noon? Why?"

"Because you were born at straight-up twelve o'clock noon. I was seven years old at the time, and I remember it clearly."

The bedroom door swung open and Hannah came in, clad in her robe. "How's my birthday girl this morning? Happy birthday, sweetheart!"

Patty Ruth bounded off the bed and hugged her mother. "I'm jus' fine! Happy my birthday to you, Mama!"

Hannah laughed. "Why, thank you."

"Mama?"

"What, honey?"

"Am I five or six?"

Mary Beth rolled her eyes and shook her head.

"Why, you're six, of course. You were born six years ago today."

"See there, Mary Beth?" she said, giving her sister a smug grin. "Mama says I'm six now. I don't have to wait till noon."

A quizzical look captured Hannah's face.

"I was explaining to her just before you came in that she wouldn't actually be six years old until noon because that's what time she was born."

"Well, technically you're right, Mary Beth."

Patty Ruth frowned. "Tech—techni—what? What does that mean?"

"It means that actually, you won't be six until noon, even though today is your birthday."

"So I have to wait?"

Mary Beth shrugged. "I wish I'd kept my mouth shut. I'm sorry, Mama."

Patty Ruth stepped close to her sister. "It's all right, Mary Beth. I don' min' waitin' till noon to be six."

To Patty Ruth, the morning seemed to drag. It was almost ten o'clock when she asked her mother for the sixth or seventh time what time it was.

"I'll be glad when you start school and can learn how to tell time, honey. It's two minutes until ten."

"How long now?"

"Two more hours."

"That long?"

"Yes, but if you go play with Tony, the time will go faster."

"How can the time go faster?"

The boys were in their room, but Mary Beth was close by and had been listening to the conversation. She laughed and said, "What do you think, Mama? Will she get better or worse as she gets older?"

Patty Ruth frowned. "Better or worse than what?"

"Never mind, honey."

"You didn' answer my question, Mama. How can time go faster?"

"Honey, it doesn't really go faster. It just seems to go faster."

"Oh. So if I go play with Tony, it will seem shorter until I'm six?"

"Yes."

"Okay!"

When noon finally came, Hannah sent Mary Beth to the

girls' room to tell Patty Ruth she was now officially six years old. The child hugged Biggie, then ran to the boy's room and made her announcement. Everyone in the Cooper family had a good laugh as they saw the excitement that filled the birthday girl.

It was just past noon when Glenda Williams and Abby Turner, Mary Beth's best friend, arrived with the birthday cake. The cake was beautiful, and Patty Ruth was more excited than ever about her party.

By suppertime, Patty Ruth was sure this had been the longest day of her life, even though she had spent a good deal of time playing in her room with Tony the Bear and Biggie. She knew the party was to begin at seven o'clock. During the afternoon she would come out of her room and ask whoever she saw first what time it was. Every member of the family was patient with her, thankful to have her back with them again.

Supper consisted of the birthday girl's favorite meal— chicken and dumplings. While they were eating, Patty Ruth talked excitedly about the party, wanting to know if everybody who was invited was coming.

"All of them said they were," Mary Beth told her.

"How many will there be?"

"Twenty-three," Hannah said. "That includes baby Larissa."

"Uncle Curly and Aunt Judy Charley are comin', aren't they?"

"Yes. And the Williamses and Abby."

"An' Larissa's bringin' her mommy an' Deputy Bower?"

Hannah laughed. "Of course."

"An' my very bes' frien'?"

"Yes. Belinda will be here, along with her parents and her brothers."

"Everyone we felt we had room for that you wanted to invite is coming," Mary Beth said. "Grandma and Grandpa O'Brien. And Pastor and Mrs. Kelly will be here."

"An' Uncle Jacob?"

"Yes," Hannah said. "And the others from the fort, Colonel and Mrs. Bateman, and the Carlins."

Patty Ruth clapped her hands. "Oh, boy! This is gonna be a fun night!"

"Now, Patty Ruth," Hannah said, "I want you to mind your manners at the party. I know you're excited, but since you're going to open the door as your guests arrive, I want you to walk when you hear the knock each time. No running. Being excited is all well and good, but a grown-up young lady of six must be well mannered and polite, or no one will want to come to her seventh birthday party. Understand?"

"Yes, Mama. I understand."

When supper was over, the boys reluctantly helped Mary Beth clear off the table and clean up the kitchen. It was near seven o'clock when the children went to sit near the fireplace in the parlor. Hannah came out of her room, stopped where Patty Ruth was standing beside Mary Beth's chair and gave her a hug and patted the little girl's red hair into place. "You look very pretty tonight, honey."

Patty Ruth smiled up at her mother, and Hannah bent over, kissed the tip of her freckled nose, and said, "I love you, baby girl."

Just then a knock sounded at the door. Patty Ruth was off at a run to answer it. Then she remembered her mother's words and stopped short. She put on her "big girl" face, moved slowly to the door, and opened it. It was snowing hard outside, and a stiff wind was blowing. Patty Ruth welcomed Gary and Glenda Williams, and Abby Turner.

As the guests continued to arrive, Patty Ruth put her best foot forward, but with each present she became more excited and had a difficult time keeping her composure.

The last of the invited guests to arrive were Curly and Judy Charley Wesson. Everyone looked on as Judy lifted Patty Ruth in her arms and hugged her, saying, "Well, lookee what we got here! We got a purty little redhead who's all dolled up and lookin' beyootiful!"

Patty Ruth hugged Aunt Judy's neck real tight.

"Well, I do declare!" Curly said when Judy put Patty Ruth down. "What a cute little thang you are! What's your name, little girl?"

"Patty Ruth."

Curly gasped, eyes widening. "What? Patty Ruth?"

"Uh-huh."

"Well, how old are you?"

"I'm six."

Curly's eyes widened the more. "Six?"

"Uh-huh."

"Do you know what I do," he said bending down close, "when I meet a little girl who's name is Patty Ruth and she's six years old? Do you know what I do?"

"Huh-uh."

"I hug 'er!"

Curly folded the small body into his arms, and Patty Ruth hugged him back.

Soon it was time to open the presents. Patty Ruth's gleeful laughter and appreciation over each gift brought gladness to the hearts of those gathered there.

Patty Ruth eyed the last beautifully wrapped gift. "Can I open this one now, Mama?" she asked, looking at Hannah.

"Certainly."

Patty Ruth tore the paper off the package and was almost speechless when she saw the beautiful doll her mother had given her. In the package were pieces of a layette Hannah had made. Patty Ruth caressed the doll, then held it while she unfolded and looked at each article that had been so carefully stitched by her mother.

Jacob tiptoed away and slipped out the door. A couple of minutes later he returned with a large object covered with an old quilt. He brushed the snow from the quilt and set the object down on the floor at Patty Ruth's feet.

"This is for you, sweetheart," Jacob said, his eyes misty. "I made it for you. I thought your new dolly might need it."

With the doll still clasped in one arm, Patty Ruth reached down and slid the quilt off. Her eyes widened even more, and her mouth formed a perfect *O* as she dropped to her knees to look at the beautiful wooden cradle.

She gave Jacob an adoring look then gently placed her baby in the cradle. She turned to Jacob then, arms opened wide, and said, "Thank you, Uncle Jacob! Thank you! I love it! An' my dolly loves it!"

After a long hug, Jacob wiped tears from his cheeks, and Patty Ruth looked around the room and said, "Thank you, everyone!"

Throughout the evening, Hannah had been aware of a strange quietness in Mary Beth. She wasn't surprised when she saw the girl suddenly leave her chair and hurry from the room.

When Mary Beth hadn't returned after a few minutes, Hannah leaned over to Glenda and whispered, "I'll be back shortly."

Hannah found the girls' bedroom door closed. She tapped lightly on the door and entered before Mary Beth could respond. The thirteen-year-old was lying face-down on her bed with her face buried in a pillow to muffle her sobs. Hannah eased onto the side of the bed and laid a hand on her daughter's shoulder.

Mary Beth turned and looked up at her. "Oh, Mama!" she wailed and threw her arms around Hannah's neck.

Hannah held her close. "I know, honey, I know. You're

missing your papa. We all miss him terribly. It's okay, sweetheart. Go ahead and cry. You've been brave for so long. You held up so well on your own birthday. It's all right to grieve. Sometimes we have to give in to our emotions and just have a good cry.

"Jesus gives us tears for a release. When we weep, He weeps with us just like He did with Mary and Martha when their brother died. In the Psalms it says God puts our tears in a bottle. He does that for many reasons, but I think one reason is to show us that when we hurt, He hurts."

Mary Beth nodded her head against her mother's breast.

"And honey, God's grace can dry those tears when you've had the release you need. And though the hurt over Papa's death is still there, God's peace is always greater than our pain."

Mary Beth hugged her mother tighter.

Hannah's own heart was breaking, but the words of comfort she had just spoken to her daughter were taking root in her own heart and soul. She silently gave thanks to the Lord for the way He had comforted her in the loss of her husband.

Slowly, Mary Beth's weeping subsided, and she eased back in her mother's grasp to look at her. "I love you, Mama," she said.

"I love you too, sweetheart."

Hannah went to the dresser and took a handkerchief out of a drawer. She eased back onto the bed and gently dried all trace of tears from Mary Beth's cheeks and swollen eyes.

"Thank you, Mama, for always knowing what I need."

A fragile smile graced Hannah's mouth. "It's the wisdom God gives a mother. You will know one day when you become a mother. And with it comes God's infinite grace to the mother who knows Him."

"But you've been through all of these heartaches yourself. Yet you always have such a joyful countenance."

Hannah brushed stray stands of hair from Mary Beth's

forehead. "We have a choice, Mary Beth. We can choose to be happy or we can choose to be miserable. I choose to be happy, and by God's grace, He allows me to be happy."

"I'm so glad the Lord let me be your daughter, Mama."

Hannah kissed her, then stood and said, "I need to get back to our guests. You stay here as long as you need to. Wash your face and touch up your hair. Come back out when you're ready. Everyone will understand."

CHAPTER FOUR

While Hannah Cooper was with Mary Beth, Gary Williams turned to the fort's commandant and said, "Colonel, word has been going around about the recent Cheyenne attack on Fort Steele. Do you know what caused it?"

Everyone's attention was now on Colonel Ross Bateman.

"Actually, Gary, Fort Steele isn't the only military post to be attacked of late."

"Really? I haven't heard of any of the others."

"The Shoshoni attacked Camp Brown up by Lander ten days ago. And just two days ago, the Blackfoot attacked Camp Stambaugh, some thirty miles south of here. But it hasn't been just the military who've been attacked. All three of the tribes I mentioned have also attacked small settlements, farms, and ranches in those parts."

"Why this increase in hostilities, Colonel?" Jack Bower asked. "The Indians don't usually expose themselves to the cold weather this time of year to wage war."

"I received a wire from Colonel Barlow a few days after the Cheyenne attacked Fort Steele. He said Chief Big Wolf had come to the fort, asking for food for his people. Barlow turned him away. The attack came just before dawn a day or so after that. They killed two sentries in the tower, then launched hundreds of flaming arrows on the fort. The stockade walls were damaged before they could get the fires extinguished."

Bower nodded. "So it was because Barlow refused to give them food?"

"That's right. Same story at Camps Brown and Stambaugh. And it's clear that the Indians are attacking the farms and ranches not only to show their anger for being turned away without food, but to take food from cellars and livestock for meat. Of course, they're killing many white people in the process."

"Well, no wonder the Indians are hungry," Captain John Fordham said. "Most of the deer, antelope, elk, and buffalo have migrated elsewhere, and the few that've stayed are hard to find."

"I'm glad, Colonel Bateman, that you had the men of the fort hunting game in early November," Dobie Carlin said. "We've still got a good meat supply."

"And I'm glad Hannah ordered what she did in early November," Jacob said. "She had the storeroom well stocked before the big snows slowed down the supply wagons. If she hadn't, we would've had to start our rationing program much sooner."

"I just hope these heavy storms let up soon," Sylvia Bateman said.

"Me, too," Doc O'Brien said. "I'm getting a little nervous about some of my medical supplies."

"Looks like we need to pray even harder than we have been," Andy Kelly said. "I think we've got another big one on us right now."

Curly nodded. "'Fraid so, Pastor. But like you've often preached, prayer changes things. I really believe the Lord is gonna clear the weather up in time to get us some more groceries before Hannah's shelves are bare."

"I like your attitude," Kelly said. "Maybe I ought to have you preach this Sunday, Curly."

The little man gasped, his eyes wide. "Oh no! I...I can talk, but I cain't preach!" There was a round of laughter, then Curly said, "Colonel Bateman, I can understand the Indians attackin' farms and ranches to steal food and livestock for butcherin', but why brave this bad weather to attack the army forts and camps?"

"It's the anger in them," Bateman said. "They're furious they were turned away when they asked the army for food. So they want to cause all the damage they possibly can. If they can kill some military personnel in the process, so much the better."

"We're not ruling out trouble from some of the hostiles in the Fort Bridger area," Fordham said. "Could come from Blackfoot, Cheyenne, or Shoshoni. Even all three."

"We're keeping our eyes peeled," Bateman said. "And I'm sending out daily patrols all around the area. Except, of course, when there's a blizzard on us. The only time the Indians won't attack is during a blizzard."

"I'm sure glad the Crow are friendly to white people," Chris Cooper said. "Especially with Chief Two Moons's village just twelve miles north of us."

"The Crow are exceptionally fierce fighters," Dobie Carlin said. "They've shown it when they've fought the Blackfoot and the Shoshoni. Neither of those two tribes want to go to battle with the Crow. I'm sure glad the Fort Bridger cavalry won't have to fight them. It's reassuring knowing that Two Moons and the other Crow chiefs are our friends."

Hannah came down the hall and stopped at the kitchen. Rebecca Kelly saw her first and said, "Hannah, is Mary Beth all right?"

"She was having a hard time about her father, but she's better now. I think she'll be out in a few minutes."

"Mrs. Cooper," Abby Turner said, "would it help Mary Beth if I went back and spent a few minutes with her?"

"I'm sure it would, honey. Go on back."

As Abby headed down the hall, Hannah looked at the candles on the birthday cake, saw that the coffee cups were ready to be filled, and the glasses contained milk for the children. "Thank you, Glenda," she said. "What would I ever do without you?"

Glenda hugged her and said softly, "It's my joy to help you. Do you want to hold off lighting the candles till Mary Beth comes?"

Before Hannah could reply, they heard Mary Beth and Abby come down the hall. The girls entered the kitchen, and Mary Beth greeted everyone with a smile.

"Would you like to light the candles on your little sister's cake?" Hannah asked.

Patty Ruth's eyes lit up when she saw the cake, and Hannah started singing "Happy Birthday." Patty Ruth blew out all six candles at once, and everyone clapped, then enjoyed cake and each other's company.

Hannah noticed that Mary Beth stayed close to her side, and she prayed that the Lord would comfort her with His peace. As the party went on, Hannah also noticed that the O'Briens were unusually quiet and a bit distracted. When the guests were preparing to leave, Hannah whispered to Doc and Edie, asking if they would stay a little longer.

Patty Ruth gave everyone a hug and thanked them for coming to her party and for the presents.

When everyone was gone except the O'Briens, Hannah told her children to go to their rooms and prepare for bed, explaining that she needed to talk to Grandpa and Grandma O'Brien in private. She asked Chris to read the Bible and pray with his siblings. Then she hugged and kissed each child, saying she would kiss them good night again later, even though they would be asleep.

The children hugged and kissed Grandpa and Grandma O'Brien, then scurried off to their rooms.

Hannah guided the O'Briens to the sofa closest to the fireplace then sat down in an overstuffed chair, facing them.

The O'Briens were almost as dear to Hannah as her own parents, and she was troubled by the unhappiness she saw on their faces. Doc and Edie had been a constant support to her and her children since they arrived in Fort Bridger many months ago.

Never once had Hannah heard them complain about the long hours or the necessity of always being available to tend to the sick or injured. They considered their work a joy, and they gave generously of their time and abilities. Often they received no pay for the work they did.

For a fleeting moment the thought crossed Hannah's mind that maybe what she read on their faces had to do with her and the baby—but she quickly dismissed it. No, this was something clawing at their hearts and bringing unhappiness.

"Hannah," Doc said, "are you having more problems with the baby?"

"No, the baby still isn't as active as before, but I'm feeling more movement each day." She felt a substantial kick just then to her ribs and smiled as she rubbed the spot. "He just made his presence known."

"You're pretty sure it's a boy, aren't you?" Edie said.

"Yes. But I haven't let on to the children."

Doc managed a grin. "I know there's a debate amongst your other four about that."

"Continually."

"Well, since it's not the baby you want to talk to us about, we're ready for whatever it is."

Hannah's eyes misted up as she leaned over, took Edie's hand, and said with a tight voice, "I don't mean to be nosy. But I love both of you, and I know something is bothering you. You're just not yourselves. You can share it with me if it will help."

Doc and Edie exchanged glances, then Edie's eyes filled with tears. "Honey…you tell her," she said.

Doc cleared his throat. "It's about our son, Patrick."

"Oh? Has something happened to him?"

"In a sense, yes. It has us quite concerned. We've told you some things about him, but I don't remember how much."

"Well, I know he's your only child, and that he's been a surgeon in Chicago since 1866. And last I heard, he isn't married yet."

"Your memory is excellent, Hannah," Edie said.

"You may recall," Doc said, "that when we came to Fort Bridger we planned to eventually retire here, and there were tentative plans for Patrick to come to Fort Bridger, work with us for a while, then eventually take over the practice. Patrick had prayed about it for some time, and each time he wrote he told us he believed the Lord was confirming that it was His will for him to come here and one day take over the practice. Then about…oh, four months ago, he wrote to say that he knew the Lord was leading him to come, and that he would be here sometime in early 1871."

"This, of course, was what we had prayed would happen all along," Edie said. "I'm proud to say that Patrick is an excellent doctor. He showed interest in medicine since he was a very small child. Before Doc became an army doctor, his practice was in a small town in Illinois. Patrick used to spend hours at the office, wanting to learn what he could about medicine. He even rode along with his father when he made house calls. We used to tease him that he had been born with medicine in his blood. Being a doctor was the only career he ever talked about.

"We had to scrimp and scrape on army pay to have the money to send Patrick to a reputable medical school, but we were able to do it, and he graduated in the top ten of his class. We were a little apprehensive when he chose to go into practice right there in Chicago. We were afraid he might get to where he liked the big city and forget that he had planned to be a country doctor."

"You know," Doc said, "the lure of the big city and the income from a lucrative practice. It could be tempting. Especially compared to the workload and the lifestyle of a country doctor like myself."

"Needless to say," Edie went on, "we were thrilled beyond words when Patrick wrote and said he was coming. He even said that nothing in the big city attracted him, and he was looking forward to joining his father where he could do the kind of medicine he had always wanted to do. He said that in a small community like Fort Bridger he felt he could make a difference in people's lives."

"A wonderful attitude," Hannah said. "But I assume something about this has changed?"

Just then Mary Beth and Patty Ruth appeared; Mary Beth was holding her little sister's hand.

Hannah excused herself to the O'Briens then said, "Girls, I thought you'd both be asleep by now. What's wrong?"

"Mama, Patty Ruth's having the same problem I was having earlier this evening. She wants to ask you something."

"What is it, honey?"

Patty Ruth dipped her head sheepishly. "Can I sleep with you tonight?"

"I'll be back shortly," Hannah said to the O'Briens.

Hannah took Patty Ruth's other hand, and the three of them headed down the hall. Mary Beth let go of her little sister's hand when she reached their room, told her mother and Patty Ruth good night, and closed the bedroom door.

Hannah led the little one into her bedroom, turned back the downy quilts, and said, "Okay, sweetie, climb in."

Patty Ruth snuggled down on what used to be her papa's side of the bed. Hannah thought she looked so small in the big feather bed. She tucked her in, kissed her cheek, and said, "You get to sleep now. I'll join you as soon as Grandpa and Grandma leave."

The child nodded with a satisfied look on her face. "Thank you for my party, Mama."

"I'm glad you liked it, honey. You get to sleep now."

Hannah stepped into the hall and closed the door, briefly leaning against it to gather her thoughts. She asked the Lord to give her wisdom as she tried to be a help to the O'Briens, then she returned to the parlor.

"I'm sorry," Hannah said as she sat down.

"Don't be sorry, dear," Edie said. "Poor little Patty Ruth. We understand."

"Now, where were we? Oh yes. I assume something about Patrick's plans to come here have changed?"

Doc's lower lip trembled. "Yes, Hannah. In early October we noticed something different about Patrick's letters, which had arrived weekly for a long time. He seemed cold toward the things of the Lord. In all of his letters he had told us what happened in his church on the previous Sunday, and he often shared something from his pastor's sermons. But suddenly there was nothing in the letters about church at all. And...and no mention of the Lord. This just wasn't like Patrick."

"So after three such letters," Edie said, "we wrote back and asked him if he had quit going to church. It was almost two weeks before we received another letter from him. And in that one he said he'd been too busy to go to church lately but would get back soon. The next letter was more than two weeks in coming, and in it Patrick mentioned that he had met a young woman named Lois Trent, and he said they were becoming good friends."

"When we answered his letter," Doc said, "we asked some questions about the girl. His next letter, which was also longer than usual in coming, hit us pretty hard. He said he wasn't so sure he should come and take over my practice. Things had changed in Chicago, and he just might decide to stay there. He didn't answer any of our questions about Lois or even mention her."

"We could tell by the tone of the letter that he was getting further from the Lord," Edie said. "When we wrote back, we asked what had happened to make him change his mind about coming to Fort Bridger."

"His reply, if you could call it that," Doc said, his voice breaking, "was vague, but there was enough in it that we could tell Patrick had become involved with this Lois Trent. There had been no mention that she was a Christian, so we figured she wasn't. But we could see that she was having an influence on him, and it wasn't good."

Edie pulled a hanky from her sleeve and wiped her nose. Tears were trailing down her cheeks. "It was the letter that came on December 8 that broke our hearts, Hannah. Patrick wrote that he had definitely decided he would not be coming to Fort Bridger. Dad would have to find someone else to take over his practice when he retired."

Edie began to sob. Hannah left her chair and wrapped her arms around the older woman. It took a few minutes for Edie to gain control. When she did, Hannah kept an arm around her.

"We wrote back to our son," Doc said, "and told him that he must not allow this Lois Trent to cause him to stray from the Lord. We warned him that God chastises His own. He will not let them get by with sin."

"I hope Patrick will heed your warning," Hannah said.

Edie sniffed and said, "We sent that letter on December 9, Hannah. We haven't heard from Patrick since."

"So you can see why we're feeling a bit low," Doc said.

"I know you've been praying hard for Patrick," Hannah said, "and I'll be doing the same. Before you head for home, let's pray for him together."

After they had spent some time in prayer, Doc and Edie thanked Hannah for caring about them.

"You need to tell Pastor Kelly about Patrick," Hannah said. "I know you probably don't want the whole church to know about this, but you really should share it with the pastor."

"We will," Doc assured her. "We'll talk to him tomorrow."

They embraced Hannah, and as Doc opened the door, Edie kissed Hannah's cheek and said, "Thank you for having such a tender heart."

Though it was still snowing hard and the wind was blowing, Hannah watched until the O'Briens reached the bottom of the stairs, then closed the door.

Hannah surveyed the parlor and kitchen. Bits of wrapping paper littered the floor, and a stray cup and saucer sat on a side table. She thought about cleaning it all up before going to bed, but she was just too tired. She stirred the fire and tossed on more logs, then blew out the candles about the rooms and extinguished the lanterns.

She slipped into Mary Beth's room, kissed her cheek, and slipped out again. She entered the boys' room and kissed them both. B.J. stirred slightly but only turned over.

She went into her own room and looked down at the sleeping little redhead. There was a slight smile on Patty Ruth's lips, and her cheeks were flushed with sleep.

"What a blessing you are to me, sweetheart," Hannah whispered. "How very proud your papa would be of you."

Hannah made fast work of washing her face and brushing her hair and slipped into a flannel nightgown that went from her chin to her bare toes. She put out the lantern on the dresser and joined Patty Ruth in the wide, soft bed. She closed her weary eyes and became conscious of the wind howling around the eaves.

Hannah thanked the Lord for her many blessings. She prayed for Patrick O'Brien, then for each of her children, asking her heavenly Father to keep them safe, well, and healthy.

She gently caressed the bulge beneath her heart and felt a strong kick, as if the little one was reassuring her that he, too, was fine.

CHAPTER FIVE

I t was a cold night in Chicago, and the windy city was living up to its name as Dr. Patrick O'Brien emerged from a burlesque theater with Lois Trent on his arm. With them were Roy Domire and Murielle Wygant.

"Brr-r!" Lois tugged at her fur collar. "It's a cold one tonight, isn't it?"

"That it is," Patrick agreed, glancing toward the carriages waiting for hire. He motioned to the driver of the nearest one and said to his companions, "Let's get out of the wind."

The men helped their dates into the carriage, then Patrick and Roy gave the driver the addresses to their homes.

As the carriage made its way through the streets lighted with gas lanterns, Lois took hold of Patrick's hand. "Thank you, darling, for taking me to the burlesque. I really enjoyed it."

"Yes, it was wonderful!" Murielle said and squeezed Roy's hand. "Did you have a good time, Roy?"

Patrick and Roy exchanged furtive glances, and Roy said something about a song he had liked.

"And how about you?" Lois asked, squeezing Patrick's arm. "How did you like the show?"

"Oh, there were…some parts that were better than others. I did like the same song Roy mentioned."

"Smells like snow out there, doesn't it?" Lois said. "We may be in for a storm."

Patrick entered his apartment, shook the snowflakes from his hat and coat, and hung them up. He rubbed his hands together and went to the potbellied stove. It was still warm. He added some coal and waited for the fire to build.

He thought of the evening he had just spent and wished he had taken Lois somewhere else. The burlesque show had been a distasteful experience. And he knew by the look on Roy's face, and by his manner, that he had found the show distasteful, too.

Patrick went to the bedroom and began to undress. His eyes fell on the letter from his parents…the letter that seemed to condemn him, the letter he had not yet answered.

He doused the lantern and climbed into bed. He knew what his parents would say if he told them the truth about Lois. Guilt was already gnawing at him because he had not spoken one word to her about Jesus Christ and her need to be saved.

But she's so beautiful, and she has such a winning way about her. I don't think I could stand to lose her.

Patrick rolled over and told himself he would answer his parents soon.

Two nights later, Roy and Murielle were with Patrick and Lois in an exquisite downtown Chicago restaurant. After they had given the waiter their orders, he asked if they would like something from the bar. Both women ordered whiskey, then looked to their escorts.

"I'll just drink water," Patrick said.

"Yeah, me too," Roy said. "Water's fine."

When the waiter walked away, Lois giggled. "What's the matter, Doctor? Afraid a little liquor will make your hands unsteady? You don't see another patient till tomorrow morning."

Patrick cleared his throat nervously and said, "I've never touched the stuff. It's a hazard to your health."

Lois laughed. "A little alcohol now and then isn't going to destroy a person's health."

"As a physician, I recommend you don't drink it at all," Patrick said. "Every alcoholic took a first drink."

"I had a conversation one time with one of those Bible-thumping, hellfire-and-brimstone preachers," Murielle said. "He quoted from the Bible about the evil of strong drink and all that. And then he tried to get me saved! I asked him why I should believe in a man who lived eighteen hundred years ago. Besides, Jesus was just like anybody else. He sinned just like we do."

Lois snickered. "And what did the preacher say to that?"

"He told me Jesus is the only begotten Son of God and that He never sinned. And I said, 'What about that time Jesus lost His temper and overturned the tables of the moneychangers and drove them out of the temple? Seems to me doing a thing like that is wrong. I'd call that sin.'"

"I guess you showed him," Lois said. "And how could anyone believe those fables about Jesus coming back from the dead? I think it was His own fault that He got the religious leaders mad at Him and got Himself crucified."

Roy chuckled hollowly but kept quiet. Patrick just stared at the centerpiece on the table.

Later, when the meal was over, Lois and Murielle went to the powder room, leaving the men at the table by themselves.

"Roy, we need to talk," Patrick said.

"About what?"

"About what's gone on here at this table tonight. I'll come by the construction site tomorrow about five minutes before twelve and buy your lunch at the Downtown Café, okay?"

"All right."

The next day brought a clear sky, and the wind had diminished to a slight breeze. Barely a half-inch of snow had fallen.

Patrick left the clinic just before noon and walked down the busy street toward the Downtown Café. He could easily see the ten-story building several blocks away where Roy was employed as a construction worker. Chicago's skyline was becoming quite impressive with so many tall buildings going up.

Patrick reached the construction site and saw Roy on a girder with two other workers on the fifth floor. Roy saw him and cupped a hand beside his mouth. "Be down in just a minute!"

Moments later, Roy joined his friend on the street, and they headed toward the café.

"I happened to run into Murielle and Lois this morning on their way to work," Roy said. "Murielle said someone in her apartment building told her this morning that the Stardust Theater is opening up with a new show Saturday night. Murielle had already told Lois about it, and they both hinted strongly that the four of us should go."

When Patrick didn't reply, Roy said, "Well? We ought to take them, don't you think?"

"Roy, let's…let's have our talk over lunch first, then we can discuss the burlesque show."

"Whatever you say."

They entered the café and found a table and ordered lunch.

"I had a hard time with Murielle's low-handed remarks about Jesus last night," Patrick began. "And with her remarks about Bible thumpers. And I have to say it was difficult to take Lois's ready agreement with what Murielle said."

Roy cleared his throat. "Well, I didn't like it either, but I didn't want to say anything that would offend Murielle…or Lois either, for that matter."

"I wanted to set them straight, but I was too cowardly to do it. You and I need to come to an agreement that we're going to talk to the girls about this. We need to explain that we didn't like what they had to say."

Roy took a bite of his food and looked down at his plate as he chewed.

"Well? Are you in agreement?"

"I don't think we should go at it too strongly, Pat. We need to be careful. It wouldn't be right to offend them."

Patrick was quiet for a moment, then said, "You know who we're acting like, don't you?"

"Hmm?"

"You and me. We're acting like Peter when he stood by the enemies' fire on the night Jesus was arrested and taken to the high priest's house. Peter stood there by the fire and three times denied the Lord. He was cowardly. And that's exactly what you and I were last night. Not only that, but we didn't even have the gumption to tell them the truth as to why we don't drink. I know what our problem is, Roy. We need to get back to church. We haven't been with God's people and under the preaching of the Word."

"I plan to get back to church someday. But not just yet."

"Not yet?"

"I love the Lord, Pat, but if I started going to church instead of spending Sundays with Murielle, she'd drop me. I've really developed an attachment to her. I think I'm falling in love with her. I just can't bear the thought of losing her."

Patrick set his coffee cup down and looked at his friend without speaking.

"Okay, so what about your feelings for Lois?" Roy asked. "Aren't you in love with her?"

"She has me wrapped around her little finger."

"You want to lose her?"

"Well, no."

"You will, just as sure as I'll lose Murielle if we get back in church. Lois will find her another beau. You want that to happen? The reason she's got you wrapped around her little finger is because you're head over heels in love with her. Just stop and think about life without her. I'm telling you, Pat, church is going to have to wait."

Patrick took another sip of coffee. "Roy, there are warnings in the Bible about God's children straying off the path and giving in to this world. God says He will chastise His children when we stray from Him, because He loves us."

"I know, but I've got to have a little fun. Church can wait. Now, what about that new burlesque show at the Stardust this Saturday night?"

"Roy, we were miserable last night listening to all the filthy language and the off-color humor. It was repugnant because we're born again and have the Holy Spirit in our hearts. I could see it on your face as well as you could see it on mine. Right?"

"Well, yeah. I'd rather it had been clean. But…"

"But what?"

"The girls want to go to the new show on Saturday night. They're going to expect it. You know…since they hinted about it to me and knew I'd be seeing you for lunch. I told them we were having lunch together."

Patrick shook his head. "Roy, before we set any more dates, I think we'd better have a talk with them about the way Jesus was ill spoken of last night."

"We could lose them both if we aren't careful."

"Maybe so, but I have to make sure they understand the truth about Jesus. I should've spoken up last night. It's been eating at me ever since. I don't know about you, but I have to talk to Lois about being saved."

Roy shook his head. "I can't do that with Murielle. I know what'll happen. I know what'll happen if you talk to Lois, too. Please, Pat. Think it over before you do anything foolish."

"Foolish? Talking to Lois about her need to know the Lord is foolish?"

Roy stood up. "I've got to get back to work."

"I've got to go too," Patrick said, rising from the table.

Neither man spoke as they walked back toward the building where Roy was working. When they reached the construction site, Roy said, "Thanks for lunch."

"You're welcome," Patrick said. "This will all work out, Roy. You just wait and see."

Roy nodded and walked away.

It was almost two-thirty when Dr. Patrick O'Brien entered the Cook County Hospital and began his rounds. He had been at the hospital a little more than an hour when he was coming out of a patient's room and saw the head nurse hurrying toward him.

"Dr. O'Brien, you're needed in the surgical wing."

"I don't understand, Mrs. Stevens. I have no operations scheduled today."

"No, no. What I mean is, you're wanted in the surgical wing. A friend of yours was just brought in on an emergency. His name is Roy Domire. He fell while working on that new ten-story building on North Avenue. He's in critical condition but conscious. They're about to do surgery on him, and he's asking for you, Dr. O'Brien."

Patrick's heart was in his throat as he ran through the hospital to the surgical wing. He paused at the desk long enough to find out which room Roy was in, then hurried in to find two nurses preparing the patient for surgery.

"Here he is now, Mr. Domire," said one nurse.

Patrick drew up beside the table and asked the nurses, "Who's doing the surgery?"

"Dr. Yarrow."

Patrick nodded, then took one nurse aside. "What's the diagnosis?"

"He's bleeding internally and has some broken bones. Beyond that we're not sure."

Dr. William Yarrow burst through the door, removing his frock. When he saw Patrick, he said, "Are you scheduled in here, Doctor?"

"No, sir. Mr. Domire is a friend of mine. I'll talk to him while you're getting ready."

Yarrow nodded and turned toward one of the closets next to the medicine cupboard.

Patrick stepped up to the table, and one of the nurses said, "Doctor, I have to begin chloroform immediately."

Before she put the cloth to Roy's nose, Patrick leaned over him and said, "I'll be praying for you."

Roy swallowed hard and said in a weak voice, "It won't do any good. I'm going to die, Pat. And…I know why. I was perturbed at you for want—wanting to square things with the girls. The Holy Spirit was convicting my heart…and I was rebelling. I was going to go my own way. God knew it. That's when I lost my balance and fell. This is God's chastisement, like you said."

"Excuse me, Doctor," the nurse said, "but I have to administer the chloroform."

Patrick stepped back, then went to Dr. Yarrow. "What do you think, Doctor?"

"The diagnosis isn't good. I'm afraid he's torn apart inside. I'll do my best to save his life, but at best his chances are slim."

"Yes, sir. I know you'll bring him through it if you can. I have some rounds to do yet. I'll be back later."

Patrick's heart felt like lead as he moved from room to room, looking in on his patients. When he had finished his rounds, he returned to the surgical wing and found Dr. Yarrow standing in the hall, talking to the nurse who had administered the chloroform to Roy. The nurse saw him coming, said something to Yarrow, then hurried away.

Yarrow's features were drawn as he said, "there was no chance for him, Doctor. He was hemorrhaging profusely. He died on the table. I'm sorry."

Tears flooded Patrick's eyes. "No reason for you to be sorry, Doctor. His death was no fault of yours."

"I know, but he was your friend. I'm sorry we couldn't save him."

Patrick nodded. "Me, too."

Moments later Dr. Patrick O'Brien left the hospital, his head lowered as tears ran down his cheeks.

Early on the evening of December 31, another blizzard swept down on the plains and mountains of Wyoming, Colorado, and Montana territories.

Lantern light in the Cheyenne City terminal building was barely visible from the train as it chugged into the depot and came to a halt. Flames flickered in lanterns on posts in the depot, giving off what little light they could. The oncoming night was a shifting, blinding dusk of black, white, and gray against the chilling wind.

Conductor Bart Wilson bent his head into the wind as he stepped off the train with a lantern in hand and directed passengers toward the terminal building. They covered their faces against the stinging wind-driven snow as they trudged toward the dim lights of the terminal.

Engineer Wally Forbes slid down out of the cab while his fireman made ready for new wood and coal to be loaded in the coal car. Two men braved the storm as they prepared to fill the engine's water tank.

Forbes and Wilson met near the engine, and both looked toward a large barn nearby where two huge doors were swung open. They could see the supply wagons emerging and heading toward the freight cars. The snow immediately began to coat the men, horses, and wagons in white.

"I'll see to the wagons, Wally!" Wilson shouted above the wail of the wind. "You go ahead and see Mr. Culver!"

Forbes hurried toward the terminal building and saw Max Culver just coming out of the Union Pacific Railroad superintendent's office.

"Good evening, sir," said Forbes, moving toward him. He saw that Culver was carrying his coat and hat. "No need to go out, sir. Bart Wilson is overseeing the unloading."

"All right. Come on into my office."

When Forbes had shed his coat, muffler, and cap, they sat down together.

"Bad one, eh?" Culver said.

"Might say that."

"Where were you when you ran into it?"

"Just inside the Wyoming border. Everything was clear all across Nebraska. Have they been able to move the wagons since we were in here a week ago?"

"Nope. We had a pretty good storm a few days ago, but the problem now is half weather and half Indians."

"Indians trying to rob the wagon supply trains?"

"Exactly. They're on the verge of starvation. Have to have a troop escort to get the supply wagons to the general stores across southern Wyoming. But the Indians are attacking ranches and farms when the weather is good, so the army has to keep the cavalry after them. There's no way the troops can escort the wagons and defend civilians at the same time."

Forbes shook his head. "That's a real problem."

"A big one. It looks like some of the forts up north are going to send some troops here so the men from Fort Russell and Fort Sanders can escort the supply wagons westward. What we need now is a break in the weather."

"Well, I sure hope it comes. Those folks out there must be about to pull their hair out."

"It has to be getting rough. We've got the supplies you brought in last week ready to go, and now with the load that just arrived we can really stock up their shelves if we can get the stuff to them."

Wally Forbes pulled his ear. "Maybe someday Union Pacific can lay tracks from here to Evanston, then we wouldn't need wagons to carry supplies anymore."

"Yeah," said Culver, smiling broadly. "Wouldn't that be good? I'm sure we'll do it. Someday."

CHAPTER SIX

On January 2, 1871, the blizzard blew eastward into Dakota, Nebraska, and Kansas, leaving clear skies and subzero temperatures in Wyoming, Colorado, and Montana.

Late in the afternoon, Chief Two Moons and a band of his warriors rode into the Crow village after a day of hunting. Anxious eyes watched from inside tepees. But only three pack horses carried game; the other nine bore no burden.

Braving the cold, the other young men of the village came out of the tepees to help dress out the carcasses.

Two Moons slid off his horse and saw Broken Wing emerge from the tepee of the aged warrior, Walking Buffalo. Broken Wing smiled at his father, then hurried to the chief's tepee and gave his mother his arm as she walked through the deep snow to see her husband.

Two Moons greeted his squaw and fourteen-year-old son. "We did not come home with much. Two deer; one antelope. But we will go out again tomorrow. We must keep hunting. The grain supply we have in store grows smaller each moon." He paused to look toward Walking Buffalo's tepee, then spoke to Broken Wing. "You are keeping the fire going for Walking Buffalo, my son?"

"Yes, Father. He is still not well. The medicine men cannot find what is wrong. He is very weak."

Sweet Blossom touched her husband's arm. "Sweet Blossom and two other squaws have been with Walking Buffalo today. You must come and see him. He cannot get off his pallet. I have not told Broken Wing, but now we know why Walking Buffalo is so weak."

"May Broken Wing come with you and Father? Please, Mother?"

"You may," Sweet Blossom said.

Two Moons turned his horse over to a young brave and walked toward the tepee with his family.

Walking Buffalo was more than ninety grasses in age. His squaw, Little Flower, had died last winter quite suddenly. The medicine men said her heart had worn out and simply stopped beating.

To Sweet Blossom, Two Moons said, "Before we go in, tell Two Moons why Walking Buffalo is so weak."

"Walking Buffalo has been eating only a small part of the food allowed him so he could leave more for others. He has been placing food in other tepees when no one was in them…especially tepees where children live. He wanted the children to have more food. We took food to Walking Buffalo at high sun today, but he refused to eat. He said we must give it to the children or others in the village who are hungry."

Two Moons laid a hand on Broken Wing's shoulder and said, "Take your mother to our tepee. I want to talk to Walking Buffalo alone."

Two Moons opened the flap of Walking Buffalo's tepee and ducked inside. The fire in the center of the tepee sent smoke spiraling to the opening above. The silver-haired warrior lay on his pallet, wrapped in heavy blankets. He looked up at his chief and tried to smile.

Two Moons knelt beside the old warrior and laid a hand on his shoulder. "Sweet Blossom told me what you have been doing."

Walking Buffalo averted his eyes from Two Moons's gaze and remained silent.

The chief squeezed Walking Buffalo's shoulder. "Two Moons appreciates Walking Buffalo's willingness to sacrifice for others, but Walking Buffalo must eat his share…must keep up his strength."

Walking Buffalo looked up at his chief and said, "It is best that Walking Buffalo die. He is no longer of use to the people of his village, nor to Chief Two Moons. He will let others have food…and pass on to walk with Little Flower and the Sky People among the stars."

Two Moons shook his head. "Walking Buffalo has much wisdom and is needed to help his chief with important decisions…and to teach the young braves about life. Walking Buffalo must eat and live."

The wrinkled one's eyes showed that Two Moons's words had touched him deeply. His lips quivered as he said, "Thank you, my chief. But with food and game so scarce, it is best that Walking Buffalo die that others might have food."

"Not true. We brought in two deer and an antelope just now. This will help. And we will go out to hunt again tomorrow. It is your chief's desire that you eat. He needs your wisdom and counsel. Walking Buffalo must not die."

"You are sincere, I know. This pleases me very much. For your sake and the sake of my people, I will eat."

A slow smile spread over the chief's features. "This is good. Two Moons will be back shortly."

Sweet Blossom and Broken Wing were in their tepee when Two Moons slipped through the opening and said, "Walking Buffalo has agreed to eat."

"This is wonderful news," Sweet Blossom said. "I will prepare him a bowl of venison broth to start."

A short time later, Two Moons, Sweet Blossom, and Broken Wing emerged from their tepee with Broken Wing carrying a lidded pot with steam escaping around the edges.

Word of Walking Buffalo's sacrifice that others might have food had spread quickly throughout the village. And though it was bitter cold, the people gathered outside the old warrior's tepee and watched as their chief, his squaw, and son entered. The people called out to Walking Buffalo, telling him they wanted him to live.

The silver-haired warrior wept tears of joy as Sweet Blossom spoonfed the broth to him.

"See, Walking Buffalo?" she said. "The Crow people love you."

At noon on Saturday, January 14, Hannah Cooper and Jacob Kates watched the crew of the wagon supply train from Cheyenne City, with the help of the cavalry escort from Fort Russell and Fort Sanders, unload goods and stack boxes in the storeroom.

The store's shelves had become frightfully bare. Hannah and Jacob had been forced to turn customers away, but the arrival of the wagons had enlivened the whole town and fort.

Many who had gathered to watch the unloading volunteered to help Jacob stock the shelves. By the time the wagons were unloaded, customers were crowding into the store.

Late in the afternoon of the same day, the Wells Fargo stage pulled into town. The only passengers were going on to Evanston, but it had been nearly two weeks since a stage had been able to get through, and a bulky canvas bag of mail was left in Curly Wesson's hands as the stage hurried on.

Curly carried the bag into the stage office and plunked it on the counter. He was pulling out handfuls of letters and small packages when the door opened and his wife came in with a grocery bag in each arm.

Judy Charley smiled, exposing the single tooth in her

upper gum, and said, "Well, honey pot, thangs are shore lookin' better around here. I got groceries an' you got mail!"

"Ain't that the truth!"

Curly sorted the mail while Judy took the groceries to their upstairs apartment. When she returned to the office, she offered to help.

"You could finish doin' this sortin'," Curly said, "'cause I gotta deliver a letter in a hurry." He lifted an envelope off the counter and held it so his wife could see it. "Jus' take a look at this!"

Judy moved closer, squinted, and said, "Oh, my! A letter from Dr. Patrick O'Brien to his ma and pa! Honey bucket, you'd better run that letter over to Doc and Edie right now!"

Edie O'Brien was at the desk in the clinic office when Curly came through the door, puffing from the cold. "Shore is nippy out there, Miss Edie," he said, closing the door quickly behind him. "Is Doc in?"

"He's making a house call at the Jones Ranch a few miles west of town. I expect him back shortly. Are you not feeling well, Curly?"

"I'm fine, but I have somethin' both of you will wanna see." He took the envelope from his coat pocket and handed it to her. "But I guess you'll jist have the edge on Doc."

Edie's eyes widened as she looked at the envelope, and her heart started to hammer.

"Me and Judy hope it's good news, Miss Edie. We been prayin'."

Edie managed a tremulous smile. "I know. Thank you."

When Curly was gone, Edie just stared at the envelope for a minute, then got up and paced around the office, tapping the letter against her fingers. Suddenly she stopped and said aloud, "Edie, this is silly. Go on and read it."

She sat down again at the desk and bowed her head. "Lord, please give me the grace to accept whatever is in this letter. You alone can strengthen me. I'm trusting You to help me."

A calmness came over her, and she picked up the letter opener and slit the envelope, then took out the letter with trembling fingers.

Sunday, December 18, 1870
Dear Mom and Dad,

I just got home from church this evening and wanted to get this letter written tonight so I can post it in the morning.

There is bad news and there is good news. I am going to give you the bad news first, for it is because of this that there is good news. The bad news is that my friend Roy Domire is dead. He was at his construction job on Wednesday and fell several stories to the ground. I was with him at the hospital just before he died. He said he knew he was dying because he had strayed from the Lord and stubbornly refused to get right with Him. He said he knew it was God's chastisement.

Your last letter had been pricking my heart, and I was starting to clearly see the error of my ways. When the Lord took Roy, I could almost see the "paddle" in God's hand, ready to chastise me for my sins, too.

I want you to know that it is all over between Lois and me. I never replied to your question about her. No, Lois is not a Christian. In fact, on Thursday—the day after Roy was killed—I went to Lois and gave her the gospel, saying I wanted her to be saved. She laughed in my face.

I broke it off right there. That night, after getting on my knees and asking the Lord's forgiveness for my backsliding (1 John 1:9), I went to the parsonage and asked the pastor to forgive me for having forsaken the church. He did, of course, and it sure felt wonderful to be back in the services today! The people were all so warm toward me.

Now I am asking the two of you to forgive me. And I know you will. Thank you!

Mom and Dad, I am leaving Chicago for Cheyenne City on January 6. Dad, I hope you still want me to be your partner, then take over the practice when you retire. If not, maybe you'll hire me as the clinic's janitor. Either way, I'll be close to both of you, which is where I want to be.

Wells Fargo tells me I will arrive in Fort Bridger on January 20, barring bad weather. I can hardly wait to see both of you and give you great big hugs! I love you with all of my forgiven heart.

Your loving son,
Patrick

Edie had to pause every few seconds to remove her spectacles and wipe the tears away. When at last she finished the letter, she dropped her head into her hands and let the tears of rejoicing flow. She suddenly raised her head, lifted her streaming eyes heavenward, and said, "Dear Lord Jesus, thank You for performing the miracle in our son's heart and life. Please forgive me for my doubts and fears. Help me not to forget that You have not given us the spirit of fear; but of power, and of love, and of a sound mind."

Anxious to share the happy news with her husband, Edie began pacing from window to window, scanning Main Street for sight of his buggy.

Only a few minutes had passed when the door opened and Dorothy Wellman came in with her son. The little boy was wailing, and a small towel was wrapped around his left hand. At the same instant, Edie saw Doc pull up to the hitch rail in his buggy.

"Come in, Dorothy," Edie said. "I saw Doc just drive up. What did Tommy do to his hand?"

"He cut it bad, Edie. He was playing with one of my paring knives when I wasn't looking."

Edie picked up the wailing boy and held him close. "It'll be all right, Tommy. Dr. O'Brien is here now. Let's get you in the back room."

Doc came in as Edie was carrying the boy toward the back door of the office. She looked past the worried mother and said, "Tommy's cut his hand."

Doc cleaned the cut and took stitches as Dorothy looked on. Edie held the little boy and talked soothingly to him. When Tommy's hand had been bandaged and Dorothy had carried him out the door, Doc turned to his wife and said, "Something's happened to you, dearie."

"What do you mean?"

Doc chuckled. "You look like the cat that swallowed the canary. C'mon, what's happened?"

Tears spilled down Edie's cheeks as she opened the desk drawer where she had placed Patrick's letter. "It's from Patrick," she said, her voice cracking.

"Well, it has to be good news because of the look in your Irish eyes."

"It is," she said, sniffling, and placed the letter in his hand.

Doc took a chair and began to read. Edie sat down next to him.

When he had read just a few lines, Doc cried out, "Oh, Mom! Oh, Mom!"

"Go on, darling. Keep reading."

After Doc finished, he and Edie wrapped their arms around each other and sobbed happily. When they could make their voices work again, they had a shouting praise meeting. The door opened and Sundi Lindgren came in. Her sky blue eyes showed puzzlement as they turned their attention to her.

"Doc…Edie…what's wrong?" she said. "I was passing by the office and heard you crying…or crying and shouting. I thought I'd better come in and see if you were all right."

"Oh, honey!" Edie said. "We're more than all right! We've never been happier!"

"That's right!" said Doc, thumbing tears from his cheeks.

"Well, how about letting me in on it?"

Doc and Edie told Sundi the story, and she rejoiced with them over the good news. At closing time, the O'Briens rushed to the parsonage and told Pastor Kelly and Rebecca, then went to the Cooper apartment and told Hannah, her children, and Jacob Kates. By midmorning the next day, everyone in town and fort had heard about Patrick's letter.

It was almost noon when Edie looked up from the desk in the office to see Colonel and Mrs. Ross Bateman come in. Sylvia's eyes sparkled.

"Good morning, Edie! Ross and I wanted to stop in and tell you how happy we are about Patrick. I know you have to be so excited. Did you and Doc sleep at all last night?"

Edie laughed. "I didn't do too well, but Doc slept like a log. But then nothing ever keeps him awake. I've told him that sometimes he sleeps so deep that when morning comes it's almost like he's had a resurrection!"

The clinic door opened and Doc came out with a young mother carrying her baby. She thanked Doc for his service and covered the baby's face to go outside. Colonel Batemen opened the door for her.

After a few minutes of talking about Patrick, Doc looked at the colonel and said, "So how goes the Indian problem?"

"Not good. We're still receiving reports almost daily of attacks, some as close as thirty miles from Fort Bridger. People have been massacred and their animals taken. I've had to beef up the size of the patrols, and I've had them out everyday except when the blizzards have been on us. I hope the show of force will keep the hostiles from attacking any outlying areas around here. Of course, I'm also keeping a strong force here at the fort in case they decide to attack the fort or the town."

"My heart goes out to the Indians, Colonel," Doc said. "I don't condone what they're doing, of course, but I hate to see them going hungry."

"I feel the same way, Doc."

"I wish we could feed all of them," Sylvia said, "but I don't know how we could ever do that."

Under a brilliant, clear sky the next morning, Chief Two Moons gathered his warriors about him in the center of the village. Arctic air filled the January morning with frost. Mercifully, there was only a slight breeze. Smoke rose from dozens of tepees, the narrow plumes lifting skyward in almost straight lines.

Two Moons told his men he would again take half the braves to hunt game and leave the other half to protect the village from attack. The Blackfoot and the Shoshoni might decide to come and take what food stores the Crow had.

The chief divided the hunting party into four large bands and reminded them they might have to travel two or three moons to find enough game to supply the village with meat. Two Moons had made the hunting bands as large as possible in case they encountered the Blackfoot or Shoshoni. Each band would go a different direction, and Two Moons would lead one of the bands himself.

The hunters spent a few moments telling their families good-bye, and Two Moons spoke tender, comforting words to his wife then turned to his son.

"Father, may I go on the hunt with you?" Broken Wing said.

The chief slowly shook his head. "No, my son. You are still too young to be a hunter."

"But, Father, you have seen what a good shot I am with my rifle. I can shoot as straight as the warriors."

Two Moons smiled. "I know my son is an excellent shot, but it takes more than this to be a good hunter. You know that every Crow young man must qualify as a warrior before he is able to be in a hunting party. And you must be eighteen grasses to begin training as a warrior."

"But Father, I thought that as the chief's son, I—"

"I cannot grant special privileges, my son. It is not in my power to change laws that came down from our ancient fathers."

Walking Buffalo stepped close and laid a gentle hand on Broken Wing's shoulder, and the boy looked into the man's tired old eyes. "The Great Spirit wants Broken Wing to stay and watch over his mother until he is of age to be a warrior and a hunter."

Two Moons looked at his son, and said, "Walking Buffalo speaks truth, my son."

Broken Wing nodded and said, "Broken Wing will do as the Great Spirit wishes."

The old man's face crinkled as he smiled. "Walking Buffalo knows such a fine boy will always do what is right."

The hunters mounted up to ride out, and Broken Wing stood between his mother and Walking Buffalo. Before Two Moons led his party out of the village, he looked back at his wife and son. Broken Wing put an arm around his mother's shoulder, and Two Moons nodded at him and rode out with the hunting party following.

Broken Wing watched his father ride away in the world of frozen white, and his mind went to the Great Spirit. Chris Cooper had told him that the Great Spirit had a Son whose name was Jesus Christ, and the only way to come to the Great Spirit was through His Son. Chris Cooper had also reminded Broken Wing that the Crow called the Great Spirit the Sky Father…and that one cannot be a father unless he has a child.

This had intrigued Broken Wing. Standing there, watching the hunting party ride away from the village, he told himself he would talk some more with Chris Cooper about this.

CHAPTER SEVEN

At Fort Bridger, the army patrols were almost ready to pull out. It was Saturday, and the officers' children, wearing brightly colored knit stocking caps, were with their mothers inside the stockade to watch the patrols ride out. The brilliant colors dotted the crowd as families huddled close and spent a few last minutes with husbands and fathers.

Frosty plumes of air lifted with every breath from humans and horses. The sound of stamping feet could be heard across the yard as they all tried to keep their feet warm. The men would be away for only two or three days, but to the waiting families, two or three days was an eternity.

A bright winter sun shone in the clear sky and gave the snow-covered ground the appearance of millions of twinkling diamonds. But a clear sky in the morning could change into a howling blizzard by evening.

Lieutenant Dobie Carlin, second in command in Captain John Fordham's patrol unit, came out of the infirmary. His wife and son were waiting for him on the porch. He placed his arms around them, and they walked across the compound to where Captain Fordham stood with his wife and children.

Dobie smiled at his commanding officer and said, "Doc Blayney says Mike and Brad can ride with us, Captain. He doesn't think it's anything serious."

Betsy Fordham glanced at her husband. "What's wrong with them, John?"

"They were both feeling a little weak and light-headed when they got up this morning. I sent them to Doc Blayney. Sure didn't want to take them out on patrol if they were coming down with something."

Moments later, Mike Serra and Brad Liston emerged from the infirmary, and the men in all units were told to mount up.

Hugs and kisses were liberally given as the officers reassured their families that all would be well. Then they mounted up and rode out of the fort. The gates immediately closed behind the last patrol. Fordham's unit headed east in the cold sunlight.

Inside the fort, the officers' children were eager to spend a little time playing outside while the sun was shining. They had been pent up for days on end while the wild wind blew and the snow fell. The children waited long enough for their mothers to give some necessary admonishments, then hurried off to play.

The wives chatted with each other for a few minutes, then parted to crunch through the snow to their warm homes and the chores that awaited them. Staying busy helped to pass the time as they waited and prayed in their hearts for the safety of their loved ones on patrol.

In the town, Deputy Marshal Jack Bower rode along Main Street toward the marshal's office. Everything around him was white and beautiful, glowing with a pearly sheen in the early morning sun. The limbs of the bare trees were softened by cushions of snow, and the street was a broad, unobstructed thoroughfare of white.

Bower rode slowly along the street and spoke to people as they greeted him. He was surprised to see his boss on the boardwalk up ahead with Heidi Lindgren on his arm. He veered toward them, hauled up and said, "Good morning, Miss Heidi."

"Good morning, Jack," Heidi said with a smile.

"Ah…pardon me, boss, but aren't you supposed to be at home recuperating?"

Marshal Lance Mangum cleared his throat. "Well, Deputy Bower, I can't stay home forever. It's time I get out and around a bit."

"Well, sir, I can understand your wanting to walk your sweetie to her shop, but don't you overdo it."

Lance grinned. "I'm not simply walking Heidi to work, Jack. I'm also going to work, myself."

"Going to work! Now look, boss, it's much too soon for that."

"I won't do anything but paperwork, but I need to be back in the office again."

"Has Dr. O'Brien approved this?"

"I…ah…I haven't really asked him for his approval. I feel good enough to do it, so there's no reason to bother Doc about it."

Jack set his worried gaze on Heidi. "What do you think about this, ma'am?"

Heidi looked at Lance and sighed. "I told him I wished he would wait another couple of weeks, but since we're not married yet, I can't boss him."

"Did you say 'since you're not married *yet?*'"

Heidi giggled. "That's what I said."

"Why, this is the first time I've heard anything about wedding bells. When did this happen?"

"Night before last," Lance said. "I popped the question, caught her in a weak moment, and she said yes."

Heidi laughed and lightly clipped Lance's jaw. "Weak moment, eh? That's what you think! I set the trap and you stumbled into it."

"Wait till I tell Julianna!" Jack said. "You two make a beautiful couple…almost as beautiful a couple as we do!"

They had a good laugh, then Heidi said, "Have you and Julianna set a wedding date yet?"

"No, but we will soon. Very soon. We'll probably be an old married couple by the time you two tie the knot. Well, boss, I'll see you at the office. I'd better go get a fire started in the stove."

"You do that."

Jack tipped his hat at Heidi and rode away.

Lance and Heidi continued on down the street and entered the dress shop. He took a few minutes to get a fire going in the potbellied stove, then pulled her into his embrace.

"The Lord has been so good to me," Lance said. "Not only did He spare my life, but He also saved me and gave me the most beautiful and wonderful woman in the world."

Heidi grinned. "Jack would argue with you on that last part."

"Well, Jack has the right to be wrong about some things. Miss Julianna is a lovely young lady, but she can't compare with you." Lance kissed her soundly, held her close for a moment, then said, "I'd better get to work."

That afternoon at the general store, Hannah Cooper was sitting on her stool behind the counter while Jacob took care of customers. Her three oldest children were at school. Patty Ruth was at the Fordham house inside the fort, playing with Belinda.

Hannah found it difficult to stay on the stool when customers were at the counter. Jacob had tried to talk her into staying upstairs in the apartment where she would be more comfortable, but she liked to feel a part of things and converse with her customers.

Dr. O'Brien had all but ordered her to stay off her swollen

feet, and so she stayed on the stool most of the time. But the hard stool was not very comfortable, and periodically Hannah got up and walked around a bit. When customer activity became heavier than usual, and Hannah saw that Jacob was swamped at the counter, she joined him to help. She soon wished she had taken Glenda Williams and Julie Powell up on their offer that morning to work behind the counter.

Hannah tired quickly as she worked at Jacob's side. He and customers alike gently scolded her until she returned with a sigh to her perch and tried to stay put.

A few moments later, Jacob noticed Hannah kneading the small of her back with her fist. Soon customer traffic lessened, and when there was a complete lull in business, Jacob turned to her and said, "Miss Hannah, how about letting me walk you up the stairs, and you lie down on your bed?"

She adjusted her position on the stool and said, "I'll be all right. I'd really rather stay here."

He grinned at her and shook his head. "You really are the stubborn sort, aren't you?"

"I don't mean to be. It's just that it's so lonely up there in the apartment."

Jacob looked toward the front door. All seemed quiet on the boardwalk outside. "Excuse me a moment," he said. "If anyone comes in before I return, have them pick out their goods and put them on the counter. I won't be long."

"What are you up to?" Hannah said. "There's a sneaky gleam in your eye."

The little man chuckled. "Just remember…if anybody comes in, I'll be right back."

The store remained quiet after Jacob disappeared into his quarters at the rear of the building. Hannah kneaded the small of her back again and scanned the shelves she could see from her perch. "We need to restock some items," she murmured, making a mental note to have Chris, Mary Beth, and B.J.

restock the shelves when they came in from school.

She heard the door to Jacob's quarters open, and he reappeared. He was smiling and still had the gleam in his eye.

"Jacob Kates, what are you up to?" Hannah asked, a curious smile on her lips.

"You'll see." He reached out both hands. "Here. Let me help you off the stool."

While she stood there, Jacob picked up the stool, marched to the back of the store, and vanished again. Hannah shook her head in puzzlement, smiling to herself.

Within a few seconds, Jacob appeared, carrying a new stool that had a cushioned seat and a back with the same thick padding and fabric.

Hannah's eyes widened, and her hand went to her mouth. "Jacob! Wherever did you get this?"

"I've been working on it for some time. I was saving it for your birthday, but April 12 is a ways off. So I decided I'd go ahead and give it to you now. Happy birthday, m'lady!" Jacob placed the stool behind the counter.

"Oh, Jacob, it's perfect! And exactly what I needed!"

She surprised him by planting a kiss on his cheek. His face beamed and blushed a bright red. "It was my pleasure, Miss Hannah. A small token of appreciation for all you've done for me."

"You are such a joy to this family," Hannah said, wiping tears from her cheeks.

Jacob took her hand and ceremoniously led her to the stool. "All right. Let's try it out, eh? C'mon. Climb aboard."

Hannah leaned back against the comfortable padding and sighed. "Jacob, this is wonderful! You may never get me off it."

"That's the idea. Just enjoy it, Miss Hannah. It was made for you out of a heart full of love."

A cold blast of air hit them as the front door opened and the three older Cooper children came in, followed by a couple of customers. All three headed for their mother to give her a hug and a kiss.

"Mama, where did you get that stool?" Mary Beth asked.

"Uncle Jacob made it for me. Isn't it nice?"

"Very nice," Chris and B.J. said.

"Uncle Jacob has been working on it for some time. He was going to give it to me for my birthday, but he decided I could use it now."

Jacob turned from the customers he was helping and smiled. "Like it?" he said to the children.

They nodded vigorously and thanked him for being so kind to their mother.

"Your mother has been more than kind to me," he said.

More customers were coming in. Among them was Mandy Carver, who smiled at Hannah and waved.

Hannah waved back then ran her gaze over the faces of her children. "I need you three to stock some shelves. Uncle Jacob has been pretty busy today and hasn't had time."

"Sure," Chris said. "I've got to run upstairs for a minute. I'll be right back."

"Me too," Mary Beth said.

"Well, I'll get started," B.J. said. He took off his stocking cap and coat and laid them behind his mother's stool. "Should I start with the sugar and flour shelves? They're usually the first ones to run low."

"That'll be fine," said Hannah, looking at him with misty eyes.

"What's wrong, Mama?"

"Come here and let me hug you again." She held her youngest son close to her heart and said, "I just saw your father's smile on your lips. You're reminding me more and more of Papa, B.J. Not only in physical resemblance but in personality."

B.J., who would be nine years old on March 13, grinned and said, "I'm proud to look like Papa, and to be like him, too.

Other than Jesus, Papa is my greatest hero."

"Hero? What do you know about heroes?"

"A lot. Mr. Carver has taught us boys in his Sunday school class about heroes in the Bible…like Abel, Moses, Abraham, David, Elijah, and Paul. But he said our greatest hero should be the Lord Jesus. When he told us that, I raised my hand and asked him if it was all right to have other heroes, like our fathers. He said yes. So…next to Jesus, my greatest hero is Papa."

Hannah wiped tears from her cheeks. "That's wonderful, honey. I'm so glad."

B.J. took off for the storeroom.

Hannah was suddenly aware that Mandy Carver was standing close by. Mandy moved closer, smiling broadly. "Miz Hannah, I couldn't help overhearin' your conversation with B.J. Abe tol' me about B.J. sayin' in Sunday school class that his papa was his next greatest hero after the Lord Jesus. He's a fine boy, Miz Hannah."

"That he is."

Mandy took a step closer, her brow furrowing. "Miz Hannah, is B.J. still havin' a hard time over his papa's death?"

Hannah nodded. "All four of them are. And for me it gets harder every time I look at B.J., the way he's resembling Solomon more all the time. And when Solomon's personality comes out in him, or Solomon's smile curves his lips, it makes it harder." She paused. "Well…it makes it harder in one way, but easier in another way, because it's almost like having Solomon here again."

Mandy bent over and hugged Hannah's neck. "You are such a brave lady, Miz Hannah. If Abe was to be taken, I don' know if I could hold up like you do."

"You could with God's grace, Mandy."

On the second day out from the fort, Captain Fordham and his thirty-two men awakened to the sound of the wind slapping at the canvas walls of their tents, though they had pitched them on the lee side of a huge pile of boulders. When they stepped out into the biting wind, the sky overhead was clear, but clouds were gathering on the western horizon.

They quickly built fires, and the men assigned to cook duty began preparing breakfast while others tended to the horses.

Lieutenant Carlin stepped up to Captain Fordham. "Sir, I looked in on Serra and Liston when I first got up. They're both running a fever. They're having trouble breathing, and they have wracking coughs."

Fordham shook his head. "I had a feeling this might happen. I wish I had left them at the fort. All they can do now is stay with the patrol and ride. There's no other choice."

"Yes, sir. We sure can't leave them here."

At breakfast, Fordham and Carlin sat together in the snow beside one of the fires and talked of spiritual things, including Pastor Andy Kelly's recent sermon on how Christians should love one another and sacrifice for each other when necessary.

When breakfast was over, the soldiers broke camp, saddled up, and continued on patrol through a world of white. Two of the pack mules were already carrying deer that had been shot the day before.

The sun's glare off the snow was blinding as it lifted higher into the azure sky. The relentless wind blew snow devils across the tops of the drifts, and the cloud bank in the west continued to increase in size.

Fordham and Carlin led the patrol, and Mike Serra and Brad Liston were directly behind them so Carlin could keep an eye on them. Both rode hunched over, their heads drooping listlessly.

The patrol had been in their saddles some two hours and were moving through a shallow valley when they saw a large Blackfoot hunting party on horseback charge over a snow-covered mound. They yapped like dogs as their rifles blazed.

Fordham pointed to a nearby stand of trees and brush and shouted, "Take cover over there!"

The army horses flung snow toward the sky as they galloped to the trees and brush. The men jumped out of their saddles and returned fire as the Indians drew near.

Carlin saw to Serra and Liston, making sure they were in as safe a spot as possible, then he bellied down behind a clump of bushes beside his captain and began blasting away at the enemy.

The battle raged, with both soldiers and warriors going down. Suddenly the hammer on Carlin's revolver clicked on a spent shell. When he rolled onto his side to reload, his eye caught movement directly behind them.

A fierce-eyed Blackfoot warrior had managed to sneak into the stand of trees and brush and was rushing toward Captain Fordham with his knife drawn.

Carlin dropped his empty gun and lunged for the warrior, driving his shoulder into him and knocking him off his feet.

They struggled in the snow, and Carlin gripped the wrist that held the knife. Fordham was about to go to the lieutenant's aid when in his peripheral vision he saw two warriors charging him on foot, their guns ready. He whirled and fired, dropping one Indian in his tracks, but the other one kept coming. It took two more shots to stop him.

Carlin still had a grip on the Indian's wrist, but the Indian was fighting back for all he was worth. Suddenly, Carlin lost his grip and felt the blade rip through his coat sleeve and bite into skin. The Indian swung the knife at him again, but this time

Carlin dodged it and sent a stiff punch to the Indian's nose. They were on their knees in the snow, and the blow rocked the Indian backward.

The warrior grunted, shook his head, and swung the knife in a deadly arc. Carlin avoided the blade again and seized the Indian's wrist, and this time twisted it violently. The Indian let out a painful grunt, and Carlin wrenched the knife from him and drove the blade into the Indian's chest. The Blackfoot collapsed and lay still.

The breath sawed in and out of Carlin's lungs as he staggered to his feet and saw his captain blasting away at more Indians. He dropped to his knees beside Fordham, picked up his revolver, and began to reload.

"Good work, Dobie," Fordham said. "If you hadn't been so quick, he'd have driven that knife into my back. Thanks for risking your life to save mine!"

Dobie snapped the fully loaded cylinder into place, fired at an Indian aboard a pinto, and dropped him into the snow. "Captain," he said, still breathing hard, "you'd have done the same for me."

"You're right about that." Fordham glanced at Carlin and saw the bloody rip in the lieutenant's sleeve. "Lieutenant, you're wounded!"

Carlin fired another shot, then looked down at the sleeve. "Oh, yeah. Guess I forgot."

"You forgot?"

"Yeah. I mean yes, sir!"

The captain looked around. When he saw no more Blackfoot warriors for the moment, he said, "Get down and I'll wrap that cut."

Carlin bent low and pulled off his coat. His shirtsleeve was soaked with blood.

Amid shouting soldiers and yapping warriors, and while bullets whined around them, Captain Fordham used Carlin's bandanna to wrap his upper left arm. When he got it tied, he checked it and said, "I think that'll stop the bleeding. It doesn't seem to be too deep."

The pinned-down soldiers fought back bravely, but their small band was outnumbered, and the battle looked hopeless.

CHAPTER EIGHT

On the second day of hunting, Chief Two Moons and his band of warriors turned south, looking for game. Periodically they glanced westward across the frozen vastness to keep check on the dark clouds. The merciless wind clawed at them without letup.

Despair showed on the chief's dark face as he turned to subchief Black Bear, who rode next to him. When he started to speak, a gust of wind momentarily took his breath away.

"I do not want to turn back to the village with only four deer, but those dark clouds are coming quickly. What does Black Bear think?"

"We are far from the village. It is best we not be caught in a blizzard here."

Two Moons nodded. "It best we—"

Above the howl of the wind they heard the sound of rapid gunfire punctuated by whoops and shouts. The sounds were coming from the far side of a rise to their left.

"We go," said Two Moons, putting his horse to a trot in the deep snow.

The others followed and quickly drew up beside their chief, who had pulled rein at the crest of the rise to study the scene below. An army patrol unit was under attack by a large band of Blackfoot warriors.

"Subchief Wolf Fang," Two Moons said. "We must help the soldier coats."

The Crow warriors jacked cartridges into the chambers of their rifles and followed Two Moons down the snow-covered slope, then opened fire as they drew near the scene of the battle.

Wolf Fang's head whipped around at the sound. His eyes widened when he saw his warriors peeling off their horses. Shouting loudly, he galloped among his men and quickly led them away, leaving a scattering of warriors lying dead in the bloodstained snow.

Two Moons led his warriors among the trees and brush and was surprised to see Captain John Fordham and Lieutenant Dobie Carlin rise from behind a bush. He recognized many of the other soldier coats from Fort Bridger.

The soldiers waved their guns in the air and lifted a loud cheer for the Crow.

"Chief, are we glad to see you!" Fordham said. "They had us pinned down and outnumbered. If you hadn't come to our rescue, they would have killed us all."

"Two Moons glad we come along. Crow are friends to soldier coats."

Dobie Carlin told the captain he would check on the wounded, who were being attended by the other soldiers. The heavy, wind-driven clouds overhead blotted out the sun as Carlin trudged through the deep snow.

When Carlin had checked on each wounded man, he turned to Mike Serra and Brad Liston. They were unscathed from the battle, but the purple semicircles under their eyes were darker than ever, and their fevers had gone higher.

Dobie headed back to report his findings to the captain and came upon Corporal Wally Beemer, who was sitting in the snow, holding his head. "Are you wounded, Corporal?"

Beemer looked up with dull eyes and covered his mouth

as he coughed. "No, sir. I…I think I've got the same thing Mike and Brad have." He coughed again. It had the same wracking sound that plagued Serra and Liston.

Captain Fordham was still talking to Chief Two Moons when Carlin drew up and said, "Sir, Serra and Liston are getting worse, and now Corporal Beemer has the same thing. He's running a fever, coughing, and is quite weak. Four of the wounded men aren't hurt too bad. The other three—Sergeant Ryan, and Privates McKee and Wallace—desperately need a doctor."

The captain looked up at the darkening sky. "We need to head for the fort. I think another blizzard is coming."

The Indian chief nodded. "Captain John Fordham is right. Two Moons and warriors are riding for village. Big storm coming. We travel together?"

"We sure will, Chief. And the sooner we get started, the better."

The two leaders announced their plans to their men, and when the dead soldiers were draped over the backs of their horses and the wounded were tied in their saddles, the whole group headed southwest.

Riding, as usual, next to his lieutenant, John Fordham lifted his voice above the wail of the wind and said, "Thank you, again, Lieutenant, for saving my life. You could've gotten yourself killed."

Carlin grinned. "My dear brother in Christ, I was only doing what Pastor said I ought to do."

"To what Scripture are you referring?"

"First John 3:16, Captain. 'Hereby perceive we the love of God, because he laid down his life for us: and we ought to lay down our lives for the brethren.'"

The Captain smiled. "Once more I thank you."

In the late afternoon the long column of soldiers and Crow warriors spotted a small herd of antelope in a snow-laden draw. The antelope had seen them first and were on the run. Soldiers and warriors alike shouldered their rifles and fired into the fleeing herd. Two antelope went down, but the others soon disappeared.

Although no new snow had fallen, when darkness came the wind was bitter cold and blowing hard. The two leaders watched for some kind of windbreak, and soon they led their men into a dense forest and made camp.

The condition of Mike Serra, Brad Liston, and Wally Beemer was worsening, and now Sergeant Bo Maxwell was showing signs of the same sickness. Fordham and Carlin talked privately inside Fordham's tent.

"Sir, I'm afraid to say it, but I think these men have influenza."

Fordham ran splayed fingers through his hair. "I've been thinking the same thing. Only I was more afraid to say it than you were."

"If we're right, why didn't Dr. Blayney recognize it in Mike and Brad when he examined them?"

"Well, from what I know about influenza, the symptoms don't always show up when the afflicted person finds he isn't feeling quite right. I'm sure Dr. Blayney simply didn't have anything definite to go on when he checked them. If he could have examined them a few hours later, he would've been able to make a proper diagnosis."

"Shall we tell the rest of the men?"

"No. Since we aren't dead sure that's what it is, let's not start a panic. If it is influenza, every man in the patrol has been exposed to it. Let's leave it alone for now."

"All right, sir."

Dawn came after a night of howling wind and bitter cold. Sergeant Sean Ryan and Private Jed Wallace were found dead, and their bodies were draped over the backs of their horses. The sick and the other wounded were hoisted into their saddles, and the long column started out. It wasn't snowing yet, but the clouds were low and heavy, and the wind had not let up.

The warriors and soldiers bent their heads into the icy blast as the horses trudged through the deep snow. Some two hours later, the clouds released their heavy burden, and the wind-driven sleet stung the men's faces.

Hour after hour they plodded through the storm. The sick soldiers were getting worse, and the wounded weren't faring much better. At times the blowing snow and sleet was so blinding they could hardly tell which direction they were going.

It was about noon when Private Ernie McKee sagged in the saddle and started to fall. The rope that held his wrists to the saddle horn went taut, and the soldier riding next to him quickly seized his arm, calling out for the procession to stop.

By the time Captain Fordham could get the column halted, McKee was dead.

While McKee's body was being draped over his saddle and tied on, Captain Fordham drew his horse up beside Two Moons. "I'm not sure exactly where we are, Chief. I know you Indians have an uncanny sense of direction, even with the landmarks covered with snow. I have a feeling we might be drifting off course. What do you think?"

"Have been thinking we should steer a bit to the right."

"All right. You guide us."

A few hours later, there was a slight break in the storm, and the captain and his men saw familiar landmarks that told them they were now just a few miles from the Crow village.

The storm was soon in full force again as they slogged on. Moments later, Two Moons pulled his horse as close as possible beside Captain Fordham and lifted his voice to be heard. "We will reach village first. Two Moons think it best that soldier coats stay in village. If blizzard continue tomorrow, it be easier for Captain John Fordham and men to stay on course in that familiar territory."

"That's a very generous offer, Chief Two Moons. I accept the invitation. We'll pitch our tents in your village."

"No need. We make room in tepees. Much thicker and warmer than army tents."

Fordham thanked the chief and rode back among his men, announcing they would stay in the Crow village for the night and that Two Moons would make room for them in the tepees.

By the time they saw the Crow village through the blowing snow, Captain Fordham was glad he and his men weren't going to attempt the twelve-mile journey south to Fort Bridger.

As they entered the village, the Crow people ventured out into the storm to welcome their chief and his hunting party home. The other hunting parties had already returned and the people had been concerned about Chief Two Moons and his men.

Two Moons explained about the attack on the soldiers by Wolf Fang and his large band of warriors, and how he and his warriors had run them off. The chief then told his people of the sick and wounded soldiers, saying they needed to give them care, food, and shelter.

A thankful Captain Fordham told Two Moons that he and his people could have the two deer and the antelope the soldiers had killed.

The bodies of the dead soldiers were placed inside a tepee, and the sick and wounded were put in other tepees and cared for by the Crow men and women. Medicine men Running Buck and Red Wolf examined them but didn't try to treat them. They made sure the men were warm and comfortable but let the soldiers assigned to them by the captain do the actual tending.

The blizzard continued in all its fury as the weary soldiers bedded down. But the fires in the buffalo hide structures warmed their half-frozen bodies.

The Crow were very hospitable to their honored guests and did everything they could to meet their needs, making them as comfortable as possible.

Running Buck, Red Wolf, and the women who watched over the sick and wounded soldiers stayed at their sides through the night. At one point, the medicine men awakened Captain Fordham, asking for permission to use their ancient medicines to help reduce the fevers of the sick soldier coats. Fordham agreed.

On the same night, while the storm raged across Wyoming's mountains and plains, Pastor Andy Kelly entered the fort's mess hall with four townsmen who were members of the church. They were accompanied by Sergeant Del Frayne. The men with Kelly were Jack Bower, Gary Williams, Justin Powell, and Curly Wesson. Before Frayne could get the door closed, the wind blew snow in around them, scattering flakes on the floor.

Colonel Bateman met the preacher and shook his hand and said, "Thank you for coming, Pastor," then shook the hands of the other men.

There was a comparatively large group of military personnel gathered in the room, sitting at the tables.

Kelly's companions took seats at the tables as the colonel led the pastor to the front of the room. Kelly noted Betsy Fordham and her three children sitting toward the front, along with Donna Carlin and her son Travis.

"Folks," said Bateman, "as you know, I asked Pastor Kelly to come and talk to us, and to bring anyone of the church who could come with him. We need all the power of prayer we can get." With that, Bateman nodded to Kelly and stepped aside.

The preacher had slipped out of his heavy coat and removed his hat. He now stood with a small Bible in his hands. He ran his gaze to the stricken faces of the two officers' wives and children, giving them a reassuring smile, and said, "We're here to unite our hearts in prayer for Captain Fordham and Lieutenant Carlin, and the men in their patrol unit. I want you to know that ever since I learned late this afternoon that they were due back, I have been praying for them. And upon asking these four men to come with me, I learned that they and their families have been praying, too. My heart rejoices to know that the other patrols are all back safely.

"I feel sure these two wise officers have led their men to hole up somewhere and wait out the storm, which is the only thing they could do. It's too easy to become lost and disoriented in a blizzard. I picture them safe and reasonably warm in their tents tonight. But we must pray this storm away. God controls the weather, just as He controls everything in nature."

Kelly's four companions and some of the army people chorused an "Amen" to that statement.

"Before we pray, I want to share some encouraging Scripture truths with you."

Kelly opened his Bible. Giving Betsy and Donna another reassuring look, he said, "In James 5:16, we have these words: 'The effectual fervent prayer of a righteous man availeth much.' A righteous man is one who knows the Lord Jesus Christ as his own personal Saviour. 'Fervent' prayer is prayer offered with intense feeling, which shows the Lord we mean business. And this will make it effectual. We will see the desired effect.

"For our encouragement," Kelly continued, "God has followed this verse with a referral to Elijah of old. He reminds us that Elijah was a man of like passions as we…and tells how he prayed that it might not rain, and the God who controls the weather heard Elijah's prayer. It didn't rain on the earth for three-and-a-half years. After that period of time had passed, Elijah prayed again and God sent the rain. So we know that fervent prayer can cause God to change the weather."

With everyone's head bowed, Andy Kelly prayed ardently,

pleading with the Lord for the safety of Captain John Fordham and his men, and boldly asked Him to stop the blizzard so they could come home.

Sniffles could be heard through the crowd as Kelly closed his prayer and went to talk with Betsy and Donna and their children.

The people gathered around them, speaking words of encouragement, and thanked the pastor for being with them. Even though the storm still howled outside, everyone had a measure of peace, knowing that God was in control.

Just before dawn, people of town and fort were awakened by the sudden silence. The wind had stopped blowing. Looking out their windows, they saw faint gray light on the eastern horizon, and stars twinkling in the heavens. The storm was over.

Word soon spread through the town of the prayer meeting Pastor Kelly had held inside the fort the night before.

At the general store, Hannah Cooper was sitting on her new stool behind the counter, making up an order to be wired to Cheyenne City for the next supply wagon train that could get through. Jacob was helping a rancher find something down one of the aisles, and Glenda Williams and Julie Powell were behind the counter, waiting on customers.

The talk in the store was about how quickly the storm had stopped after the prayer meeting. Whenever someone passed close by her, talking about it, Hannah took advantage of the moment by speaking up and giving praise to the Lord for answered prayer. Even some who were known to be blatant unbelievers gave her no argument.

Jacob rejoined Glenda and Julie behind the counter and was also waiting on customers when banker Lloyd Dawson and barber-mayor Cade Samuels drew up in front of Hannah.

She looked up and smiled, saying, "Good morning, gentlemen. Beautiful day, isn't it?"

"Sure is," said Dawson.

"Mm-hmm," agreed Samuels. "It sure is."

"We just saw Pastor Kelly, Hannah," said Dawson. "He was coming from the fort. There's no word yet on the missing patrol."

Hannah's mind went to Betsy and Donna. She wanted to go and do what she could to comfort them but knew she dare not try to walk through the deep snow to the fort. "The Lord will bring them home in His time," she commented. "I'm sure of it."

Both men nodded.

Dawson said, "Hannah, did you send the letter to your brother-in-law about my offer to loan him money to start a newspaper here?"

"I didn't get it out as soon as I wanted to, Lloyd. Shortly after we talked about it, Patty Ruth was abducted and my mind was completely on her until she was brought home on Christmas Eve."

"I can sure understand that," said Dawson.

"But I did send a letter to Adam the last time there was a stagecoach in here to carry the mail to Cheyenne City."

"Good. I sure hope he will come."

"Me, too," said the mayor. "The newspaper will be good for the town."

"It sure will," said Hannah. "And I would love to have Adam, Theresa, and little Seth living in Fort Bridger. There's about to be another member of the family, too. In fact, the baby may have already been born. The way the mail has been delayed lately, there could be a letter just waiting to be delivered, announcing the child's birth."

"Well, I'm sure it will mean a lot to you to have them here, if they come," said Dawson.

"More than I can tell you," Hannah said with a smile.

Business slowed down shortly after Dawson and Samuels

left the store, and when Jacob turned to check on Hannah, he saw that she had left the stool and was nowhere to be seen.

Glenda noticed him looking around for her and said, "Jacob, I think she's back in the storeroom. Probably needed to check on something, since she's making up the order."

"I'll go see about her," said the little man.

Jacob found Hannah counting flour sacks. "Miss Hannah," he said softly, "I could do this for you, you know."

"You were busy, Jacob. And besides, I have to get off the stool now and then to stretch my legs."

"All right. But how about letting me do the counting?"

"Okay. You count, and I'll write."

When they had made inventory of the needed items, Jacob said, "I heard you and Mr. Dawson and Mr. Samuels talking about your brother-in-law coming here to start a newspaper."

"I'd love to have them here, Jacob. Adam is a lot like Solomon. And Theresa is so sweet."

"When you were talking to Mr. Dawson and Mr. Samuels about it before Patty Ruth disappeared, I overheard part of the conversation. Did I hear right that Adam is editor-in-chief of the *Cincinnati Post*?"

"Yes."

"And he is Solomon's younger brother?"

"Mm-hmm. Solomon was thirty-six when he…when he died. Adam is thirty-four."

"That's really something," said Jacob. "Thirty-four years old and editor-in-chief of such a large and prominent newspaper. I've known of the *Cincinnati Post* for years."

"Adam is a sharp young man."

"He has to be to have reached that position at such a young age. I hope he will take Mr. Dawson up on the loan offer and establish a paper here."

"Me, too."

"I was thinking…do you know Adam and his family well, Miss Hannah? I mean, since they live in Cincinnati and you and your family lived in Independence, Missouri?"

"I know Adam better than I know Theresa and little Seth. When we lived in Independence, and Adam was single, he lived in Kansas City. Because of this, the older children and I got to know Adam quite well. He went to Cincinnati to take a job with the *Post* about seven years before Solomon and I decided to come west. It was in Cincinnati that Adam met Theresa.

"After they married, they came to Independence about once a year before Solomon and I struck out for Fort Bridger. The children and I don't know Theresa and Seth as well as we would like, but what times we did have together were good."

"Well, I sure hope they'll come," said Jacob.

Hannah smiled. "The children and I have made many wonderful friends here, and we wouldn't trade them for anything, but it would be nice to have some family living close by. I feel a very close kinship with Adam, Jacob. As I said, he's a lot like Solomon. And I would like for my children to have their uncle near them. He couldn't take Solomon's place, but he could be a strong male influence in their young lives. Especially for the boys."

Jacob nodded.

"I'm really making it a matter of prayer," said Hannah. "I want the Lord to send them here."

Suddenly they heard Glenda calling Jacob's name.

"The girls must need my help for something, Miss Hannah," he said. "I'll walk you to your stool."

"Never mind," she said, smiling. "You go on. I've got a couple of things to check on, first."

Moments later, when Hannah returned to the counter, she found the store teeming with people.

Hannah greeted customers who were near the counter as

she struggled onto her stool. She noticed two officers from the fort come in; Captain Derk Sparrow and Lieutenant Anthony Udall. She caught their eye as they weaved their way past the three lines of customers at the counter. She motioned for them to come to her.

As they drew up, Hannah said, "Any news on Captain Fordham's patrol?"

"No, ma'am," replied Sparrow, whose wife, Lila, was the church organist.

"How are Betsy and Donna holding up?"

"We really don't know," said the captain. "We haven't seen them since the special prayer meeting in the mess hall last night."

"I'd like to go to them," said Hannah, "but in my condition I'm a bit fearful to try to walk through the snow."

Jacob's ears had picked up the conversation. Turning from the customer he was helping at the counter, he looked at Hannah and said, "Excuse me for butting in, Miss Hannah, but don't you try walking to the fort. You could fall and hurt yourself or the baby…or maybe both."

"I know," Hannah said with a sigh. "But Betsy and Donna might need me."

"Tell you what, ma'am," said Captain Sparrow, "Lieutenant Udall and I will walk you to the fort and back if you'll trust us to hold onto you and keep you from falling."

"Sure will," put in Udall.

A big smile broke over Hannah's lovely features. "All right!"

She saw a frown form on Jacob's brow.

Slipping off the stool, Hannah gave the little man a pat on the arm and said, "Jacob, dear, I'll be better off by far to go see Betsy and Donna than to stay here and be frustrated, wondering how they're holding up under the strain. These two big strong men will help me…and more importantly, God will keep His secure hand on me. I'll be just fine."

"Well, all right. When you put it that way, how can I argue with you?"

CHAPTER NINE

Lieutenant Anthony Udall helped Hannah put on her cloak. She fastened it tightly under her chin and pulled the hood up over her head, then slipped on the fur-lined mittens Sweet Blossom had made for her. She was already wearing her warm boots, for every time the door opened to let a customer in, a blast of frigid air entered.

She took a deep breath and said to her escorts, "All right, gentlemen, I'm ready."

Jacob looked up from tabulating a bill for a customer and said, "You be extremely careful, little lady."

"I'm in good hands, dear Jacob."

"How long are you planning on staying?"

"Probably until midafternoon."

"What about lunch?"

"I'm sure whichever lady I'm with at noontime will see that I don't starve."

"All right. I just want you to keep up your strength."

Anthony Udall chuckled. "Jacob, you'd have made somebody a good mother."

"You will walk her back?" Jacob said, running his gaze over the faces of the army officers.

"We will," Sparrow said as they escorted Hannah toward the door. "I promise."

Jacob had shoveled the snow off the boardwalk in front before opening the store. All the same, Sparrow and Udall gripped Hannah firmly, even before they reached the end of the walk. Moments later they passed Dr. O'Brien's clinic, and the doctor happened to be looking out the window. He knocked on the window to get Hannah's attention, then smiled his approval.

Soon they were at the fort. The sentries in the tower called down a greeting as another sentry opened the gate.

"Which place do you want to visit first, ma'am?" Udall asked.

"Since the Fordham house is closest, you can leave me there first."

"When should we come for you?" Sparrow asked.

"Let's wait and ask Betsy. She'll probably want me to eat lunch with her."

"Fine," said the captain. "We'll come whenever you say."

They walked on to the Fordham house, and the two men carefully helped Hannah onto the porch.

When Betsy responded to the knock on her door, her eyes brightened at the sight of her friend. "Oh, Hannah, it's good to see you! Come in! You, too, gentlemen."

Suddenly Donna Carlin appeared with little Belinda Fordham at her side. "Hannah!" she said. "You shouldn't have ventured out in this snow!"

"It was no problem," Hannah said, as Betsy led her inside, followed by the officers. "These gentlemen escorted me from the store, and they will take me back. I was going to visit both of you, but since Donna's here, I'll just see you at the same time. I had to know how you're both holding up."

"We're drawing strength from each other," Betsy said. "Donna's been here since Travis and my boys left for school. Can you stay till they come back, Hannah? We'd love to have you here for lunch."

Hannah looked up at the men. "Would three-thirty be all

right? That way I'd be home shortly after my three oldest ones get there."

"Of course," Captain Sparrow said. "Three-thirty it is."

When the officers were gone, Hannah bent over and hugged Belinda, who wrapped her arms around Hannah's neck.

"Where's Patty Ruth, Miss Hannah?" the five-year-old asked.

"She's staying at Miss Julianna's house today, helping her take care of little Larissa."

"I really like it when Patty Ruth stays here with me."

"I'm glad you do, honey. She loves to come here."

Both women helped Hannah remove her cloak and then sat her in the rocking chair closest to the crackling fire.

Betsy went to the kitchen and returned with a steaming mug of fragrant tea for Hannah, who took a sip and felt the welcoming warmth all the way down to her stomach. Betsy and Donna sat on the edge of their rockers, looking at her questioningly, their faces troubled.

Suddenly Hannah smiled, realizing their concern was for her. "I'm fine. Don't worry about me. What I want to know is, how are you two?"

Betsy's eyes filled with tears. "It's been a bit rough. We've prayed together, and we're trusting the Lord to bring our husbands back to us safely."

"It helps to have each other to lean on," Donna said. "And it helps having you with us."

Betsy nodded. "Yes, Hannah. Thank you so much for coming."

"I had to. I love you both. I thought maybe I could encourage you."

Donna wiped tears from her cheeks. "You already have."

Hannah took a sip of tea, then said, "I wanted to go over a verse of Scripture that has been a tremendous blessing to me. You probably both know it, but I'd like for us to look at it together."

"I'll get my Bible," Betsy said. As she left the room, she took Belinda by the hand. "Come on, honey. Let's find you something to play with while Mommy and Miss Donna and Miss Hannah talk."

"Is Daddy gonna come home soon?" they heard the child ask.

"Yes, honey. We're trusting Jesus to bring him home real soon."

When Betsy returned, Bible in hand, she sighed and said, "This whole thing has taken its toll on all three of my children. Belinda is so close to her father and—"

A sob escaped her throat. Hannah and Donna put their arms around her, then Donna broke down, too. Hannah had an arm around each of the women, holding them tightly.

While both women used hankies to dry their faces, Hannah said, "Let's go into the kitchen and sit at the table."

At the table, Hannah opened Betsy's Bible. "I know it's terribly hard to have your husbands out there in that wilderness of snow and not to know where they are, or if they're all right. But let me remind you that God knows exactly where they are, and He's watching over them."

Both women nodded, dabbing at their tearstained cheeks.

"Listen to Joshua 1:9," Hannah said. "'Have not I commanded thee? Be strong and of a good courage; be not afraid, neither be thou dismayed: for the LORD thy God is with thee whithersoever thou goest.'"

Betsy lifted a trembling hand to her mouth.

"Do you see?" Hannah said. "Wherever God's children are, He is with us. And because He is with us, we can be strong and of good courage…and He doesn't want us to be afraid or dismayed. He's with John and Dobie wherever they are, as well as with us where we are. We must trust Him to remove our fears and take care of John and Dobie."

Betsy tried to smile as she said, "I just need more faith, Hannah."

"We all do, honey. And there's just one place to get it. 'Faith cometh by hearing, and hearing by the word of God.' Romans 10:17. Let's ask the Lord to increase our faith with His Word."

Many tears were shed as Hannah led her two friends in prayer. She thanked the Lord that He knew where John and Dobie were and that He was with them at that very moment, even as He was with Patty Ruth when she was kidnapped. She thanked the Lord that He had brought Patty Ruth back unharmed when it looked as if they would never see her again, and that He was going to bring John and Dobie home, safe and sound.

At the Crow village another one of the wounded men had died, and Sergeant Bo Maxwell was now as sick as Wally Beemer, Brad Liston, and Mike Serra. All four were feverish, though Captain Fordham believed they would have been worse had they not been treated by the Crow medicine men, who now approached Chief Two Moons to give him their report.

"Do Red Wolf and Running Buck know what sickness has overtaken the soldier coats?" Two Moons asked.

"We have decided," Running Buck said, "that it is what white men call a cold."

"Your sick men are welcome to stay with us until they are better," Two Moons said to Captain Fordham and Lieutenant Carlin, who stood close by.

"We appreciate that, Chief," Fordham said, "but it would be best if we took them home so Dr. Blayney can treat them."

"You seem worried. You think this illness other than a cold?"

"We're afraid it might be influenza, but we're not sure," Fordham said.

Two Moons's eyes widened. "Influenza bad disease. Two Moons hope it not influenza. His people have been exposed to it."

"If it is influenza, we are very sorry that you and your people have been exposed."

Two Moons laid a gentle hand on the captain's shoulder. "Captain John Fordham, Two Moons and his people your friends. No matter what, we would have taken sick men in to help them."

"Chief, we thank you for being our friend. And if this proves to be influenza, I can tell you that Dr. Blayney will gladly come and offer his medicine to any of your people who come down with it. I realize your medicine men may object, but Dr. Blayney will come if you will allow him to."

Two Moons nodded silently.

"Now, Chief," Fordham said, "we must mount up and head for the fort. I appreciate what your people have done to help our sick and wounded. We are going to leave the meat with you that we had intended to take with us to the fort. You have been so very kind to us, and we know you need it."

"I and my people thank you, Captain John Fordham."

A half hour later, the Crow people stood in the deep snow and watched as the soldiers rode away.

It was almost three-thirty when Ryan and Will Fordham and Travis Carlin crossed the compound with the other officers' children as they came home from school. Captain Sparrow and Lieutenant Udall appeared at the Fordham house at the same time the boys drew up. Hannah was ready, and after greeting the boys and telling their mothers and Belinda good-bye, she was escorted across the compound. Just as they moved out the gate, they saw three children running toward them.

When Chris, Mary Beth, and B.J. drew up, they wanted to know if their mother was all right. Hannah assured them she was fine.

Jacob was there to meet them when they reached the door

of the general store. He had been on edge ever since Hannah had left. He expressed his appreciation to Sparrow and Udall, then asked what they knew about Corporal Lenny Croft being down with influenza.

"How'd you find out, Jacob?" Sparrow asked.

"Sergeant Wilkins was in a few minutes ago and told me."

"Well, Anthony and I just learned about it before we went to the Fordham house to escort Hannah home."

"Is this confirmed by Dr. Blayney as influenza?" Hannah asked.

"Yes, ma'am," Udall said. "And, of course, now Dr. Blayney fears it was influenza that Mike Serra and Brad Liston were coming down with before they left."

Sparrow looked at his companion. "Well, Lieutenant, we'd best get back to the fort."

Hannah thanked them again, and they left.

Jacob looked down at Hannah's boots and made a clicking sound with his tongue. "You need to go upstairs, get those wet boots off, and rest."

"They are a bit wet, aren't they?" Hannah said, eyeing the boots.

"And the hem of your dress is wet too," Mary Beth said. "What about your stockings?"

"Well, they could be a little damp."

"Uncle Jacob is right, Mama," Chris said. "You need to go upstairs and rest."

"I'm not that tired. It was invigorating to be able to go and help Betsy and Donna."

"That's all well and good," Mary Beth said, "but you are chilled and wet. You need to put on some dry things and have a good rest with your feet elevated."

"That's right," Chris and B.J. said.

Hannah looked at the four worried faces peering at her and said, "All right."

Instantly B.J. was on one side of her and Chris on the other. Mary Beth led the way toward the rear door.

Jacob shook his head and chuckled when he heard Hannah say, "I'm not an invalid, you know."

Corporal Ed Harms and Private Jed Simmons were in the gate tower at the fort when movement on the snow-laden hills to the north caught Simmons's attention. He picked up a pair of binoculars and put them to his eyes, turning the focus knob.

"It's Captain Fordham's patrol!" he said. "They…they've got some bodies draped over horses' backs, and it looks like some are either wounded or sick. They're bent over in their saddles."

"I'll go tell the colonel!" said Harms, dashing down the stairs.

Colonel Bateman was pleased to hear the news, and he told Corporal Harms to run and tell Mrs. Fordham and Mrs. Carlin. Moments later, the entire fort—except for Corporal Croft and two more men who had just been diagnosed with influenza—welcomed the patrol at the gate.

Betsy and Donna and their children waited patiently at the front of the crowd, thanking the Lord that John and Dobie were home safe and sound. It was not so for several in the patrol.

Dr. Robert Blayney was there, running his gaze over his soon-to-be patients. He spoke briefly to Fordham and led the way after the captain directed some of the men to take the sick and wounded to the infirmary. Fordham called to the doctor, saying he would be there in a few minutes. He then smiled at his family and pointed toward Colonel Bateman.

Betsy nodded, understanding that he had to make a brief report to the colonel first.

Dobie Carlin spoke to the colonel while he was dismounting from his horse, then dashed to Donna and Travis. Tears of joy and relief were shed as they clung to each other.

Betsy held Belinda in her arms while Ryan and Will flanked her closely on each side. They watched and listened as John gave a concise report to Bateman of what had happened.

When they heard about the Blackfoot attack, Betsy whispered to her children, "The Lord has been so good to spare your daddy."

"Let's talk more about it later, Captain," Bateman said, casting a glance at Betsy and the children. "Right now, your family wants to see you. And after you've had your reunion, I'd like for you to tell all these people the story you just told me."

"Yes, sir," said John, saluting. Then he rushed to his wife and children.

Belinda extended her arms to her father as he came near, and John took her in his arms and huddled close with Betsy and the boys.

Moments later, John stood with Belinda in his arms and told the people of the fort how Chief Two Moons and his warriors had saved the patrol from the Blackfoot war party, had taken them in and sheltered and fed them, and had cared for their sick and wounded.

When the captain finished speaking, Colonel Bateman said, "Folks, we need to show Chief Two Moons and his people our deepest gratitude!"

Voices rose in agreement.

Corporal Jess Cummings approached the colonel and saluted, saying, "Colonel, sir, I just came from the infirmary. Dr. Blayney asked me to come and ask if you would send someone to Dr. O'Brien. The wounded men need attention faster than he can give it to them."

"Of course," Bateman said. "You go, Corporal. Tell Dr. O'Brien how serious it is, and that I am asking him to come and help Dr. Blayney as soon as possible."

"Yes, sir," Cummings said, and hurried away.

As the corporal ran down Main Street toward the O'Brien clinic, he told people all along the way that the missing patrol was back. When Cummings entered the doctor's office, Edie was at the desk.

"Ma'am," said Cummings, somewhat out of breath, "the missing patrol has returned and—"

"Oh, praise the Lord! Are they all right?"

"Well, that's why I'm here, ma'am. Some of the men were killed and others wounded in an attack by a Blackfoot war party. And we have some very sick men. Dr. Blayney desperately needs Dr. O'Brien's help. Colonel Bateman told me to come and ask if Dr. O'Brien would come and help as soon as possible."

Edie shoved her chair back. "Doctor is with a patient at the moment, but he should be through shortly. What about Captain Fordham and Lieutenant Carlin?"

"They're fine, ma'am. Just fine."

She rounded the desk and hurried into the back room. Cummings could hear her talking to her husband, though he couldn't make out what she was saying.

Presently, Edie returned and said, "Doctor will come just as soon as he is through with this patient, Corporal."

"Good. I'll tell the colonel and Dr. Blayney. Thank you, ma'am."

By the time Dr. O'Brien arrived at the fort's infirmary, word had spread through town of the missing patrol's return, and townspeople were flocking to the fort to learn what had happened. Pastor Andy Kelly and Rebecca arrived, along with Hannah Cooper and her children, and many of the church members. They joined Kelly in praising the Lord for the patrol unit's safe return, then Kelly led them in prayer for the sick and wounded, and for the families of the troopers who had been killed.

In the infirmary, the doctors tended to the wounded men first. When they were stabilized, they turned their attention to the four sick men.

"Dr. Blayney," O'Brien said, "I hate to say this, but we just might have an influenza epidemic on our hands. I saw two patients earlier today who had these same symptoms."

Blayney sighed. "I'm afraid you may be right."

The doctors were administering salicylic acid to the four men when Colonel Bateman entered the infirmary. He paused at the cots where the wounded men lay and saw that they had been bandaged and given proper care. He went next to the doctors and said, "So what's the verdict here?"

"Influenza, sir," Blayney said. "I believe we've got the wounded men stabilized, and Dr. O'Brien agrees they will be all right in time. But we have what could be the beginning of an influenza epidemic. I've got three other men with the disease, and Dr. O'Brien has two patients who have just come down with it."

"Are you sure?"

"I'm afraid so, sir. We'll quarantine these men with the others in the adjacent room, but it really won't do much good now. All the men in the patrol unit have been exposed."

"I told my patients to go home and stay in bed," O'Brien said, "but they've been around others today. Besides, they have families. It's going to be impossible to stop it from spreading now."

Blayney sighed. "I guess we have our work cut out for us."

Colonel Bateman ran his gaze between the doctors and said, "I've heard of influenza taking lives. How dangerous is it?"

"When people with influenza die," said Blayney, "it is actually from the pneumonia that comes as a result of it. With salicylic acid we can ward off pneumonia by keeping fevers down. It's really amazing that none of these men here are on the verge of pneumonia…the way they were exposed to the cold weather. The Crow gave them good care. They kept their fevers down with their own primitive methods, which don't always work. But these men are not nearly as sick as they could have been by now."

"We owe Two Moons and his people a lot," Bo Maxwell said.

"They might well have saved our lives," Mike Serra said.

"No question about it," Dr. O'Brien said. "I fear now that the Crow people will come down with it, since they've been exposed. If an epidemic should break out in the village, many of them could die."

"Dr. Blayney," Bateman said, "Captain Fordham took the liberty of offering your services to the Crow if any of their people come down with influenza…that is, if Chief Two Moons and his medicine men will allow it."

"That's fine. I'll be glad to help them."

"I'll be glad to help too, Doctor," O'Brien said. "There's no way we could ever repay Two Moons and his people for what they did."

CHAPTER TEN

On the fourth day after Captain Fordham and his men had left the Crow village, medicine man Red Wolf was kneeling over Running Buck, who lay close to the fire, wrapped in blankets. His body was shaking, and he was very weak.

Running Buck's squaw, Morning Bird, stood close by, nervously wringing her hands.

Red Wolf looked up at her. "Running Buck has white man's disease. Morning Bird will bathe him in cool water to bring the fever down, just as we did with the soldier coats. Red Wolf will prepare sargigruag weed tea to help relieve Running Buck's aches and pains."

Morning Bird frowned. "Will it not cool Running Buck enough simply to remove the blankets? Is cool water on his skin necessary?"

"Water is necessary. We learned this from the soldier coats. Lieutenant Dobie Carlin said that cold air does not penetrate to the bloodstream the same as cool water."

Red Wolf went to his tepee for the sargigruag weed. When he returned, Morning Bird was bathing her husband in cool water. The tea was brewed, and when Running Buck was once again wrapped in blankets, Red Wolf began administering the tea.

The sound of a handclap came from outside the tepee, followed by their chief's voice.

Morning Bird opened the flap. "Please come in, Chief Two Moons."

The chief stepped inside, looking somber. "Is this white man's sickness?"

Red Wolf nodded.

"The squaws who tended the soldier coats are sick," Two Moons said. "They have the same symptoms as Running Buck. They need Red Wolf, too."

The medicine man sighed. "I will go to them after Running Buck drinks this sargigruag tea. I fear sickness will pass to others in the village."

"Should we send for Dr. Robert Blayney?" Two Moons asked.

Red Wolf looked into Running Buck's dull eyes. "What do you think?" he asked.

Running Buck moved his head back and forth slowly. "No. It is best that we use Crow ways and medicine."

Red Wolf looked up at his chief. "I agree with Running Buck."

At Fort Bridger, more people had come down with influenza in both the fort and town. Dr. Blayney stayed busy at the fort's infirmary, and Dr. O'Brien's clinic was a beehive of activity as he and Edie cared for the sick who came to them. Dr. O'Brien was also making house calls.

Early one morning, he entered the Wells Fargo and Western Union office. Curly and Judy Charley Wesson were behind the counter and seated at the desk.

"Wal, good mornin', Doc," said Curly, stepping to the counter.

Judy greeted him and left her chair to move up beside her husband. "Whut can we do for ya?"

"I need to send a telegram."

Curly picked up a pad and pencil. "Who are we sendin' it to?"

"Wyoming Pharmaceutical Company in Cheyenne City."

"Uh-oh! Is it gittin' that bad?"

"We've got to get a shipment of salicylic acid here as fast as possible. Both Dr. Blayney and I are running low. How are you two feeling? Any light-headedness, weakness, sore muscles?"

"None at all."

"Me, neither," Judy said.

"Good. I hope it stays that way."

"Okay, Doc," Curly said, poising his pencil to write. "You want this to go to the Wyomin' Pharmaceutical Company in Cheyenne City. Any particular person?"

"Yes. Raymond Yager."

Curly nodded. "How do you spell his last name?"

"Y-A-G-E-R."

Curly scribbled it down. "All right. Now, exactly what do you wanna say?"

"You can word it. The message is that the town and fort are on the verge of an influenza epidemic, and both Dr. Blayney and I are in need of salicylic acid. We need a large shipment…at least forty pounds. Mr. Yager is to put it on the next wagon supply train or stagecoach that comes to Fort Bridger from Cheyenne City. He can send it all to me and I'll see that Dr. Blayney gets his share."

Curly was writing as fast as he could. "Uh, Doc, how do you spell sal—sal—that acid?"

Doc grinned. "Salicylic, Curly. S-A-L-I-C-Y-L-I-C."

When the wire had been sent, and Doc was paying for it, he said, "We need to pray that the next supply train or stagecoach won't be delayed by bad weather. Without the salicylic acid, many people here could die."

"We'll shore be a-prayin' 'bout that, Doc," Judy said.

The doctor headed back down Main Street, and a gust of wind plucked at his hat and almost pulled it from his head. He glanced toward the west and saw dark clouds gathering. "Please, Lord," he said, "don't let anything keep that medicine from getting here soon."

Doc neared Cooper's General Store and reached into his shirt pocket for the list of things Edie had written down. There were many customers in the store when Doc stepped inside. Hannah was on her feet beside Jacob behind the counter, taking care of a long line of customers. On Jacob's other side was Mandy Carver. Three long lines had formed in front of the counter.

Some of the customers greeted Dr. O'Brien as he walked past them and moved between two rows of shelves. He saw Carlene Bledsoe at the far end of the aisle bent over, coughing. Doc hurried toward her and saw that her face was flushed.

"You don't look so good, Carlene," he said, concern showing on his ruddy features. "That cough sounds bad." Doc laid a palm on her brow. "And you have a fever. Have you had chills?"

"Well, maybe a little."

"Headache?"

"Yes."

"Pain in your muscles and respiratory tract?"

"Well, yes. Especially in my lungs when I cough."

"Carlene, I want you to go home right now and get in bed. Why haven't you been to see me or sent Dan over to tell me that you're sick?"

"I haven't had time, Doc. I've been awfully busy doing inventory at the store. Dan…well, Dan told me this morning that he would come and get you to look at me, but I told him I would be all right."

"Well, you're not all right. And as your doctor, I'm ordering you to go home and get in bed. You need rest to get over influenza. I'll come by shortly and give you a strong dose of salicylic acid. You tell Dan that I want you bathed in cool water right away. That fever must come down."

"Yes, sir," Carlene said as she mopped sweat from her brow.

Doc looked into the basket Carlene was carrying and noted the items she had already chosen. "What else do you need, Carlene? I'll help you so you can get home quickly."

A few minutes later, Doc held Carlene's basket in one hand and lightly gripped her arm with the other and escorted her to the counter area. When Carlene had made her purchases, Doc said, "I'll see you shortly at home."

Carlene nodded and headed for the door.

"Hannah, I need to talk to you in private for a moment," Doc said.

"What is it, Doc?" Hannah asked, as he led her away from the counter. She glanced back at her customers.

"I'm concerned about you working in the store with this influenza epidemic on us. Carlene has it, and you were exposed by her being in the store. And no doubt there have been others in here who have come down with it. If you get influenza, Hannah, it could be very bad for both the baby and you."

"Doc," Hannah said, lowering her voice, "I'm grateful for your concern, but this store is my responsibility."

"But can't you get some of the other women to help Jacob so you can stay in your apartment and not be exposed further?"

"Doc, I can't ask others to put themselves at risk so I can avoid it."

"Why not? They're not pregnant. You could have more complications than they if you come down with influenza."

Hannah shook her head. "I can't ask my friends to do what I won't do myself. I'll get plenty of rest, Doc, and I'll eat well. Hopefully, I'll escape it."

Doc set his jaw. "You are a stubborn woman, Hannah Marie Cooper!"

Hannah patted his round cheek and said, "I'll be fine, Dr.

Frank Harvey O'Brien. Now if you'll excuse me, I have to get back to my customers."

Doc sighed. "You're from Missouri, right?"

"Yes. Why?"

"Now I know where they get the idea of the stubbornness of a Missouri mule!"

Hannah grinned at him and walked away.

Doc went to the shelves to pick up the items Edie wanted him to bring home.

At the counter, people in line were talking about the Crow Indians' unselfish deeds when they helped Captain John Fordham and his men.

"What they did was a marvelous thing," Hannah said as she took her place once again and began totaling a customer's purchases.

"Tell you what," Jacob said, "I never had been around North American Indians until I came here. I've really come to admire and appreciate Chief Two Moons and his wonderful people. They have always been so friendly when I've seen them here in town, and—"

"Just hold on there, Jacob!" snapped Jason Drumm, a silver-haired farmer.

"Did I say something wrong?" Jacob said softly.

"You shouldn't be praisin' those bloodthirsty savages! You oughtta hate 'em like any decent white man does!"

Mandy's eyes opened wide as she sent a glance at Hannah. Jacob's face reddened.

"When those heartless savages act like they're friends of the white men, it's only a front, Jacob! You and Hannah oughtta have enough sense to figure that out. Those red devils hate whites, and they'll massacre us without a tinge of conscience when they get the chance!"

"That's right, Jason!" another farmer said.

"All you folks better listen to me!" Drumm said. "Those

redskins are born killers! I don't trust anybody unless they have white skin!"

Mandy Carver's eyes blinked wide, then resentment flared in them.

"Jason, you have hurt Mandy's feelings," Hannah said. "The statement you just made is totally unkind and unseemly. Just because a person's skin is not white is no reason to be prejudiced against them. You owe her an apology."

"Mrs. Cooper, you don't really know me," a woman in Hannah's line said. "My husband and I are ranchers several miles north of here, and we've only been here once since you opened your store. I'm sorry for this man's rude statement about white skin. I have no ill feelings toward black people. But let me say this, Mrs. Cooper. You seem to have such a soft spot in your heart for Indians. Maybe you should go live in Dakota for a while, where my husband and I grew up. I could tell you some stories about the atrocities of the Sioux Indians against the whites there. If you'd seen what I have, you wouldn't be defending Indians!"

"Ma'am, the Indians were in Dakota Territory long before white men set foot there," Hannah said. "They were here in Wyoming a long time before we invaded it, too. If white men hadn't stolen the Indian's land and killed their buffalo by the thousands, they would never have met with Indian opposition. Those early explorers, like Jim Bridger—for whom this town and fort are named—stole no land, nor did they slaughter buffalo simply for their hides. They were befriended by the Indians, and none of them were massacred. But let's face one unalterable fact. We are the intruders, not the Indians."

"That's right, Hannah," Ray Noble said. "We have no reason to hate the Indians."

"Yeah," Charles Goodman said. "Especially the Crow, who have proven themselves to be our friends, no matter what this guy Drumm says."

Other voices sided with Goodman.

"Bosh!" Drumm said. "I say Two Moons is a sneakin' hypocrite! He'll cut your throat the first chance he gets! Every dirty Indian ought to be run out of this country…or buried in it! This land was meant for white men!" His hard gaze fastened on Mandy's face. "And I do mean white people!"

Mandy's eyes filled with tears. Hannah took hold of her hand.

"Jason, God made all the races," Jacob said, "and a person shouldn't be prejudiced against another. I'm considered a white man, though my skin is darker than the average Caucasian, and by race I am a Jew. I know what prejudice is. I grew up in New York City, and I've often suffered persecution because of my race." He turned to smile at Mandy, then looked back at Drumm. "This dear lady and her family know what it is to suffer because their skin is black…and that persecution is dead wrong! And it's just as wrong for the Indians to be persecuted because their skin is red."

The store was silent as a tomb.

Mandy's tears now streamed down her cheeks, and Hannah put an arm around her shoulder.

Jason Drumm started to speak again, but Jacob pointed a finger at him and said, "Wait just a minute." He ran his gaze over the faces of the small crowd and said, "The day President Abraham Lincoln signed the Proclamation of Emancipation—January 1, 1863—he rejoiced for the slaves. Every man, woman, and child who lives under the American flag should live free of prejudice, whoever they are and whatever race they may be or what color of skin they may have."

"You're right, Jacob," Mandy said, wiping tears and speaking through quivering lips. "God did make all the races, and one race shouldn't be prejudiced against another."

The majority of customers in the store spoke their agreement.

Jason Drumm looked at Mandy and said, "God made the races, eh?"

"That's right."

"Hah! How do you know there is a God?"

Doc left his place in line and stepped up to Drumm. "How do you know there isn't?"

Drumm cleared his throat uneasily and mumbled, "I'm an agnostic."

"Oh, so you're one of those fellas who says the human mind can know nothing for sure beyond the material world."

Drumm's voice was just above a whisper. "That's correct. I don't know if God exists."

Hannah spoke up. "Mr. Drumm, I notice you speak softly on this subject. I've found other agnostics who do the same. You say you don't know if God exists, but you're afraid to say it loudly in case God might hear you."

There were snickers in the crowd, and Drumm's face turned crimson.

"Let me help you with your problem, Jason," Doc said. "Can you really look around at the universe with its countless stars, the planets, the sun, the moon, and this marvelous earth with all of its wonders, and tell me God didn't create it?"

"I don't know," Drumm said, keeping his voice subdued. "Maybe those fellas Lamarck and Darwin have it right. Maybe man is alone in the universe. Maybe it all happened by that big explosion billions of years ago."

"Maybe?" Doc said. "Seems there are a lot of maybes in your way of thinking." He reached into his vest pocket and took out his pocket watch. "Tell me about this watch, Jason. Did it have a designer…a watchmaker?"

"Of course."

"You're right, it did. And you know what? It keeps perfect time."

"So what?"

"You are aware that men of the sea use the stars to navigate across the great oceans of this world. The stars are in perfect timing as they travel their courses up there, right?"

"Yeah, I suppose."

"You know, not long ago at the watch factory where this timepiece came from, some fool tossed a lighted stick of dynamite into a storeroom where there were boxes of crystals, minute and hour hands, springs, and the other pieces it takes to make a watch. That dynamite exploded in the storeroom…and the pieces flew together and here's my watch! All from that explosion!"

Again there was snickering among the crowd.

Jason Drumm scowled. "Don't insult my intelligence, Doc."

"Why not? You insulted mine when you said maybe Lamarck and Darwin have it right. Maybe it all happened by that big explosion billions of years ago. If this watch had to have a designer, a maker, then so does this universe. We can predict the exact days each season will begin. We can predict the exact time the sun will rise and set every day, even as the seasons change. We have figured out that in the earth's precise timing, every four years we have to add a day to the year to keep our calendars right. Are you telling me that maybe this universe and its precision came from an explosion, when you agree that it couldn't happen to this watch? Are you telling me that maybe there was no designer…maybe there was no world maker who put it all together? Maybe there is no God?"

All eyes were on Drumm. He cleared his throat again and said, "Well…uh…you've given me somethin' to think about, Doc."

"Jason…" Hannah said.

He turned to look at her. "Yes, ma'am?"

"God does exist. And He loves you. He showed it by sending His only begotten Son, the Lord Jesus Christ, into the world to shed His blood on Calvary's cross and die for our sins. Jesus is the one and only way for sinners like you and me to be saved from God's wrath and go to heaven when we die. And Jason…"

"Yes, ma'am?"

"I love you, too. And I would love to talk to you sometime in private about Jesus Christ."

Drumm nodded and said, "Maybe sometime, ma'am."

"Maybe?"

"Well, I'll come and talk to you after I think all of this over."

"All right. Now, we can all get back to business here once you've apologized to Mandy for your remark about not trusting anybody unless they have white skin. What reason has Mandy or her husband ever given you not to trust them?"

"Well…uh…none, ma'am."

"Good. Now, let's hear that apology."

Jason looked at Mandy and said, "I'm sorry, Mrs. Carver. I…I was wrong to say that."

"I accept your apology, Mr. Drumm. And please, let Hannah or Doc or any of the other Christians here talk to you about Jesus. You need to know Him."

"All right, folks," Hannah said. "Let's get back to business here!"

Doc gave Mandy the money for his purchases, then leaned in Hannah's direction and said, "I've probably got an office full of people waiting to see me, so I don't have the time to try and talk sense into your stubborn head."

Hannah smiled at him but said nothing.

There was an admiring look in Doc's eyes as he reached over and gave her a loving pat on the hand. Then, with a shrug of his tired bent shoulders, he picked up his purchases and made his way out into the gathering storm. As he leaned his head into the wind, there was a prayer on his lips for Hannah Cooper.

CHAPTER ELEVEN

When it was closing time, and the last customers were leaving, Jacob followed them to the door and hung the Closed sign in the window, noting the dark lowering clouds and strong wind.

Behind the counter, Mandy sighed and said, "It's been a busy day."

"Thank you for your help, honey," Hannah said. "I wish you'd let me pay you."

Mandy shook her head. "No, ma'am! It's my pleasure to help." She gave Hannah a hug. "Thank you for takin' my part with Mr. Drumm today."

"You don't have to thank me, honey. What Mr. Drumm said was uncalled for, and you had an apology coming."

"She most certainly did, Miss Hannah," said Jacob, who had returned to the counter and was now locking the cash drawer.

Hannah smiled at the little man. "I'm sorry for the persecution you've suffered in your life, Jacob. Jews are very special people to me."

"Really?"

"My Saviour is half-Jew, you know. His mother was a Jew. Of course, His Father is God, for He was virgin born."

Jacob smiled weakly. "I have to be honest, Miss Hannah. My people have been very prejudiced against Gentiles, too."

"I guess everybody's guilty of it at one time or another."

"You're right about that." Jacob looked at the two women through eyes filmed with tears. "Hannah, Mandy, I'm glad I can say I feel no prejudice against anybody in the world. And that includes the Indians, which was what started our discussion today. And Miss Hannah, if there is such a thing as a real Christian on this earth, that Christian is you. Here I am, a Jew by nature and by religion, but you took me in and gave me a home and a job."

Hannah blushed and lowered her eyes.

"You are so right, Jacob," Mandy said. "This lovely lady is the sweetest Christian I know."

"You two are too kind," Hannah said. "I'm only a sinner saved by the grace of God, and my greatest desire is that everyone around me should come to know my precious Lord Jesus."

"God bless you, honey," said Mandy, hugging her.

Jacob looked on as Hannah hugged Mandy back and kissed her cheek. He knew he was included in the "everyone around me."

On January 11, 1871, Dr. Patrick O'Brien watched the landscape as the train began to slow for Cheyenne City. A few puffy clouds were visible in the azure sky, and the sun was glistening on a world of white.

Patrick looked at his reflection in the window and thought, *Pat, you'll have to move slow and not let Dad feel pushed in any way. And you must never let him feel that he's not needed. Go to him for advice, even when you already know the answer.*

"Lord," he said, "please give me wisdom, and guide me as I enter this new phase of my life."

The engine bell started ringing as the depot came into view. When the wheels rolled to a stop, Patrick noted how bundled up the people were, and that the vapor from their mouths was instantly whipped away by the wind.

Moments later, overnight bag in hand, Patrick followed other passengers toward the front door of the coach. He felt the cold air hit him, pulled his hat down a little tighter, and stepped from the train.

He followed the other passengers into the terminal and stopped to look through frosted windows at the Union Pacific workmen as they braved the cold to unload the baggage. He heard some of his fellow passengers talking to relatives who had come to pick them up and learned that another fierce blizzard had hit two days earlier.

When the workmen finished setting the baggage on the platform, Patrick went back outside to ask that his luggage be brought inside. Then he went across the terminal to the ticket window.

"May I help you, sir?" the man behind the counter said.

"Yes, please. I just came in on the train from Chicago, and I'm scheduled to take a stagecoach to Fort Bridger. Where will I find the Wells Fargo office?"

"It's just a block south down the street, sir."

Patrick thanked the man and left the terminal.

The rotund, middle-aged Wells Fargo agent was waiting on a customer when Patrick entered the office. He looked at the new arrival and said, "I'll be with you in a few minutes, sir."

Patrick made his way to the potbellied stove in a corner of the office and listened as the agent gave the customer a detailed description of the most recent blizzard to hit Wyoming.

In a few more minutes, the agent looked toward Patrick and said, "I can help you now, sir."

Patrick smiled as he moved up to the counter. "I'm Dr. Patrick O'Brien. I just came in on the train from Chicago, and I have a reservation for tomorrow on your stage to Fort Bridger."

"Oh, yes, Dr. O'Brien."

"Is the stage leaving on time in the morning?"

"Ah…no, sir. All of our stagecoaches got caught in the blizzard that hit us two days ago and won't be back in Cheyenne City for several days. I'm sorry, Dr…O'Brien, did you say? Are you related to Dr. Frank O'Brien in Fort Bridger?"

"He's my dad. I'm going there to become his partner in the clinic. Do you know him?"

"Not personally, but I was contacted yesterday by Raymond Yager of the Wyoming Pharmaceutical Company here in town. He received a wire from your father the day before the blizzard hit, saying that the town and the fort are on the verge of an influenza epidemic."

"Oh, no!"

"Your father and the army doctor are in desperate need of salicylic acid."

"Yes, that's crucial for influenza."

"They asked for at least forty pounds of it to be put on the first supply train or stagecoach heading to Fort Bridger from Cheyenne City."

"People could die if that salicylic acid doesn't get to Fort Bridger in time. Do you know anything about the wagon supply trains?"

"I know that the train you just came in on is carrying food, supplies, and ammunition to be transported by wagon across southern Wyoming to towns and forts. One of those supply trains is set up to carry a big load of goods just to Fort Bridger. However, none of the supply trains will be going any time soon."

"Because of the blizzard?"

"Well, the snow would have slowed them up some, but that's not the reason they won't be going."

"So, what is it?"

"Indians. There's been an uprising by the Cheyenne, the Blackfoot, and the Shoshoni. Mostly they're after food. It's been a tough winter so far. The wagon supply people don't dare send their wagons out without protection from the army. Forts Russell and Sanders, which ordinarily provide the escorts, have all their troops occupied fighting the hostiles. Until the hostiles can be subdued or driven away, none of the wagons will be going."

"So what about your stagecoaches? When they come in, will you be sending them on their routes?"

"Once they're here, yes. Since it's food the Indians are after, they haven't been bothering the stages. But again, it's going to be several days before they can get back here, because of the snow."

"Is there somebody here in town who would sell me a horse, and a saddle and bridle?"

"You don't mean—you can't mean that you'd try to ride to Fort Bridger on a horse, do you? Not this time of year."

"That's exactly what I mean. I'm a doctor, and I know how serious influenza can be. That salicylic acid has to be delivered to my dad and the army doctor as soon as possible."

"I sure hate to see you try it, Doctor."

"I have no choice. Who would sell me a horse?"

"Well, the town hostler would."

"And where do I find him?"

"His name's Ned Stokes. His stable is two blocks north of here on this same street. You can't miss him. Sign's got his name on it. But I really hate to see you strike out alone on horseback this time of year. Another blizzard could hit at any time. And even if it didn't, you're several days from there, and the cold is murderous. Not to mention that if Indians see you, they might decide to kill you and take your horse."

"I'll have to chance it. Where do I find the pharmaceutical company?"

"It's over on the next street…Second Street. Two blocks north."

"Thanks for the information. And what did you say the man's name is?"

"Yager. Raymond Yager. He's the manager."

"All right. Now, I need to know if I could leave my luggage with you to be sent to Fort Bridger on the first stage that goes there…whenever that might be."

"Sure. How much you got?"

"One medium-sized trunk and two large suitcases."

"We can handle it."

"Good. I'll go see if I can hire someone to cart it over here."

When Patrick's luggage was in Wells Fargo's care, and he had purchased fifty pounds of salicylic acid, he entered the office of Ned Stokes carrying his overnight bag and the heavy cloth sack that contained smaller sacks of salicylic acid.

The office was unoccupied, but Patrick could hear voices coming from the rear of the building. He left his belongings on a chair and moved through a creaky door into the connected barn. His attention went first to a giant of a man who stood watching another man pound a nail into the hoof of a stout gelding. Next to the gelding stood a pack mule.

The massive man, who wore a full beard and heavy buffalo-hide coat, said, "Ned, you've got another customer."

The hostler hit the nail a final lick, stood erect, and looked at Patrick. "Howdy, sir. I'm Ned Stokes. What can I do for you?"

"I can wait till you're done," Patrick said. "This gentleman was here first."

"I'll be a while with him. I've got to put three more shoes on the horse and a full set on the mule. Gus won't mind if I take a few minutes for you."

"'Course not." Gus's voice was so deep it sounded as if he were speaking from a cellar.

"I just need to buy a good horse," Patrick said.

Stokes looked him up and down. "You're not from these parts, are you?"

Patrick smiled. "No, I'm from Chicago." He removed his right glove as he moved toward the hostler and extended his hand. "I'm Dr. Patrick O'Brien. I'm on my way to Fort Bridger to join my father as partner in his clinic there."

"A doctor, huh? We sure could use more of you fellas out here in the West."

"That's for sure." Gus stepped up to Patrick and extended a meaty hand. "I'm Gus Wolfskill."

Patrick's hand was lost in Gus's. He smiled up at him and said, "Glad to meet you, Gus."

Ned Stokes frowned. "Excuse me, Doctor, but you said you're on your way to Fort Bridger. You mean now?"

"Yes, sir. I need to buy a good horse, and a saddle and bridle. I'm planning on riding out first thing in the morning. I was supposed to go on a stagecoach tomorrow, but as you probably know, there aren't any around."

"Well, I've got nine or ten horses out back for you to pick from, but you really shouldn't strike out across the prairie alone. It'd be too dangerous this time of year. Those storms can come in awfully fast. Not only that, but the Indians are killing white people with a vengeance right now. They're hungry, and they seem to think we're supposed to feed 'em. They might not bother a lone white man, but it isn't worth the chance. My advice is to wait till you can take a stage."

"Can't. I have to get to Fort Bridger as soon as possible."

"Is it worth risking your life over?"

"It is. There's an influenza outbreak in Fort Bridger and they desperately need salicylic acid, which I'll be carrying with me."

"But if you end up freezing to death or becoming a target for Indians, you won't get it there anyhow, Doctor."

"I've got to take the chance, sir."

Stokes shook his head, looked at Wolfskill, and said, "He's about as stubborn as you, Gus." Then he said to Patrick, "I've been trying to talk Gus into waiting till spring before he heads across the prairie, but he's bent on going."

Gus laughed hoarsely. "Ned, I've been across them plains in January before. And there have always been Injuns…and I'm still kickin'."

"You're heading across the plains, Mr. Wolfskill?" Patrick said.

"Yep. I'm on my way in the mornin'. Meetin' up with some trapper friends in the Uintah Mountains in about ten days."

"Uintah Mountains. Where are they?"

"Due west of here. Southwest of Fort Bridger 'bout thirty miles…maybe a little less. I was about to ask if you'd like to ride with me. I'd be with you most of the way. Be about twenty miles from Fort Bridger when I'd have to veer southwestward toward the Uintahs."

"That would be great! I'd really appreciate it. Those people in Fort Bridger would, too. I've just got to get that medicine to them."

Gus chuckled. "Well, now, that'd put a feather in my cap if I sorta helped you get that medicine to them sick folks, wouldn't it?"

Patrick smiled. "I guess you could say that."

"Okay. Tell you what, Doc—can I call you Doc?"

"Sure."

"All right. And no more of that Mr. Wolfskill stuff. Mr. Wolfskill was my dear ol' daddy. I'm just Gus."

Patrick laughed. "Okay, Gus."

"Now, as I was about to say, Doc…I've got my food packed in sacks over there in the corner. There'll be plenty for both of us. I've got a tent for campin' at night. Plenty big enough for the two of us. Only thing…you'll have to get yourself a bedroll and a good pair of high-top boots. Them city slicker shoes will get your feet froze off."

Patrick looked down at his shoes. "Where do I find boots and a bedroll?"

"I can take you while Ned's puttin' shoes on my animals."

"Thanks. And, really, I'd like to pay you for the food I eat."

"No need, Doc. Be my pleasure to feed you. Let's go get the stuff you need."

Ned Stokes shook his head. "You guys are really gonna head across that prairie, aren't you."

"I'll pick out my horse when we get back, Mr. Stokes," Patrick said.

When Patrick and his new friend returned to the stable, Stokes was just finishing up with the pack mule. Patrick picked out a bay gelding under Gus's advice and also a saddle and bridle.

As Patrick was paying him, Stokes said, "Tell you what, fellas, to save you hotel money, I'll let you sleep here on the office floor tonight."

"We'll just take you up on it," Gus said. "It'll give Doc a chance to try out his new bedroll without the cold comin' at him."

They ate supper in a local café, and Patrick found himself a bit uncomfortable with Gus's profanity-laced conversation. Patrick liked the big man, though, and was plenty glad to have him as a traveling companion. After supper, they returned to the stable office and began to lay out their bedrolls.

"You got a gun, Doc?"

"Gun? No."

"You mean you were gonna ride across that prairie without a weapon?"

"Well, actually, it hadn't crossed my mind."

Gus chuckled. "Believe me, it would about the time you had to fight off a pack of hungry wolves or defend yourself against blood-hungry Injuns."

Gus pulled a Colt .45 revolver from his gear. The gun was in a holster with the belt wrapped around it. He handed it to Patrick and said, "Here you go, Doc. It's my spare. You can wear it till we part ways." He grinned from ear to ear. "You do know how to use one of these, don't you?"

Patrick eyed the weapon in his hand and said, "I've never even held a gun, much less fired one."

Gus threw back his head and laughed. "You really are a city slicker. I'm gonna have to toughen you up!"

Patrick chuckled good-naturedly. "While you're doing that, mountain man, I'll teach you some finesse!"

"Guess I could use some of that, all right!" Gus paused, then said in a serious tone, "I'll teach you how to use the gun, Doc. We'll have a lesson or two when we get out on the prairie. Now it's time to slip into these bedrolls and get ourselves some sleep."

"You go ahead, Gus," said Patrick, reaching into his overnight bag. "I'll douse the light in a few minutes."

Gus had his boots off and was about to slip into the bedroll when he spotted the black Book in Patrick's hand. He watched Patrick sit down close to the lantern on the desk and open the Bible. Quietly, Gus slid into his bedroll, then lay there, observing.

Patrick read for about ten minutes, then closed the Bible, laid it on the desk, and put out the light. He felt his way in the dark and slipped into the bedroll.

"You read the Bible a lot, Doc?" Gus asked.

"Yes, sir."

"I…uh…I've never even looked inside one."

"Really? Why not?"

"I don't know. Just never had the urge, I guess."

"Well, you need to get the urge and read it. It's God's Word. This is how He communicates with us. The Bible has all the answers to the big questions."

"Big questions? What big questions?"

"The ones the philosophers and the so-called wise men are always trying to answer. You know: who we are; where we came from; why we're here; where we're going."

There was a long silence. Then Gus said, "Doc, by where we're goin', you mean where we're goin' when we die? Like heaven or hell?"

"Precisely, Gus. It's one or the other, forever."

"Well, I'll tell you right now, I don't believe in hell."

"That's strange. I've heard you use the word numerous times today."

Dead silence.

After a few minutes, Patrick said, "Good night, Gus."

"Good night, Doc."

After a minute or so, Gus said, "Doc, you still awake?"

"Mm-hmm."

"Have you ever ridden a horse?"

"A few times when I was a kid."

"Been that long, eh?"

"Yes."

Gus chuckled.

"What's funny, mountain man?"

"I hope you've got some salve in that medical bag of yours. Are you ever gonna be sore by the time we make camp tomorrow night!"

CHAPTER TWELVE

The sky was heavy with clouds when Patrick O'Brien and Gus Wolfskill rose from their bedrolls at the break of dawn. Gus frowned as he looked at the sky through the hostler's window, but he told Patrick they would go ahead and prepare to leave and see how the weather looked after they'd had breakfast.

When they left the café, the sun was just breaking over the horizon, spreading light into the widening space of open sky beneath heavy gray clouds.

"Looks like we can ride, Doc."

"Let's do it then," Patrick said.

The physician and the mountain man rode out of Cheyenne City, pointing their animals due west. The pack mule bore Patrick's overnight bag and the salicylic acid.

The snow was deep, and the horses trudged at a steady pace. There was little talk between the two men as they concentrated on keeping warm. The sky had cleared completely, and the glare off the snow was blinding as they rode across the white world of prairie. Patrick noted that Gus barely squinted.

By noon Patrick's inner thighs were beginning to feel tender. By evening, he was in pain. He walked gingerly as he helped Gus set up camp and pitch the tent.

Gus chuckled. "Legs hurtin', Doc?"

"You might say that."

"You got some salve in your medical kit?"

"Yes."

"You'd better get some on your legs. You've got to be back in that saddle in the mornin'."

Morning came bright and clear, and after a target lesson with the Colt .45, Patrick approached his horse with dread.

"Might as well mount up and get it over with, Doc." Gus was already aboard his mount, with the pack mule's lead rope in his gloved hand.

Patrick lifted his foot into the stirrup, swung into the frozen saddle, and settled in with a groan.

By midmorning, the sun actually gave off a small measure of warmth.

While the animals plodded through the two-foot depth of snow, Gus asked about Patrick's past. Patrick talked about his childhood and growing up years and told Gus that his father had been an army doctor. They talked for some time about the Civil War.

Patrick then told about his internship at Cook County Hospital, his practice at the downtown Chicago clinic, and his desire to come to Fort Bridger to help his father and eventually take over the practice.

"Well, Doc, that's wonderful," Gus said. "I'm sure your parents are really lookin' forward to havin' you with 'em."

"That they are. And I'm looking forward to it, myself."

The only sound for the next few minutes was the breathing of the animals and their hooves crunching through the snow. Gus finally broke the silence.

"Doc, in all of this history about you and your comin' to Wyomin', you haven't said a word about a wife or a sweetheart."

"I'm not married, Gus. No sweetheart left behind in

Chicago, either. I've dated lots of girls, but just haven't found the right one to marry. What about you? Is there a Mrs. Wolfskill somewhere? I'd also like to know what made you want to live the life of a hunter and trapper."

Patrick glanced at his traveling partner and saw sadness in the man's eyes.

"I'll tell you about Mrs. Wolfskill in a little while," Gus said. "But let me answer your other question first."

Gus said he had always loved the great outdoors. He had come west from Kentucky in his teen years with an uncle who had taken him in when his parents died. He and his uncle spent a lot of time in the Bighorn Mountains of northern Wyoming. It was there that he saw his uncle killed by a huge grizzly. Gus had come upon the scene of the attack when his uncle was nearly dead. He shot and killed the grizzly but was unable to save his uncle's life.

"After I buried my uncle I wandered southward, huntin' and trappin' in the Medicine Bow Mountains west of Laramie. Just a few years ago I was loadin' a bundle of furs on my pack mule—a different one than this one—when a cougar leaped at me from a tall rock. My horse, here, had given me a split-second warnin'. I was able to pull my big huntin' knife just before the cat hit me. I plunged the blade full-heft into his middle, but he clawed and mangled me before he died. Most of the scars are on my chest and stomach. Some are hidden here beneath my beard."

"Whew, you must've been bleeding pretty bad!"

"I was, Doc. I was so weak I couldn't move. I was just lyin' there on the ground, bleedin' to death, unable to help myself. I opened my eyes to see a small band of Cheyenne Indians standin' over me. They patched me up and took me to their village. Their chief's name was White Bear, and his young daughter, Pretty Face, nursed me back to health. We fell in love and were married by tribal custom. Pretty Face became my huntin' and trappin' partner, and we had a wonderful life together. After about a year and a half of marriage, she told me we were going to have a child. I was so excited I could hardly contain myself."

"I can imagine so," Patrick said.

"When she became large with child, she stayed in her father's village while I went on with my huntin' and trappin'. One day, when I was sellin' furs to a tradin' post near Laramie, soldiers from Fort Russell attacked White Bear's village to punish him for one of his war parties havin' wiped out a wagon train. Pretty Face—" Gus's voice faltered. "Pretty Face took a bullet, Doc. It hit the baby first, then lodged against her backbone. She and the baby were dead when I got back to the village." Gus turned his head away.

"I'm sorry about your wife and baby," Patrick said.

Gus nodded as he put a gloved hand to his eye. "I get to thinkin' that I'm past cryin' about it, Doc, then I up and shed tears again. Forgive me."

"Don't ever be ashamed of tears, Gus. I know it isn't supposed to be manly to cry, but don't you believe it. Jesus Christ is every inch a man, and He wept many times, according to the Bible."

Gus nodded but kept his face pointed straight ahead and urged his horse on.

When they made camp that night in a shallow draw, they cooked a meal and drew warmth from the small circle of flames.

"Doc, I hope I didn't talk your leg off today," Gus said as they sat beside the flickering fire and ate.

"The way these thighs are hurting, I sort of wish you had."

Gus let out a guffaw and slapped his leg.

"Seriously, you didn't talk my leg off," Patrick said. "I'm glad I learned so many things about you and from you. However, I did want to mention something."

"And what's that?"

"Well, when you were talking today you kept using two words—*damn* and *hell*. Do you realize, my friend, that a person who dies without Jesus Christ is damned to hell?"

The mountain man's face flushed bright red. "Well, I…uh…I've talked that way since I was a kid. Learned it from my pa and other men."

"Gus, I'm not trying to be a smart aleck or anything, but profanity is built on mocking the things of God. All of us were born sinners because we're descendants of Adam and inherited his sinful nature. We're at enmity with God and use language that attacks the things that are holy or that are connected with God and eternal things. So we're sinners by nature, but let's be honest, we're also sinners by choice. Isn't that right?"

Gus nodded. "Yeah, that's right. We choose to do wrong."

"Now, here's the thing, Gus. We must have our sins forgiven and cleansed by the Lord, or when we die we go out into eternity to face Him in our sins, and that will land us in hell. God will not allow sin into heaven. Can I read you something from the Bible about that?"

"Sure."

Patrick went to get his Bible from his overnight bag and hurried back to the fire. Gus was throwing more wood on the fire and stirring up the coals. Patrick sat beside Gus this time and said, "Let me read you a brief passage from Romans chapter 3: 'For all have sinned, and come short of the glory of God; being justified freely by his grace through the redemption that is in Christ Jesus.'"

The wind tugged at the pages of Patrick's Bible, and he laid his palms on them to prevent them from tearing.

"Gus, we've already agreed that all human beings are sinners."

"Yeah."

"Now, look here," Patrick said, holding the page so Gus

could see it clearly by the light of the fire. "It says when a sinner is justified, he is justified freely by God's grace. Salvation is not by works or religious deeds. Salvation is by God's grace. You can't earn it, you can't deserve it, and you can't buy it. It's free. And notice where redemption is found. What does verse 24 say?"

Gus leaned closer to the page. "It says redemption is in Christ Jesus."

"Do you know why?"

"Well, I suppose it's because He's the one who died for sinners on that cross."

"So you know about that?"

"Mm-hmm. I told you, I've heard some Bible."

"Well, that's the gospel, Gus. Christ died for our sins, He was buried, and praise His name, He came back out of the grave on the third day. The price for our redemption was paid when Jesus shed His blood and died for us. For you, for me, and for all mankind."

"For me?" Gus said, swallowing hard. "You mean Jesus actually died for me…personally?"

"When He went to the cross, He went there for you, personally. He shed His blood on the cross so He could wash away all your sins. Right here in this same passage, in verse twenty-five, God makes it clear that you must have faith in the blood of Jesus to be saved. If you will trust the one who shed His blood for you, repent of your sin, and call on Him to save you, Gus, He will do it."

The big man tugged nervously on his beard.

"Do you understand?" Patrick asked.

"I believe so. I just need some time to think it through."

"Of course. If I can answer any questions for you, please ask."

"All right. Thanks, Doc."

After they had bedded down inside the tent, Gus lay awake. The Scriptures Patrick had given him kept running through his mind.

The next morning at breakfast, Gus asked some questions about the difference between grace and human effort. Patrick answered from the Word, making sure Gus understood clearly. Gus only nodded, then told Patrick he needed to give him another lesson on how to use the Colt .45.

When Gus was satisfied that Patrick was catching on sufficiently, they mounted up and rode westward again. It was another clear day, though the temperature was below zero.

Patrick prayed in his heart, *Lord, I know You are working in Gus's heart. Please let me lead him to You before it's time for us to part. Dear Lord, thank You for Your patience with me. When I was astray, I had no burden for souls. It feels so good to be walking close to You again.*

As the day progressed, Patrick noticed a change in Gus. Although the big man did a lot of talking, the usual profanity was absent. Twice he slipped but immediately caught himself and apologized.

That night, inside the tent, while both the wind and nearby wolves howled, Patrick told Gus about the circumstances in his life that brought him to the place of repentance and faith.

Gus listened politely, then said, "Doc, I'm glad you found what you needed."

"It wasn't *what* I needed, Gus," Patrick said softly. "It was *who* I needed. Jesus is the only one who can save sinners, and He is the only one who can satisfy our souls. We not only need Jesus here in this life but in the next one. All sinners need Him, Gus, including you. And we'll need Him when judgment comes. Only those who have opened their hearts to Him here on earth will escape the wrath of God."

The big man was quiet for a moment, then said, "Good night, Doc."

"Good night, Gus."

Patrick fell asleep within a few minutes, but while the wind and the wolves continued to howl, Gus was having a battle in his soul. He was finally able to get to sleep, but only after a long struggle with himself over his lost condition.

Dawn brought another clear sky, though the temperature remained below zero. After breakfast, Patrick was given another lesson in the use of the Colt .45 and was starting to hit his targets at least half the time.

Gus patted him on the back and said, "I'm proud of the way this city slicker is takin' to the gun!"

Patrick snapped the cylinder shut and said, "Well, I'm glad to make the old mountain man proud."

They laughed together, mounted up, and once again headed west. Patrick's thighs were still quite tender, but the pain was easing some.

It was coming up on noon. A brilliant sun reflected strongly off the snow.

"So how long till your dad retires and you take over the practice?" Gus asked.

"Can't say for sure, but I'd say it'll be another year or so. Maybe two. But I can wait. Just getting to work with Dad will be a pleasure. Mom, too. She's his secretary, receptionist, and all-around helper."

"Is your mother Irish, too?"

"Oh, yes. Her maiden name was Rafferty. She's—"

Patrick's words were cut off by the sound of yapping Indians and the crack of rifle shots on the frigid air. A half-dozen dark-skinned riders in buckskin came toward them from behind a snow-laden mound to their right. Bullets plowed the snow, zipping all around them.

Gus's horse nickered shrilly and the mule made a whining sound. Patrick's horse tossed his head and whinnied. Patrick whipped the Colt .45 out of its holster.

"Wait a minute!" Gus said, raising both his arms to make

hand signals. "Put the gun away! I'm trying to show them I'm friendly toward them and know their sign language."

The lead Indian raised his rifle over his head and barked a command to the others. The firing stopped. The Indians kept coming, pushing their horses hard through the deep snow.

"Smile, Doc," Gus said. "Look friendly. These are Blackfoot. They probably think the bundles on the mule's pack are full of food. Blackfoot are allies with the Cheyenne. Since I was married to a Cheyenne, I think I can persuade them not to kill us. You pray. I'll try to negotiate."

Patrick started praying silently but it didn't still his heart fluttering in his chest.

When the Indians drew up, their faces looked hard as stone. The leader edged closer to Gus, eyeing him warily, his mouth a thin, brutal line. He stared at Gus for a long moment. When the Blackfoot started conversing in the Cheyenne language, Gus used it, too, and spoke to the leader.

Patrick listened, carefully watching the faces of the Indians. He didn't understand a word Gus said until the mountain man spoke his name.

The leader spoke a few words back, then Gus talked some more. When he had spoken for some two or three minutes, the leader turned and conversed with his warriors.

Gus spoke to Patrick in a low tone. "The leader's name is Many Scalps. I told him my name and explained that I was married to Chief White Bear's daughter. I also told them that Pretty Face was killed when white men's army attacked White Bear's village. I told him that I'm still a friend to the Cheyenne and to their allies. Many Scalps is not sure I'm telling the truth about being married to Pretty Face."

"So what happens if he decides not to believe you?" Patrick whispered.

"You just pray that he does!"

The conversation went on between Many Scalps and his men.

"What are they saying now?" Patrick asked.

"Shh, hold on."

One of the warriors was saying something to Many Scalps. Most of the warrior's nose was missing, and a hideous scar ran down his cheek. Finally, Many Scalps nodded at the warrior, then turned back to Gus. His face had lost its stony expression.

Many Scalps said something lengthy to Gus, then Gus smiled and nodded, speaking back in Cheyenne.

Many Scalps turned to talk to his men again, and Gus said to Patrick, "The warrior's name is No Nose. He told Many Scalps and the others that he had been to White Bear's village on several occasions and knew Pretty Face well. He also told them that he remembered seeing her standing beside me in front of her father's tepee. He has assured Many Scalps that I am speaking the truth."

"Good for him," said Patrick, breathing a sigh of relief.

Many Scalps turned back to Gus with a smile and spoke again. Then the Blackfoot turned their mounts to ride away.

Gus waved and said, "Wave, Doc. Many Scalps said he will let us live because I am a friend of their allies, the Cheyenne."

Patrick waved enthusiastically, saying, "Praise God!"

When the Indians were out of earshot, Gus released pent-up air from his lungs and said, "I'm sure glad No Nose had seen me with Pretty Face."

As Gus and Patrick rode on, Patrick thanked the Lord in his heart for sparing their lives. He also prayed again that the Holy Spirit would work in Gus's heart and draw him to Jesus before they parted.

The cold day wore on, and finally the sun set behind the western horizon. While there was still light in the sky, the travelers pitched their tent and started a fire. There was only a slight breeze as they huddled next to the fire and ate their supper of beans, elk jerky, hardtack, and strong coffee.

Gus shook his head and said, "We had us a real close call

today, Doc. A real close one. If No Nose hadn't seen me with Pretty Face, or if he hadn't been ridin' with Many Scalps today, we'd both be dead right now."

Patrick took a sip of the strong coffee and looked at his friend as the light of the flames danced on his rugged, bearded face.

"Gus, if Many Scalps and his warriors had killed us today, tell me where you'd be right now."

Gus's mouth seemed frozen shut. After a lengthy silence, he said, "Well, Doc, according to your Bible, I'd be in hell."

Patrick let the man's own words hover in the cold air a moment, then said, "Is the Bible true, Gus?"

The mountain man blinked at the tears welling up in his eyes and nodded. "Yeah, Doc. I know it's true."

"God was good to see to it that No Nose was in that war party today, wasn't He?"

Tears began spilling down Gus's cheeks and into his beard. "Yeah, He sure was." He laid his tin plate down and said, "Doc, I want to be saved. Right now."

The rest of supper was put on hold as Patrick O'Brien had the joy of leading his friend to Christ. After Gus had called on the Lord to save him, he shed more tears, telling Patrick that he was so relieved to know that all was right between him and God, and that heaven was his eternal destination.

On January 23—eleven days after they had left Cheyenne City—the two brothers in Christ came to the fork in the snow-packed trail where Patrick would continue on to Fort Bridger and Gus would head for the Uintah Mountains. The mountains' jagged, snow-capped peaks touched the sky in majestic beauty in the distant southwest.

It was midmorning as both men dismounted. Gus tied the overnight bag and the sack of salicylic acid behind Patrick's saddle.

Patrick squinted against the sun's glare off the snow, looking due west, and said, "So, it's about twenty miles?"

"Just beyond those rollin' hills. Keep a steady pace and you'll be in Fort Bridger before sundown."

Patrick laid a hand on the huge man's shoulder. "Thank you, Gus, for inviting me to ride with you. It might have been a long time before I got this medicine to Dad if I'd waited for the wagon supply train to go, or even a stagecoach."

"It's been my pleasure, Doc."

Patrick started to unbuckle the gunbelt. "Almost forgot to give this back to you."

"Why don't you just keep it? You might need it between here and Fort Bridger."

"I don't think so. Besides, it's your spare."

"Really, Doc, I can get by with—"

"No. If I need a gun when I get to town, I can buy one. You can't buy a gun in those mountains."

Gus took the holstered gun, wrapped the belt around it, and stuffed it in his gear. When he turned around, Patrick was holding out his Bible.

"Something else you can't buy in those mountains. I told you before we went to sleep last night how important it is for you to read the Word everyday for your spiritual growth."

"Yeah, but I can't take your Bible, Doc."

"It's not my Bible anymore, dear brother," Patrick said, pressing it into Gus's meaty hand. "It's yours now. I can buy another one in town."

Touched by Patrick's generosity, Gus thanked him for leading him to Jesus, and put a bear hug on the doctor he would never forget.

When they were in their saddles, Patrick said, "Gus, if you ever get a chance to drop into Fort Bridger, I'd sure love to see you again."

"Might happen. But if we never meet again on this earth, one thing for sure—we'll be together forever in heaven."

CHAPTER THIRTEEN

On Wednesday, January 18, Julianna LeCroix awakened and wondered what she had heard that brought her out of a deep sleep. She glanced at the window and could tell by the dim light that dawn was breaking.

Thirteen-month-old Larissa, who lay in her crib next to the bed, made a fussing sound. Larissa was usually a happy baby, and she normally cooed when she awakened.

Julianna left her bed and bent over the crib. A chill settled around her heart when she saw that Larissa's chubby cheeks were flushed. Julianna picked her up and pressed the baby's face to her own. The heat of fever radiated from Larissa's tiny body as she let out a wail.

Julianna folded Larissa close to her breast and tried to quietly soothe the baby. A feeling of dread washed over her. The baby's lungs were already weakened from her earlier bout with bronchitis.

She wrapped Larissa in a heavy, double-folded blanket, carried her down the hall to the parlor, and took another blanket along in her free hand. She laid Larissa on an overstuffed chair and then stirred what embers were still alive in the fireplace. Soon the fire was going. She laid on several logs, then picked up the fussing baby and headed for the kitchen.

Julianna placed the extra blanket on the kitchen table and

laid Larissa on it. "Mommy will take care of you, sweetheart," she said.

Julianna built a fire in the kitchen stove and put a pan of water on to heat up. She paced the floor with the baby in her arms, speaking softly in an attempt to soothe her. Larissa's fussing was growing louder, and she was coughing.

Soon the water was steaming. Julianna held Larissa in one arm and poured hot water into a basin she had placed on the table, then added cold water to make it tepid. She laid the baby on the blanket next to the basin, stripped off Larissa's nightclothes, and eased her down into the water.

Larissa wailed while her mother crooned softly to her. When it had no effect, Julianna prayed, "Lord, I know how important it is to reduce her fever, but I have nothing else to use. Please help me. Give me wisdom. Don't let this precious little one suffer. Thank You that You love her more than I do and will do what is best for her."

Julianna talked to Larissa and kept her in the water until it became cool. When she lifted her out of the basin, she could tell Larissa's fever had come down some. Julianna took the towel from the back of the chair next to the stove. It was warm and comforting, and Larissa snuggled into it when her mother wrapped it around her pudgy little body. Her fussing lessened, and finally she went quiet.

Julianna sat down in a rocker near the stove and tried to get Larissa to nurse, but the baby had no interest and squirmed away.

"All right, sweetie. We'll try again later."

In hushed tones, Julianna hummed a lullaby. Minutes later, Larissa's eyes began to droop, and soon she dozed off.

Julianna glanced out the kitchen window and saw the bright sunlight reflecting off the tops of the snow-covered trees in the backyard. She tried to shift into a more relaxed position, and Larissa stirred, but settled back to sleep again. The warmth from the stove and the steady rocking soon had Julianna nodding off.

Suddenly she was startled awake by a wracking cough, and the baby began wailing again, then choking and coughing intermittently. The baby's breathing was labored, and Julianna could hear a slight wheezing.

"Steam treatment," Julianna said to herself, rising from the rocker. "Just like Dr. O'Brien had me do when she was sick before."

Julianna dropped a couple more logs into the cookstove and placed a teakettle full of water on it. She went to the pantry and took out the jar of peppermint camphor she had used before and poured a measure into the teakettle. She then went to the linen closet and took out a large towel.

After what seemed an eternity, the teakettle began to whistle. With the squirming baby in her arm, Julianna set a pad on the table, placed the teakettle on it, and made a tent with the towel over both of their heads, praying all the while that the steam would ease her little daughter's discomfort.

There was a knock at the back door, and Julianna called out, "Yes, darling, the door's unlocked! Come in!"

Jack Brower stepped into the kitchen and rocked back on his heels. "Julianna, what's the matter?"

"Larissa's got influenza symptoms."

Strong arms slid around her and the baby on her lap. "When did this come on her?"

"She woke me up right at dawn, fussing. She was running a fever then. I bathed her in tepid water, and it cooled her down some. The only other thing I could think to do was give her this steam treatment."

"As soon as you're through, we'll take her to Doc O'Brien."

"We don't dare take her out in the cold, Jack. But I'd like you to go to the clinic and tell Dr. O'Brien Larissa's symptoms, and if she can take salicylic acid, to send some home with you."

"Whatever you say, honey. I'd like to give both of you a hug before I go."

"We're just about through here."

"Then I'll wait."

When Julianna removed the towel, Jack bent over them and elicited smiles from both of the women in his life.

At the clinic, Doc and Edie were swamped with people who needed their care. Edie was in the examining room when Jack entered the crowded office, and Doc was just coming out with a mother and her teenage daughter. Their coughs blended in with the rest of the hacking sounds in the office.

Doc looked at the deputy marshal. "Are you coming down with it, Jack?"

"No, sir. It's little Larissa. She has a fever and is coughing, and she's been pretty fussy. Julianna didn't want to bring her out in the subzero temperature. She asked me to come and find out if Larissa can take salicylic acid, and if so, to bring some back to her."

"Julianna did the right thing," Doc said, "especially since Larissa had that bronchitis problem a few months ago. We're running low on salicylic acid. I'm having to ration it out. Dr. Blayney's doing the same thing at the fort. But I'll give you a small portion. Tell Julianna to give it to the baby one teaspoon to a full cup. She should start her on it immediately."

"I'll tell her."

"Is Larissa's cough bad yet?" Doc said as he headed to the door of the back room.

"From what Julianna said, I think it is."

Doc paused at the door. "Julianna probably still has some peppermint camphor from the bronchitis episode. Tell her to start giving Larissa steam treatments. At least three a day…and to bathe her in tepid water at least twice a day."

"She's already given her one bathing, Doc. And when I got there, she was giving her a steam treatment."

"Good. Be right back."

The doctor returned a moment later with a small envelope of salicylic acid powders and placed it in Jack's hand. "Tell Julianna that I commend her for her good thinking. And I want to know how Larissa is doing. Please tell me how she responds to the treatments by tonight, okay?"

"I'll come by and give you a report."

"Good. See you then."

When Doc returned to the examining room with an elderly patient, he took Edie aside and told her about Larissa LeCroix. Shaking his head, he said, "If we don't get that shipment of salicylic acid soon, it's going to be disastrous."

Late that afternoon, Curly Wesson entered Cooper's General Store and approached those working behind the counter. "Howdy, Mrs. Bateman, Jacob. Is Hannah in the store?"

"She's upstairs in the apartment," Jacob said.

"She not feelin' well? I hope she hasn't come down with the influenza."

"She's fine. But Doc O'Brien asked her not to expose herself to people, with so many coming down with it."

"Well, that's best. I shore 'preciate you helpin', Mrs. Bateman, so's Hannah can stay up there like Doc said."

"It's my pleasure. The other ladies who come in and help feel the same way. We love Hannah and want her to stay healthy."

Curly nodded. "That's good. Jacob, the telegraph lines are workin' again and I've got a telegram here for Hannah. Be all right if I take it up to her? Purty important. It's from her supplier in Cheyenne City."

Jacob excused himself to the customer he was waiting on

and said, "That depends. You havin' any influenza symptoms?"

"Nope. Shore don't."

"How about Judy?"

"Nope. She's fine."

Jacob smiled. "Then it's all right for you to go up."

Curly laughed. "Tell you what, Jacob. I'm right proud to see that you're so pertective of Hannah."

"I owe that sweet lady a lot, Curly. I'll do anything I can to keep her from getting sick."

"Curly, come in! It's wonderful to see you!" Hannah motioned for the little man to come inside out of the cold, then closed the door after him. "To what do I owe this visit, Curly?"

"Well, you owe it to the fact that neither Judy nor yours truly has any symptoms of the influenza."

"I don't understand."

"It's like this, honey. They got the telegraph system to workin' again. You know it went out after that blizzard the other day." He pulled a yellow envelope from a coat pocket. "Well, I have this here telegram for you from your supplier in Cheyenne City, but that stubborn Jacob Kates put me through a question and answer session down in the store before he'd let me come up here to see you."

"Oh? About what?"

"He wanted to know if'n either Judy or me had any influenza symptoms. When I assured him we ain't had none, he give me permission to come up."

Hannah laughed. "That Jacob is an old grandmother, but I love him for it!"

"I wish this was good news, honey, but it ain't," Curly said as he handed the envelope to Hannah.

Hannah took the envelope and opened it. The wagon train bearing her last order had been delayed indefinitely for a lack of military support. Once the Indians had been driven off or subdued, the wagons would roll again.

Hannah sighed. "Well, I'm going to have to start rationing the sale of food in the store, like I did before."

Curly removed his hat and ran a palm over his bald head. "This is bad, Hannah. I shore hope the army gits the Indian problem under control purty soon. We really need them wagons movin'. And that ain't all. I'm concerned 'bout them stagecoaches that have been held up because of the last blizzard. Doc O'Brien has ordered a shipment of salicylic acid from his medical suppliers in Cheyenne City, but since both the supply trains and the stages ain't runnin', there's no way the medicine can git here."

"Maybe they'll at least get the stages running again, since the weather seems to have taken a turn for the better the past few days."

By the next day, the number of children and adults down with influenza had both doctors so busy they had to enlist help to care for them all.

Dr. Blayney had asked every officer's wife who was not down herself—or caring for her own sick children—to help him. The infirmary was packed with the most serious cases, while those not so serious were being taken care of in their homes or in the barracks.

Dr. O'Brien had Pastor Kelly and his wife, Rebecca, assisting him with many of the sick who had been put on cots and mattresses in the fellowship hall of the church. Some of the women of the town were also helping out and working in shifts.

Ordinarily Sundi Lindgren got out of bed with a bound and didn't slow down until she crawled beneath the covers at bedtime. But this morning she just wanted to lay in bed.

"All right, Sundi," she finally said aloud, "let's get out of this warm bed and start our day."

She threw back the covers and had taken only a couple of steps when a chill ran through her. She walked down the hall to the washroom and heard Heidi getting out of bed as she passed her room.

Sundi's mind seemed a little foggy, and she felt the onset of a headache behind her eyes. But she had to get to the school-house early to get the fire going in the potbellied stove before the children arrived.

Sundi was drying her face when she heard Heidi coming down the hall.

Heidi smiled at her little sister and said, "Good morning, Sundi! This is Friday! You get two days off after today."

Sundi looked at her over the towel pressed to her face. "Yes, just think of it. Two days off. That's why I'm glad I'm in the teaching profession rather than running a dress shop where I'd have to work six days a week."

Heidi cocked her head, studying her sister. "Honey, are you feeling all right?"

Sundi patted her face with the towel. "Just a little tired. Why?"

"You look peaked."

"Really? I'm sure my color will come back when I get out there in that cold air."

Sundi forced herself to eat her usual breakfast with Heidi, though she had no appetite. But the hot tea felt good when it went down.

She tried to convince herself that she was feeling better as she put on her coat, hat, and mittens. She hugged her sister as usual, went out the door, and trudged down the street toward her beloved schoolhouse.

The one-room frame structure was cold when she entered

and headed for the potbellied stove. She could see her breath almost as easily as she had seen it outside.

While Sundi was getting the fire started, her head went light, and she was so dizzy she had to sit down. The headache was now full strength. After a few minutes, she started to get out of the chair to put more logs in the stove, but all of her strength had drained away. She pressed a palm to her brow and felt perspiration.

When the first group of children arrived at the school, they found their teacher sitting at her desk, holding her head in her hands.

Mary Beth Cooper rushed ahead of the others and drew up to the desk. "Miss Lindgren, are you all right?"

"I...have a bad headache, Mary Beth."

Chris and B.J. moved closer.

"She all right?" Chris asked.

"Headache," Mary Beth said.

Sundi forced a smile. "I'll be fine. All of you sit down at your desks. As you know, there's to be a history test this morning. Why don't you look over chapter seven in your history books until it's time for school to start?"

Travis Carlin sat down at his desk next to Chris Cooper. "Miss Lindgren doesn't look so good," he said.

"She's got a headache," Chris said. "Must be a bad one."

Sundi looked up at the clock on the back wall. "It's eight-thirty, children. Looks like we have more students missing today than yesterday. Mary Beth, will you ring the bell for me this morning, please?"

"Yes, ma'am." Mary Beth left her desk and went to the small vestibule at the front of the building. Another student came in just as she took hold of the rope and began ringing the bell.

She was almost back to her desk when two boys came running in, out of breath. They cast a worried glance at their teacher, but Miss Lindgren rubbed her temples and said, "Josh, Mark, I'll excuse your being late this morning."

"Thank you, ma'am," they said, and quickly removed their mittens, caps, and coats.

"Mary Beth, would you come to the desk for a moment, please?" Sundi said.

"Yes, Miss Lindgren."

Sundi lowered her voice so only Mary Beth could hear. "I really am not feeling well. I think…I think I may be coming down with influenza. I've got to go home. Will you take over for me?"

Worry captured Mary Beth's features. "Of course, but I don't think you should try to walk home, Miss Lindgren. Maybe I should send someone to fetch Grandpa—I mean, Dr. O'Brien."

"That might be best. I'll tell everyone that I have authorized you to take my place today. You can go ahead and give the history test. The questions are in this folder right here on the desk. After that, you can teach them the other lessons I have here in my notebook."

"I can handle it, ma'am. Let me get a couple of the boys to help you to another chair so I can use your desk."

"All right, after I speak to the class."

Sundi explained the plan to the class, asking them to cooperate with Mary Beth. Luke Patterson volunteered to fetch Dr. O'Brien and hurried out the door, putting his coat on as he went.

Chris Cooper and Travis Carlin helped their teacher to another chair, and when they had returned to their desks, Mary Beth began the history test.

Some twenty minutes later, Luke returned with Marshal Lance Mangum. Dr. O'Brien had so many new influenza patients that he couldn't come. Mangum had borrowed a horse and buggy from someone on the street.

The O'Briens were ready for Sundi when she arrived. They had the marshal carry her into the back room and place her on one of the examining tables. Lance said he was going to the dress shop to tell Heidi of Sundi's condition.

Edie worked on other patients nearby, while Doc examined Sundi. Moments later, Edie drew up to the table and patted Sundi's hand, saying to her husband, "Does she have it, Doc?"

He nodded. "All the symptoms. Fever, chills, weakness, headache, dizziness, and pain in her muscles and respiratory tract."

"Oh, my. What about your students, honey?" Edie asked.

Sundi's voice was faint as she replied, "I...I have Mary Beth taking my place. She can finish the day all right and proceed on Monday if she has to."

Edie smiled. "Well, since Mary Beth is planning on being a teacher, this will be good experience for her."

"Yes. She's going to be an excellent teacher. She does a superb job of teaching when she has gone with me to the Crow village on a Saturday."

"Edie," Doc said, "I'll give Sundi a dose of salicylic acid, then I need you to bathe her in cool water. We've got to get her fever down quickly."

As soon as Doc had administered the medicine, Edie drew a curtain around the table. Moments later, Heidi came in and was allowed to stand by Sundi while Edie continued to bathe her. When Edie was finished, Doc returned, placed a thermometer in Sundi's mouth, then led Heidi to a far corner.

"She's pretty sick," he said. "I'm not going to send her to the church for care there. I want to keep an eye on her here."

"Thank you, Doc. I'll be back after I close the shop this evening."

By late afternoon Sundi's fever had not gone down, and Dr. O'Brien shook his head as he looked at the thermometer in his hand and walked away from the table where Sundi lay. Edie, who was tending a child on a cot nearby, saw the look on her husband's face and left the child momentarily. She moved to his side and looked up into his eyes.

Doc ran splayed fingers through his thick mop of silver hair and sighed. "Honey, her temperature is still rising. It's almost a hundred and three."

"Oh, dear."

"The salicylic acid doesn't seem to have had any effect."

"And my bathing her hasn't either."

"No."

"Then I'll bathe her again in a few minutes."

"All right. I'll give her another dose right now. We've got to bring her temperature under control. If we don't…"

CHAPTER FOURTEEN

The sun was setting when Dr. Frank O'Brien returned to the back room where Sundi lay. Edie and Heidi stood beside her. "Well, there's no one else in the office," he said. "Looks like we may get a break in the number of new patients."

"Didn't I hear someone come in while you were in the office?" Edie asked.

"It was Chris, Mary Beth, and B.J. They came to see about their teacher."

A slight smile formed around the thermometer in Sundi's mouth.

"Bless their hearts," Heidi said as she wiped perspiration from her sister's brow. "Those are special children."

"Sundi," Doc said, "Mary Beth said to tell you that she has everything under control at school and she will have new lessons ready for Monday."

Sundi nodded.

"And all three of them said to tell you they love you, and the whole family will be praying for you."

Edie patted Sundi's arm. "We all love you, sweetie. And we're praying."

Doc removed the thermometer from Sundi's mouth and studied it for several seconds.

"Well, tell us," said Edie.

"It's exactly a hundred and three," Doc said, a glum look

on his face. "Went up a fraction. We've got to keep bathing her every hour, all night."

Sundi closed her eyes.

"Doc," Heidi said, "I'll do it."

"No, Heidi. You can take the first few hours, then Edie can take a shift, and I'll take the third shift."

Heidi shook her head. "No. You two need to get a good night's sleep. You've been working long and hard as it is, and no doubt you'll have new cases to deal with tomorrow, let alone the attention you'll have to give the ones who are already sick. I'll do the whole night."

Doc sighed and rubbed his eyes. "I know it will do no good to argue with you."

"You are so right. Now, go on. You two take the rest of the night off."

"We've got to give Sundi another dose of salicylic acid first," Edie said.

They heard the outer office door open and close.

"I'll see who that is," said Doc, heading for the office door. "You go ahead and give her the powders."

When he stepped into the office, Doc was surprised to see his colleague from the fort. "Well, hello, Doctor. What can I do for you?"

"First I want to know how Miss Lindgren is. Some of the fort children told their parents about her being sick and that Marshal Mangum had brought her to the clinic."

"Well, she's a sick young lady, Doctor. We're having a hard time getting her fever down. She's at a hundred and three right now."

"I'm sorry to hear that. I'd offer some salicylic acid, but I'm out."

"We've still got a small supply. We've been giving it to her and bathing her in cool water, but her body's not responding to it. The only thing we can do is keep trying."

"Yes. If you need help, I can—"

"No, no. Heidi's going to stay with her all night."

"Oh. Good."

"Was there something else?"

"Yes. When I was told about Miss Lindgren coming down with the influenza, they also said that Mary Beth Cooper is taking her place."

"That's right."

"I know Mary Beth is quite capable of handling the job for a brief time, but I think in light of how sick Miss Lindgren is, and the fact that so many of the schoolchildren are already down sick, maybe you and I ought to suggest to the school board that they simply close the school until Miss Lindgren and her students can resume the normal schedule."

"I agree. It'll cut down on the continual exposure for the children, too. I guess you probably heard that Pastor Kelly has canceled the church services Sunday."

"No, but I think it's wise. He's already got the fellowship hall full of patients, I understand. No sense exposing people any more than necessary."

"I have to make a house call in the morning at the Bledsoe's to see how Carlene is doing. Since Dan is chairman of the school board, I'll tell him we both recommend that the school be closed until this epidemic is over. I'm sure Dan and the rest of the board will do what's best for the children."

Sunday morning came bright and clear, but the subzero temperature still held Wyoming in its grip.

As happened quite often, Jacob Kates was at the Cooper breakfast table. Although food supplies were limited, Hannah and Mary Beth had prepared a nourishing breakfast of oatmeal and biscuits. Oatmeal was not the family's favorite item for breakfast, but it stretched a long way, and Hannah enhanced the flavor by adding some maple syrup on top of each mounded bowl. Using a little of her secret supply of cocoa, she saw to it that each child had a steaming mug of the chocolate delight.

The Coopers talked a few minutes about how they would miss going to church, then Mary Beth brought up the responsibility she would face at school the next day. In spite of the reason for it, she was obviously relishing being the substitute teacher.

While secretly feeding Biggie a part of her biscuit under the table, Patty Ruth said, "Mama?"

"Yes, honey?"

"Since I'm six years old now, can I go to school? I want to see Mary Beth teachin' the class."

"No, honey. You can't go to school until next fall, because your birthday came after October thirty-first."

"Not even if it's just to watch my big sister teach?"

"No. Besides, it's best that you not be exposed to the influenza any more than necessary."

The little redhead's brow puckered. "Is that why Pastor Kelly didn't have church today? So folks wouldn't be 'sposed to the 'fluenza?"

"Yes."

"I'm surprised they haven't closed the school too," Chris said.

"Maybe the school board figures all the students have already been exposed in one way or another," Jacob said.

They ate quietly for a few minutes, then Jacob said, "I was going to mention to you, Miss Hannah, that Glenda, Rebecca, and Nellie told me after closing the store yesterday that some of the customers complained to them about rationing the food and supplies. Just like I told you it was on Thursday and Friday."

"I'm sorry we have to do it, but folks will just have to understand. I'm trying to be fair to all of my customers by rationing how many items they can buy."

"That's what I told them, and I know the ladies did, too."

"Mama," Chris said, "if the supply train doesn't come soon, you'll have to close the store, won't you?"

"That's right. We've been praying. It's in God's hands. We have to trust Him to take care of the matter."

Hannah noted that B.J. was slumped in his chair, just stirring his oatmeal around in the bowl. And he had not touched his hot cocoa, which he dearly loved.

"B.J., are you not feeling well?" she asked. "You usually gobble your food down, even if it's oatmeal, and ordinarily you would've asked for more cocoa by now."

The boy laid his spoon down. "I've got a headache, Mama. And I feel weak and achy...and there's a tight feelin' in my chest."

Mary Beth left her chair, rounded the table, and laid a palm on B.J.'s brow. "Mama, he's got a fever," she said almost in a whisper.

Hannah sighed and said, "Well, so far we've escaped the dread disease, but it looks like it has decided to visit the Cooper household. B.J., you go get back in your nightshirt and climb in bed. I'll be in shortly."

B.J.'s lower lip quivered as he pushed his chair back and stood up. "I'm sorry, Mama. I didn't mean to get it."

Hannah got up from her chair and laid a hand on his brow. "Of course you didn't, sweetheart. You've got a fever, all right. Hurry, now. Get back in bed. I want you to stay under the covers, even though you feel hot. We'll deal with this as we do everything else in our family. We'll lay our burden on the Lord, and with His help we'll work through this together. Don't you worry. Just rest."

"Mama," Patty Ruth said, "are we all gonna get the 'fluenza?"

"I hope not, honey. Sometimes people are exposed to it

but never get it."

Little sister sent a worried look to her brother. "I'm sorry, B.J."

He gave her a wan smile and headed toward his room.

"Mama," Chris said, "should I go get Grandpa?"

"I was about to ask if you would, honey. He's got his hands full, so it may be a while before he can come. In the meantime, I'm going to bathe B.J. in cool water and see if I can bring that fever down."

Chris pulled on his coat and darted out the door.

"Patty Ruth and I will clean up the table and do the dishes, Mama," Mary Beth said. "I'd offer to bathe B.J. for you, but I'm sure he wouldn't want his sister to do it."

Jacob chuckled. "Brothers are like that. Miss Hannah, I've got to go down and stock some shelves for tomorrow. If you need me, please send Chris down."

"Thank you, Jacob," she said, managing a tiny smile.

Over an hour had passed before Chris returned and found his sisters sitting in the parlor by the fireplace. Biggie was next to Patty Ruth, getting his ears rubbed. The ecstasy of it showed on his little black-and-white face.

"Mama's just putting B.J. back in bed, Chris," said Mary Beth, rising from the couch. "Did you get to see Grandpa?"

"He was making house calls when I got there, but Grandma told me to wait. When he came in, he said he would come as soon as he could, but he had to check on Miss Lindgren and the other patients he's keeping at the clinic. He'll be here soon, though."

"That's good."

"Grandpa told me something else, too. He and Dr. Blayney discussed the epidemic Friday night, and they decided the school should be closed."

A pang of disappointment shot through Mary Beth.

"Grandpa said he talked to Mr. Bledsoe about it earlier this morning, and Mr. Bledsoe agreed. So there won't be any school till the epidemic is over. I know you were looking forward to doing the teaching, sis, but it's really best to close school down, don't you think?"

Mary Beth nodded slowly. "Since Grandpa and Dr. Blayney say it is, then I have to agree."

"It won't be long till spring; then you can teach at the Crow village on Saturdays again, with Miss Lindgren."

The sound of footsteps came up the outside stairs.

"That's probably Grandpa," Chris said as he headed for the door.

"Hello, youngn's," Doc O'Brien said as Chris opened the door. "How's B.J. doing?"

Mary Beth spoke first. "Mama gave him a bath in tepid water, Grandpa, but he's still pretty hot. I'll take you back to his room. Mama's with him."

Both Chris and Mary Beth asked about Miss Lindgren.

Doc shook his head. "She's very, very sick. Please keep praying for her."

"We will," Chris said.

Mary Beth led the physician down the hall, and they stopped in front of the door to the boys' room, which was closed.

"Mama, Grandpa's here," Mary Beth called.

"Bring him in, honey."

Doc followed Mary Beth into the room, and Hannah rose from where she was sitting on the side of B.J.'s bed. "I appreciate your coming, Doc. How's Sundi?"

"Not good. Her fever just won't go down. She was running a hundred and three last night, and now it's almost half a degree higher."

"Oh, my."

"Keep her in your prayers. She's delirious at times. Heidi stayed with her all night, bathing her in cool water every hour, but nothing is helping. Let's check this boy," he said, moving to the bed.

B.J. held a thermometer in his mouth, while the doctor pushed, pressed, and squeezed on his body, and Hannah reported what B.J. had told her about his symptoms.

"Hannah, I hate to tell you this, but I don't have any salicylic acid to give B.J. I'm out. So is Dr. Blayney. I used the last I had this morning to give to Sundi and three children I'm keeping at the clinic. They're running exceptionally high fevers, too."

"We'll just have to keep him cool with water, Mama," Mary Beth said. "I'm sure Chris will be glad to help."

"Of course," Chris said.

Doc nodded. "Good. I was about to tell you that bathing him often in tepid water is the only recourse you've got. There won't be any more salicylic acid till Wells Fargo can get a stagecoach here from Cheyenne City."

As he spoke, O'Brien removed the thermometer from B.J.'s mouth and read it. "Well, not as bad as it could be. He's right on a hundred degrees."

Hannah ran her fingers through B.J.'s thick hair. "It's high enough that Chris and I are going to dip him in the tub four or five times a day and bathe him with washcloths in between. Whatever it takes to bring his fever down, we'll do it."

"That's good," Doc said. "Uh…Hannah, I need to talk to you in private for a moment, if I may."

"Of course." Hannah turned to locate Patty Ruth and saw her standing in the hall, just outside the door, with Biggie beside her. "Patty Ruth, you and Mary Beth go to your room. Chris, you stay here with your brother. Grandpa and I will go talk in the parlor."

Hannah and the doctor sat down, and Doc looked at her

with concern in his eyes. "Hannah, dear, you mustn't wear yourself out taking care of B.J. I know Chris will do what he can, but since I know you quite well, I know you'll carry the load. You can't do it. You need to get Glenda or one of the other ladies to come in and help."

"But Doc, I can't ask someone else to come and help me take care of my child. With Chris's help, I can handle it."

"But you'll wear yourself out. I'm concerned that you've now been exposed to influenza and you're more likely to get it if you become tired and weary."

"I'll be careful, Doc. But I must take care of my son."

O'Brien sighed, shaking his head.

"I really will be careful not to get too tired. I promise."

O'Brien gave her a cautionary look and said, "I'll be back tomorrow to check on B.J. And while you're dipping him and soaking him with washcloths, pour as much water as you can down him, so he won't dehydrate. And give him plenty of broth, too."

"I will."

She and the doctor returned to B.J. and Chris, and Hannah called for the girls to come out of their room.

Patty Ruth dashed up to the open door of B.J.'s room, with Biggie beside her, and said, "Mama, I can help you take care of B.J. now that I'm 'sposed to the 'fluenza, can't I?"

"No, honey. You haven't been close to B.J.'s face like Chris and Mary Beth and I have. You haven't even been in the boys' room since B.J. got sick. So we'll keep it that way. I don't want you to come into his room. We've all been exposed, but from what I've learned about influenza, to actually breathe the same air up close to an infected person increases the chances of getting it. Isn't that right, Grandpa?"

"Your mama's right, Patty Ruth. The smaller the room, the more breath from the sick person you get. No sense taking chances. It's best that you don't come into the room where B.J.

is."

The six-year-old nodded, then looked down at the little rat terrier. "Did you hear that, Biggie? You can't go into the boys' room 'cause you might get 'fluenza."

Dr. O'Brien had been gone little more than an hour when there was a knock at the door of the Cooper apartment. Hannah and Chris had just taken B.J. out of the galvanized tub in the boys' room, and Chris was helping him dry off while Hannah adjusted the covers on B.J.'s bed and fluffed the pillow.

"Mama, Aunt Glenda is here," Mary Beth said through the closed door.

Hannah smiled at Chris. "Your Grandpa," she whispered, then called out, "Glenda, I'll be right there. Chris, straighten up the room, will you? I can tell you right now that Aunt Glenda will be in here."

She tucked the covers around B.J.'s shivering body, then picked up a bowl off the dresser and spooned a few drops of warm broth into his mouth and got him to drink a cup of water. As she set the empty cup on the dresser, she said, "Try to sleep now, sweetheart. I'll be back to look in on you in a little while."

B.J. nodded and closed his eyes.

Hannah helped Chris finish straighten the room. At the door, she paused to look back at her ailing son and said to Chris, "I hope he'll sleep till it's time to bathe him with wash-cloths. I'll have you do that in an hour, honey. In the meantime, why don't you go down to the store and see if there's anything you can do to help Uncle Jacob?"

"Okay. I'll be back in an hour."

In the kitchen, Hannah moved to the table where Glenda sat alone. She gave her friend a wan smile.

"I told Mary Beth to keep Patty Ruth occupied," Glenda

said. "I'm here to take care of B.J. for you."

Hannah bent over and hugged Glenda. "I love you for it, but this isn't necessary. Between Chris and me, we'll take care of him. Besides, you shouldn't be exposed."

"Honey. I've already been exposed. I've been helping Nellie Patterson take care of her three children. They've all got it."

"I'm sorry to hear that. Are they bad?"

"Only Willa. Her temperature is pretty high. The boys are sick but aren't experiencing such high fever. So you see, I've already been well exposed. I am here to take care of B.J. so you can rest."

"How did you find out B.J. was sick?"

"A little bird told me."

"Mm-hmm. And is the little bird's name Dr. Frank O'Brien?"

Glenda shrugged. "The little bird told me not to reveal his identity. So what's the status on our sick boy?"

"Chris and I just bathed him. I got a few drops of broth down him, and he's trying to sleep."

"All right. I want you to go into your room, get on that bed, and rest. I'm here to do everything I can to keep you from overdoing. I'll help Mary Beth cook, and if there's washing to be done, I'll take care of it."

"But Glenda—"

"Don't 'but Glenda' me. I mean it. If you come down with this stuff, it could be disastrous."

"I know, I know. But this is my child who is so sick. I have to do everything I can. God will take care of my unborn baby and me."

Glenda looked into Hannah's tired eyes and said, "Tell you what. Before I send you to your room, I want you to sit down here at the table. I see you have some hot water on the stove. You're going to drink some tea...then you're going to lie down."

Hannah eased onto a chair and put her elbows on the table. "You're hard to deal with, Mrs. Williams."

"Oh, you haven't seen just how hard I can be. Do what I tell you, and you'll never know."

Moments later, Glenda placed a hot mug of tea before Hannah, then spooned some sugar into it. "Drink it all, Hannah Marie. It will give you some energy."

Hannah released a grateful smile. "Glenda, thank you for being such a good friend."

Glenda bent down and kissed her cheek. "You don't have to thank me for that, honey. That's just the way it is."

Hannah napped for about half an hour. When she opened her eyes, the house was exceptionally quiet. She got up from her bed and went to the hall. The door to the boys' room was closed. She was about to open it when she saw her daughters coming toward her from the kitchen–parlor area.

"Mama," Mary Beth said, "you didn't sleep very long."

"I'll do better later. Is somebody with B.J.?"

"Aunt Glenda and Chris are giving him his sponge bath."

"We were bein' real quiet so you'd sleep a long time, Mama," Patty Ruth said. "I told Biggie not to make no noise, and he didn'."

Hannah looked down at the little dog. "You're a good boy, Biggie."

He wagged his tail and ejected a tiny whine. Hannah bent down with an effort and patted his head. Then to the girls she said, "I'll check on B.J."

She found Chris and Glenda drying B.J. with a towel. "How's he doing?" she asked.

"His temperature doesn't seem any higher," Glenda said. "Aren't you up awfully soon?"

"Yeah, Mama, we were hoping you'd stay down till lunchtime."

"You need to drink lots of water, honey," Hannah said as she looked down at B.J.

"I have been, Mama. Chris gave me a big drink before he and Aunt Glenda started with the washcloths."

"Good. Do you feel any better?"

"No."

She stroked his hair. "You will pretty soon."

Glenda took Hannah by the hand, led her into the hall, and said, "As you can see, we're taking care of B.J. Now, I want you back on that bed. And this time you stay there till we wake you up for lunch."

"I suppose that's an order, General?"

"Yes, ma'am, Private Cooper. It's an order."

At noon, Mary Beth prepared lunch with Glenda's help. When Mary Beth entered her mother's room, Hannah was already awake. They walked toward the kitchen together, and Mary Beth reported that Aunt Glenda and Chris had given B.J. another bath about an hour ago.

When lunch was over, the girls told their mother to sit down with Aunt Glenda in the parlor. They would do the dishes and clean up the kitchen. Chris left to help Jacob in the store.

Glenda read the look in Hannah's eyes as the two women sat near the fireplace.

"Honey, don't worry about B.J. He's going to be fine."

Hannah sighed. "I'm thankful he doesn't seem any hotter, but of course I would like to see his temperature drop. I just wish we had some salicylic acid. And I'm very concerned about Sundi. Did Doc tell you about her?"

"Yes. I'm so sorry she's having deliriums. I keep thinking of that shipment of salicylic acid sitting there in Cheyenne City, waiting for a stagecoach to show up."

"Me, too. We've got to pray it in here."

"Let's talk to the Lord about it right now."

Both women shed tears as Glenda led in prayer, asking the Lord to take care of all the sick ones in town and fort, especially now that the salicylic acid was gone. She prayed earnestly for Sundi Lindgren, asking God to bring her out of her delirious state, and she prayed for B.J.

CHAPTER FIFTEEN

Monday morning came with a partly cloudy sky and continued subzero temperatures.

At the O'Brien clinic, Heidi Lindgren stayed busy behind the curtain, bathing her sister with cool water so Doc and Edie could take care of other patients.

It was midmorning when Edie said, "Heidi, Pastor Kelly is here to see about Sundi. He wants to pray over her."

"Of course," Heidi said. "Let me cover her up, then you can bring him in."

When the pastor was escorted to the back room, he greeted Heidi, then looked down at Sundi, who was tossing her head back and forth and mumbling incoherently.

"Oh, Pastor, I'm so frightened," Heidi said, anxiety showing in her face.

"I understand. You look awfully tired, too. Doc told me you've been with her all night."

"I can't leave her. If we only had the salicylic acid…"

"I know, Heidi. Let me pray over her."

Kelly asked God to spare Sundi's life and keep her from any permanent harm. He also prayed for B.J. Cooper and others who were ill and asked that somehow the Lord would rush the shipment of salicylic acid to Fort Bridger. When he closed the prayer, Heidi said, "Is B.J. quite ill?"

"Not as bad as your sister and some others, but I just

learned about B.J. from Doc. He saw the boy earlier this morning, and his temperature is a hundred and one. I'm going to see him right now. I'll be back to check on Sundi later."

"Pastor, this could be dangerous for Hannah and her baby."

"That's Doc's biggest concern. Pray for Hannah, won't you?"

"Of course. And you tell her I'll be praying."

"I sure will."

"Oh, hello, Pastor," Glenda Williams said as she opened the Cooper apartment door. "Please, come in."

"Hello, Glenda. Doc told me you stayed here all night," Kelly said as Glenda closed the door behind him.

Glenda shrugged. "Had to. I love this family, and I had to make sure B.J. was taken care of and that Hannah got her rest."

"God bless you, Glenda."

"He has."

"May I see B.J. now?"

"He's awake, so I'm sure that would be fine. He's not very talkative, but I'm sure it will be an encouragement for him to see you. Hannah's asleep. Chris and Mary Beth are down in the store, doing what they can to help Jacob. Patty Ruth is—"

"Right here, Aunt Glenda!" said the little redhead, rushing to the pastor.

Kelly and Patty Ruth had a good hug, then the little one looked around and said, "Did you bring Miss Rebecca with you?"

"No, honey. She's working at the church, taking care of sick people."

"Oh."

"There's a bit of good news," Pastor Kelly said as he and Glenda walked toward B.J.'s door.

"Well, I'm ready for it."

"We've been able to send some of our sick ones home

today, and Doc told me of several others who are doing better."

"Wonderful! Praise the Lord."

"Amen. The ones who are better had the benefit of salicylic acid. My concern now is for those who've gotten sick recently and need salicylic acid so desperately."

"Like Sundi. You said you were just there. How is she?"

"Still delirious. Still running a temperature of just over a hundred and three."

Glenda opened the bedroom door and stepped in ahead of the preacher. She went to stand over B.J., who opened glazed eyes to look up at her. "Honey," Glenda said, "Pastor Kelly has come to see you."

The boy tried to focus on the familiar face.

Kelly leaned over him. "We're praying for you, son. The Lord is going to make you well again."

B.J. pressed a weak smile on his lips and nodded. "Pastor...please pray extra hard for Mama. I...don't want her to get this."

Kelly took the boy's hot hand. "Let's pray for her right now, B.J."

When Kelly and Glenda were leaving the boy's room, Kelly said, "Would you tell Hannah for me that Heidi said she's praying for her, and for B.J.? And please tell her that if she needs me, to send Chris to get me anytime, day or night."

"I'll tell her, Pastor. And thank you again for coming by."

Chris and Mary Beth came up to the apartment at noon and ate lunch with their mother and Glenda.

"Grandpa will be very pleased to learn of the rest you're getting, Mama," Mary Beth said.

"Well, now that I'm rested up, I can relieve your Aunt Glenda from her load."

Glenda shook her head. "No, ma'am. I know Jacob's had

his hands full downstairs and needs Chris and Mary Beth, so I'll keep doing what I've been doing. You can help me dip B.J. in the tub again after lunch, then you're lying down again."

The jut of Glenda's jaw told Hannah she might as well not argue.

The lowering sun was near the tops of the hills due west of Fort Bridger when a lone rider trotted his horse into town, his eyes darting back and forth as he rode down the snow-laden street. The rider reined in at the hitch rail when he saw the shingle:

O'BRIEN CLINIC
FRANK O'BRIEN, M.D.

The man dismounted, his heart pounding, and untied the heavy cloth sack from his saddle and crossed the boardwalk. He entered the office and saw several people sitting on straight-backed chairs. Some had children with them. There was no one at the desk.

At that moment, Edie O'Brien came from the back room and stood stock still when her eyes fell on the tall man with the cloth sack in his hand. "Patrick!"

"Hi, Mom," he said with a smile, setting the sack on the floor.

Edie rushed to her son with open arms. Everyone in the office looked on with pleasure as mother and son enjoyed their tender reunion.

Edie wiped tears from her cheeks and said, "Your father's making a house call on a small child who's very ill. I expect him back any minute. The epidemic has gotten pretty bad, son. We've completely run out of salicylic acid, and so has Dr. Blayney at the fort. We have some patients who may die for lack of it."

A smile spread over Patrick's face as he bent down and

lifted the cloth bag. "Well, you're not out of it anymore, Mom. Here's fifty pounds of it!"

Edie drew in a sharp breath. "Oh, praise the Lord! Fifty pounds?"

"Exactly."

"Well, how did you— Did you come in on the stage?"

"No, they're not running yet. I came on horseback. I'll explain later."

Even as Patrick was speaking, they both saw Doc move past the window, medical bag in hand. Doc opened the door, and his eyes grew wide at the sight of Patrick. Then father and son were in each other's arms. Doc mumbled something no one understood, then they pounded each other on the back and finally stepped back to look into each other's face.

"When did you get here, son?"

"A few minutes ago."

"The stage is running again! Good!"

"No, Dad. I came in on horseback. All the way from Cheyenne City."

"You what?"

Edie moved up close. "Show him what you brought, Patrick!"

Patrick picked up the sack. "Fifty pounds of salicylic acid, Dad."

Doc's jaw slacked, and more tears flooded his eyes. "Praise be to God! But, how did you— You say you rode all the way from Cheyenne City? You must've met up with Ray Yager. How—"

"It's kind of a detailed story. I know you have patients to attend, so I'll fill you and Mom in later. What can I do to help?"

"First thing, son, is to take about twenty pounds of the stuff to Dr. Blayney at the fort. You need to meet him, anyway. Hurry back, though, won't you?"

"I will."

"Then ol' Dad will put you to work. That is, unless you're too saddlesore."

Patrick chuckled. "I'm fine."

"Good. Well, we've got a very sick young lady in the back room who needs the salicylic in the worst way. She's our schoolmarm. The entrance of the fort isn't hard to find. Just follow Main Street on out north, and you'll come to it. I can't tell you how good it is to see you, son."

"Same here, Dad."

When Patrick arrived back at the clinic, his mother was with Heidi behind the curtain surrounding Sundi Lindgren. Doc had just finished with a patient and was following him into the office to bring in the next one.

"Dr. Blayney was ecstatic to get his hands on the salicylic, Dad," Patrick said. "Now, what can I do here to help?"

"I need you to take some of it to an eight-year-old boy. His name's B.J. Cooper. I haven't had time to get over there. Give him a good dose and leave his mother a generous supply. Show her how much to give him each time. Her name's Hannah. She's a Christian, and a mighty good one."

Patrick smiled. "Just tell me how to find the house."

"Did you notice Cooper's General Store when you rode into town?"

"I did."

"The Coopers live in the apartment upstairs. The entrance is at the back. Just go around to the alley, climb the stairs, and knock on the door."

"I think I can handle that."

Hannah came out of her bedroom late in the afternoon and found Glenda in the kitchen. There was a big pot of beef stew simmering on the back of the stove and a small pot of beef broth heating up for B.J.

Glenda turned and smiled. "Feel rested?"

"Very much. The stew smells good. I—" Hannah noticed one of her small satchels sitting by the door. "What's this?"

"Do you remember our conversation when you first got up this morning?"

"Well, most of it."

"You made me promise that I would go home to sleep in my own bed tonight."

"That's right."

"And as you know, I wouldn't make my best friend a promise and not keep it."

"I know you wouldn't. But that's my satchel over there by the door. How does that figure in?"

"Well, I'm taking Patty Ruth home with me after supper to spend the night at my house. I figure that'll give you just a little more of an edge on getting a good rest tonight. I'll bring her back in the morning. The satchel has her nightgown and some other necessities in it."

Hannah shook her head and smiled. "Glenda, you are the absolute limit. You don't need to take Patty Ruth and keep her for the night."

"Yes, I do. No arguments. She and I have already settled it."

Hannah sighed. "Are Chris and Mary Beth still down in the store?"

"Mm-hmm. This broth should be warm enough. Would you like to see how much you can get down B.J.? I'll proceed with supper."

Glenda poured broth into a small bowl and handed it to Hannah, who took a spoon from a cupboard drawer. "I assume Patty Ruth is in her room?"

"Yes. She's been a good girl all day."

B.J. was awake when Hannah entered the boys' room.

"Hi, sweetheart," she said, setting the bowl on a small table nearby. "Mama's got some broth for you. Let's prop you up with the pillow."

B.J.'s feverish eyes followed her every movement. Suddenly he coughed, and a dreadful wheeze followed. Hannah's brow furrowed.

"When did you start sounding like that?"

The boy coughed again and wheezed. "Little while ago."

Hannah pulled the quilts back and placed her ear on B.J.'s chest. Even her untrained ear caught the low rumbling sounds that didn't belong there. She lingered in that position for a few moments and silently prayed for grace.

She lifted her head and smiled into B.J.'s questioning eyes and tucked the covers up around him. "It will help you feel better if you can get some of this broth down," she said, taking bowl and spoon in hand. "Will you try it for me?"

He nodded, and Hannah dribbled a few drops into his mouth. With a grimace, he swallowed it, then reluctantly opened his mouth for more.

"That's my boy," Hannah said.

B.J. was able to down several spoonfuls, then Hannah dipped a washcloth into the pan of water on the dresser and placed it on his brow. Almost at once it was warm from the fever. Finally, B.J. fell into a fitful sleep. Hannah dropped into the chair near the bed and closed her tear-filled eyes.

"Please, Lord," she whispered, "I need even more grace."

She placed her hands on the curve of her swollen belly and was rewarded with a resounding kick. "Thank you, little one," she said softly. Tears trickled down her cheeks, both from worry and relief.

B.J. turned and twisted in his sleep, and Hannah lovingly patted his flushed cheek and stepped out of the room, closing the door behind her. She was almost to the kitchen when there was a knock at the door. Hannah hastened her pace, telling Glenda that she would get it. She opened the door to find a tall, attractive man standing before her.

"Mrs. Cooper?" he said, smiling.

"Yes?" Hannah knew at once that he was Patrick O'Brien, a combination of both his parents. He favored his father the most, and the same Irish twinkle was in his blue eyes.

"My name is Dr. Patrick O'Brien, ma'am. I apologize for my appearance. I've been on the back of a horse for days, and I just arrived in town. I'm Dr. and Mrs. O'Brien's son."

"Yes, I can tell. Please, come in. My children and I are very close to your parents. We've been expecting you, but not until the stages were running again."

Patrick stepped inside. "When my train arrived in Cheyenne City, I learned that all the stagecoaches out of that office were stranded all over Wyoming. The agent knew that Dad had put in an order for salicylic acid and told me about the influenza epidemic. He put me in touch with Mr. Yager of Wyoming Pharmaceuticals, and I bought fifty pounds of salicylic acid from him. And I bought a horse to get here. Now, I need to get this medicine into your boy."

Hannah clapped her hands together. "Thank God you're here, Doctor! B.J.'s condition seems to worsen by the hour."

Hannah introduced Glenda to Patrick, then started down the hall toward the bedrooms.

"I'll need a little water and a cup to mix it in," Patrick said.

Glenda quickly brought a cup of water, and while Patrick was mixing the powder, Patty Ruth moved past her mother to stand beside him and look up at him with bright blue eyes.

"Hi. I'm Patty Ruth. You're Grandpa's son, aren't you?"

"Ah...I guess so. Grandpa sent me with some medicine for B.J. Is he your brother?"

"Yes, sir. Are you gonna make him well?"

"I'm going to do my best."

"You look like Grandpa."

Patrick flicked a questioning glance at Hannah.

"My four children and your parents have adopted each other," Hannah said, smiling.

"I see. Well, Mom and Dad love children, that's for sure."

Glenda kept Patty Ruth with her while Hannah led Patrick down the hall to B.J.'s room. A deep, hoarse cough met their ears when Hannah opened the door.

Patrick sat down on the edge of the bed, mug in hand. "Hi, B.J. I'm Dr. Patrick O'Brien, Grandma and Grandpa O'Brien's son. Not feeling so good, huh?"

"No, sir. Not too good."

"I've got some medicine here that will help you. Let me lift your head a little, and let's see if you can drink it all for me."

It took B.J. a few minutes, but finally the mixture was down.

"Good boy," the doctor said. "Your mother's going to give you more later. And when she does, you drink it all for her, just like you did for me, okay?"

B.J. nodded.

Patrick handed the mug to Hannah and pulled a stethoscope from his coat pocket. "I'm going to listen to your lungs, B.J.," he said while warming the stethoscope with his hand. "I need to know just how congested you are."

He gently pressed it to the boy's chest and listened intently as he moved it from spot to spot. After what seemed a long time, he said, "There's quite a bit of congestion, but no sounds of pneumonia. The salicylic treatment should begin to take his fever down within a few hours."

"Thank the Lord there's no pneumonia," Hannah said. She then told the doctor about the tepid water baths and wet cloth treatments she had given B.J.

Patrick pressed experienced fingers all over the boy's upper torso. "That was about all you could do, Mrs. Cooper, other than pump liquids down him."

"Glenda and I have done that too, Doctor."

Patrick rose from the bed and turned to Hannah. "A couple of other things. I suggest you make a mild mustard plaster and put it on his chest. If you have any honey, dissolve it in warm water or weak tea and encourage him to sip on it. Dad and Mom told me of the shortage of food and supplies you're experiencing at present, but if you should have some lemon drops in the store, they might help soothe his throat and quiet his cough."

"I have both the mustard leaves and the lemon drops in the store," said Hannah, reaching down to stroke her son's damp hair. "I've got a jar of honey in the cupboard. I'll see that he gets all three."

Patrick smiled down at B.J. "With all of this tender loving care, you should be feeling better soon, son."

B.J. coughed, then said weakly, "Thank you for comin', Doctor."

Hannah added her own heartfelt thanks. Patrick then explained the dosage of the salicylic acid she should give him, and how often.

When they stepped out into the hall, Glenda and Patty Ruth were there. Patrick spoke encouraging words concerning B.J.'s soon recovery.

When Patrick had been gone only a few minutes, Chris and Mary Beth came in from the store. Hannah told them about Dr. Patrick O'Brien's visit and of his encouraging words about B.J. She asked Chris to go back down to the store and bring up some mustard leaves and lemon drops.

Mary Beth spotted the satchel by the door and said, "Is someone going somewhere?"

"Your little sister is spending the night with Aunt Glenda and Uncle Gary," Hannah replied.

Patty Ruth looked to Glenda, who smiled and said, "I already talked to your mama about it, honey. It's fine with her."

The child looked back to her mother, a worried look on her face. "If you'd rather I stayed here with you, I will, Mama."

"No, honey. It's fine."

"But if you need me—"

"It's all right, sweetheart. Mary Beth and Chris can help me with anything I need. Aunt Glenda and Uncle Gary would really like to have you for a night."

"That's right," Glenda said. "We'll be very happy to have you. You can sleep in the spare bed in Abby's room. She would like the company, and besides, I can really use your expert help in the kitchen."

Patty Ruth's visage brightened. "All right. I'll come, Aunt Glenda."

When supper was over, Hannah helped the little redhead into her coat, cap, and mittens. Patty Ruth hugged her sister and oldest brother, then hugged her mother, asking her to tell B.J. she would have hugged him if he wasn't sick.

Glenda led Patty Ruth toward the door, and the child chattered on about the things she would do to help Aunt Glenda in her kitchen.

Glenda turned and said, "Now, Hannah, if you should need me anytime in the night, send Jacob or Chris. All right?"

Hannah nodded.

"I mean it."

"I know you do."

"Promise you'll send for me if I'm needed?"

"I promise."

Patty Ruth hugged her mother one more time, then Glenda took her hand again to lead her down the stairs.

When Glenda and the chattering Patty Ruth disappeared, Hannah closed the door and turned to her two oldest children. "Well, we've got some work to do. I'll mix up the mustard plaster, Chris, if you'll do the dipping job. And Mary Beth, I'll need some more broth."

"Mama," Mary Beth said, "I'm so glad the Lord had it all planned that Dr. Patrick would be in Cheyenne City at just the right time to bring the salicylic acid. He's such a wonderful God!"

"He sure is, honey," said Hannah, tears filling her eyes.

"Jesus never fails," Chris said.

CHAPTER SIXTEEN

When Patrick returned to the clinic, he found his mother putting a sign in the window that told anyone seeking the doctor to go upstairs.

"Closing time, Mom?" he said as she opened the door and let him in.

"We have to do it now and then," she said, hugging him tight. "I'm so glad to have my boy here."

"And your boy is so glad to be here," he said, bending down to plant a kiss on her cheek.

"So how's B.J. doing?"

"He's still pretty sick, but there's no sign of pneumonia."

"Oh, praise the Lord for that!"

"The salicylic is going to help him immensely."

Frank O'Brien came into the office from the back room. "I heard what you said about B.J. and no pneumonia, son. That's a relief. Is he coughing much?"

"Quite a bit. I told Mrs. Cooper to put a mild mustard plaster on him. His congestion is still loose so I'm sure we caught it in time. He's going to feel a lot better in another day or so."

"Praise the Lord!"

"Amen, Dad. Say, could you tell me where Mr. Cooper is? Hannah didn't mention him."

"I should've told you," Doc said. "I was in a hurry to get

that salicylic to B.J. and forgot to mention it. Solomon Cooper was killed last August when the Coopers were coming here from Independence, Missouri, in a wagon train. Rattlesnake got him."

"Oh. I'm sorry to hear that."

"You saw that Hannah is great with child…"

"Yes."

"She's due mid-March."

"I didn't say anything to her, Dad, but it sure crossed my mind that if she gets influenza while carrying that baby…"

"I know. I've done what I could to get her to be very, very careful about letting herself be exposed."

"But with it right there in the house, she's going to be fortunate if it doesn't strike her."

"Well, at least if it does, thanks to you we've got plenty of salicylic acid to treat her with."

"The Lord had his hand in that for sure. When there's time, I want to tell you and Mom about the mountain man I had the joy of leading to the Lord on my ride from Cheyenne City."

"We'll want to hear all about it," Edie said. "It's so good to know you're walking close to the Lord again. I'm so happy about that."

"Me, too," Doc said.

Patrick chuckled. "Nobody's as happy about it as I am."

Edie ran an arm around her son's slender waist. "Dad wants to take you back and let you see our sick little schoolmarm, honey. While he's doing that, I'm going upstairs to cook you up a good meal."

"Hallelujah! Mom's home cooking again!"

"It's still the best in the world, son," Doc said.

Edie preceded her husband and son into the rear of the building and went up the stairs to the apartment. Doc led Patrick past the few patients who lay on cots and took him toward a curtained-off table. Before they reached it, Patrick's ears picked up delirious mumbling coming from behind the curtain.

"We have one sick girl here," Doc said in a low tone. "We still had salicylic when she came down with it, but it didn't seem to help at all. Her name is Sundi Lindgren."

"Sunday? Her name is Sunday, like the day of the week?"

"No. S-U-N-D-I. It's Scandinavian."

"Never heard it before. It's pretty."

"And so is she. Sundi has a sister named Heidi, who owns the town's dress shop. Both are fine Christian young ladies and faithful, active members of our church. Heidi has been at her sister's side ever since she came down with the influenza. I'm talking about nearly seventy-two hours. She finally came close to collapsing, and I had to have Marshal Mangum come and carry her home."

"You had to resort to the law to get her to leave her sister's side?"

Doc grinned. "Well, not exactly. Heidi and the marshal are engaged to be married."

"Oh. Well, that's better."

"Come on, Patrick," Doc said, holding aside the curtain.

When they stepped into the curtained enclosure, Sundi was tossing and turning and mumbling deliriously. Doc and Edie had strapped her down so she wouldn't fall off the table.

"We've had a hard time getting the salicylic acid down her since she went delirious on us," Doc said, "but when I checked her fever about half an hour ago, it still hadn't gone up. She's been running a tad over 103 degrees."

Patrick winced. "Thank God it hasn't gone any higher."

"I've been so swamped with other patients that I haven't had the time to give her the care she needs. Heidi's help was invaluable, but she's not medically trained. I'm going to turn Sundi over to you, Pat. Do all you can to make her better."

"I'll be glad to, Dad. Have you gotten any salicylic in her since I arrived with it?"

"Maybe two ounces while you were at the fort…just after I sent Heidi home. It would be good if you could get some more down her right now."

"And how about cool water treatments?"

"Heidi has used sponge baths often enough that it's been about as good as dipping her, which we just couldn't do."

"I'll do what I can before Mom calls me for supper. Just show me where you keep the salicylic."

Doc led Patrick to the large medicine cabinet, pointed out the bags of salicylic acid, and showed him where the utensils were kept. "I'll check on my other patients, then go on upstairs. It'll probably be close to an hour before Mom has supper ready."

Patrick went to work making a fresh mixture of salicylic acid in a cup of warm water, then entered the curtained enclosure. He set the cup and spoon on the small cart beside the table and picked up a cloth and used it to dab perspiration from Sundi's face. She was still quite restless.

Patrick then dipped the spoon in the mixture and, holding her head still with one hand, put the spoon to her lips. A little of the liquid went into her mouth but most of it spilled down her chin. He used the cloth to sponge up the wetness and tried once more. The same thing happened.

He used his left hand to pinch her lips into a pucker and poured a spoonful past them. This time she gagged slightly, but he saw her throat move. He puckered her dry lips again and poured in another spoonful, which Sundi swallowed.

His father's voice came from the rear of the room. "Pat, I'm going upstairs now. I'll holler when Mom's got supper ready."

"Okay, Dad, I'll be listening."

Patrick continued until Sundi finished the whole cup. He patted her lips with a fresh cloth and a smile curved his mouth.

"Thank you, Lord…and thank you, Miss Lindgren."

He stood there for a moment and studied the young schoolmarm. "I wonder what color her eyes are. Probably blue, since her hair and skin are so fair."

Sundi's cheeks were flushed a deep red from the fever, and a sheen of perspiration once again covered her face. Patrick dipped the cloth in a small basin of water on the cart and wiped her face and cracked lips. She moaned and turned her head from side to side.

"It's all right, Miss Lindgren," he said leaning close. "You're going to get better. In fact, I have an idea that just might help lower that fever. I'll be right back."

Patrick rummaged around in the supply closet and found a small bucket. He went out a side door, filled the bucket with snow, and hurried back inside. He packed snow in cloths and tied them to Sundi's wrists and pressed them to her jugular veins.

When dawn broke over Fort Bridger, Hannah Cooper was sitting on the edge of B.J.'s bed, giving him a sponge bath. Mary Beth had stayed with him until one o'clock in the morning, giving him a dose of salicylic acid and pressing wet cloths to his face, neck, arms, and wrists. She was replaced by Chris, who was determined to stay with his little brother for the rest of the night.

Hannah had risen from her bed at four o'clock and sent Chris back to bed. Though he protested, she insisted it was her turn to look after B.J. After Chris had gone to bed, Hannah replaced the mustard plaster with a fresh one and continued to bathe the sick boy with cool water. She awakened B.J. from time to time to give him sips of tea laced with honey and to pour down more salicylic acid mix.

Hannah caressed a hot cheek and whispered, "Mama

loves you, B.J. With the Lord's help, this family and the doctors are going to get you well."

At dawn Hannah left the side of the bed long enough to douse the lantern on the dresser. B.J. had drifted off in a seemingly restful sleep since taking his last dose of salicylic mix. Hannah gave him a long, loving look, then wearily sank down into the overstuffed chair beside the bed. *I'll just close my eyes for a few minutes while he sleeps,* she thought.

Hannah awakened with her chin on her chest and saw that it was sun-up. Suddenly her ears picked up a different sound. She looked at B.J. The wheezing had lessened, and he was breathing much easier. Hannah reached out a trembling hand and placed it hesitantly on the boy's forehead. His fever had broken.

"Praise the Lord," she said. "Thank You, Father, for Your healing hand on my boy!"

B.J. was still sleeping, and his mother couldn't take her eyes off him. She watched his chest rise and fall in rhythmic motion, thankful for each breath he took.

The door opened, and Chris—who had slept on the couch in the parlor—whispered, "Mama, Mary Beth has breakfast almost ready. You go eat with her, and I'll stay with B.J." He focused on her face. "Mama? Are you all right? You look pale."

Hannah smiled as she ran the back of her hand across her forehead and said, "I'm fine, honey. B.J.'s fever has broken. Isn't that wonderful?"

"Really? He's better?"

"Yes! The Lord answered our prayers! He's breathing much better, too."

"That's great! Now, you go eat breakfast and I'll stay with him. And after breakfast I want you to go back to bed. Mary Beth and I will take care of B.J."

"Jacob is going to need your help in the store. Aunt Glenda will be here soon with Patty Ruth. She, Mary Beth, and

I can trade off sitting with B.J. In between my shifts, I'll lie down and rest."

There was a sudden sound of voices from the kitchen-parlor area. Glenda and Patty Ruth had arrived. B.J. stirred and opened his eyes, and Hannah leaned toward him.

"Good morning, sweetheart. Your fever's broken. How do you feel?"

B.J. smiled his lopsided grin and said, "I feel better, Mama."

Chris moved up beside his mother and smiled down at B.J. "Hey, little brother, it's good to see you looking better."

"Thanks, Chris. But I think you need to make Mama go to bed. She looks awful tired."

Hannah rose from the chair and a wave of dizziness washed over her. She grabbed the back of the chair for support.

"Mama!" Chris rushed to her and wrapped his arms around her.

Hannah gripped the back of the chair with one hand as she waited for her equilibrium to return. Just then the bedroom door came open, and Glenda stuck her head in.

"Hey, how's my boy feeling this—" She saw Hannah and drew in a sharp breath. "What's wrong, Chris?"

"She got dizzy all of a sudden."

Glenda reached out a hand and pressed it to Hannah's cheek. "Honey, you've got a fever, and you're white as a sheet!"

"All…all I need is to lie down for a while. I'm just tired. I'll be fine. The Lord answered prayer. B.J.'s fever is broken. He's breathing better, too."

Glenda took hold of Hannah's arm and said, "That's wonderful, but you're going to bed now, young lady! No arguing. I mean it."

Hannah saw the worry on her children's faces. "Now listen, children. Don't you fret. I'll be fine once I get some rest."

"I know you're tired, Hannah," Glenda said, "but weariness

doesn't bring on a fever. Chris, let's get your mother to bed. Then I want you to run over to the clinic and bring back one of the doctors."

Together, Glenda and Chris led Hannah from the room. Mary Beth and Patty Ruth ran down the hall ahead of them, and by the time Hannah reached her bedroom, the girls had turned down the covers on the bed. Hannah let the feather mattress embrace her as she lowered herself into it. Chris left his mother in Glenda's care and dashed out of the apartment, pulling on his coat as he went.

Hannah started giving directions to Glenda and Mary Beth on the continued care of B.J.

"Mama," said Mary Beth, brushing her mother's hair from her damp forehead, "Aunt Glenda and I know B.J. isn't out of the woods yet, and we'll see that he's taken care of. But our main concern now is you. If you have the influenza—"

"Honey, if I do, Grandpa O'Brien has plenty of salicylic acid to treat me. Don't you worry."

Patty Ruth moved up close, stroked her mother's cheek, and said, "I love you, Mama. I don't want you to be sick."

Glenda laid a hand on the child's shoulder. "Your mama will get the best of care, I promise. And Hannah, you must concentrate on taking care of yourself and that precious little bundle you're carrying."

Hannah's eyes drooped. "I'm so tired. I just need some rest, and I'll be..." She had drifted into a restless slumber.

Edie O'Brien was in the clinic office showing a mother how to mix the salicylic acid with water when the door opened and Chris Cooper came in. She saw the fearful look on Chris's face and excused herself momentarily to the woman.

"What's wrong, Chris? Is B.J. worse?"

"No, Grandma, he's better. But Mama's dizzy and has a

fever. She's coming down with the influenza!"

"Oh, my! Wait just a moment; I'll be right back." She returned seconds later and said, "Chris, Grandpa is busy right now with a patient, but Dr. Patrick says he will be right with you. He's working on your teacher at the moment but is almost done."

"Thank you, Grandma."

Dr. Patrick O'Brien stood over Hannah, thermometer in hand, and said, "Your temperature is an even one hundred degrees. I brought more salicylic, so you should have plenty. Glenda or Mary Beth will mix it up right away. I want you to have a full cup every two hours."

Hannah nodded, her eyes heavy.

Patrick turned to Glenda and Mary Beth. "I'm going to show you ladies how to make snow packs and put them on her wrists and jugular veins. You can intermittently use sponge baths. Chris, will you keep a supply of snow handy?"

"Yes, Doctor. I'll bring in a couple buckets right now. I'll be helping Uncle Jacob in the store, but I'll make sure it doesn't run out."

"Good boy." Then he said to Glenda and Mary Beth, "If you follow my instructions, I believe it'll keep her fever from getting bad. An exceptionally high fever would be very dangerous for her and the baby."

Chris brought in the snow, and Patrick showed Glenda and Mary Beth how to make and apply the snow packs.

"I'm sure my dad will be here to see Hannah before the day is out," Patrick said as he put on his coat and hat. "If somehow he can't make it, I'll be back. I'm putting in most of my time on Miss Lindgren, but if something happens and you should need me, please let me know."

"Thank you, Doctor," Glenda said.

"Yes, Doctor," Mary Beth said. "It's nice to have you in Fort Bridger."

Patrick smiled as he buttoned up his coat. "I know why my parents love the people here."

"Doctor, how is Miss Lindgren?" Mary Beth asked.

"Well, there's no marked improvement yet, but now that I can give her more attention than Dad was able to give her, I have high hopes that her fever will break soon."

Patrick returned to the clinic and continued the snow pack treatment on Sundi. His father came in, having made a quick house call on a sick infant, and asked Patrick about Hannah. He said he would go see her himself in about two hours. He wanted Patrick to stay with Sundi.

Later, Doc returned from the Coopers' to report that Hannah's temperature had not risen any higher. He hoped this was a sign she wouldn't become too ill.

Heidi Lindgren came in, looking a bit weary but much better than she had the day before. She was happy to meet Patrick and to learn that her sister was under his special care. Patrick showed Heidi the snow pack treatments he thought would eventually help bring down Sundi's fever. Heidi patted her sister's arm and thanked Patrick for the good care he was giving her. Then she left, saying she would be back in the morning before going to her shop.

Patrick had to leave Sundi's side a few times through the day to help his father with other patients, but each time he hurried back to tend his special patient. All three of the O'Briens were kept so busy the rest of the day that there was no time for lunch.

Just after noon, Doc O'Brien was able to allow four of his patients to be taken home by their families. The salicylic acid had done its job. By the time the sun was setting, the other three patients were released, leaving Sundi Lindgren as the only patient in the clinic.

When darkness fell, at long last the clinic was quiet. Sundi was resting more comfortably.

The delicious aroma of food began to waft into the clinic, and Patrick headed for the stairs leading up to the apartment. His stomach was growling; it had been a long time since breakfast.

The kitchen was warm and cheery, with a bright fire burning in the shiny cookstove. Patrick's mother was at the cupboard, putting the final touches on their simple meal.

"Where's Dad?" he asked.

"In the bedroom, putting his slippers on. I think his feet are hurting him."

"No wonder, as much as he's been on them today."

"You look pretty worn out, yourself, Dr. O'Brien Jr." She opened her arms. "Let your mother give you a big hug."

Patrick welcomed the hug, then sat in his chair at the table, and Edie went back to her work.

Doc came into the kitchen wearing his sheepskin slippers. Edie smiled at him and said, "Well, now that Dr. O'Brien Sr. has put in an appearance, we can have supper."

"Dr. O'Brien Sr., eh? I feel more like Dr. O'Brien, the hundred-year-old patriarch."

Edie began ladling large portions of spicy vegetable soup into the blue bowls she had used when Patrick was a child. She placed the bowls on the table, and Patrick closed his eyes, sniffed, and sighed. "Oh, Mother, dear, have I ever missed your cooking!"

Edie placed a plate of warm bread before her two men. "Well, when you get serious about some young lady, you'd better make sure she can cook."

"Hah! Since I'll be living close by, it won't make any difference whether she can cook or not. We'll just eat all our meals at your house."

Edie placed a crock of butter and a small tub of honey on the table. "She might not like that, son."

"Oh yes, she will. I'll school her good before we get married."

Doc chuckled. "This I want to see."

"It seems like ten years since we ate breakfast," Patrick said.

"More like twenty!" Doc said. "Lead us in prayer, son, and we'll eat."

After prayer, Patrick went to work on the soup and bread, taking gulps of hot coffee between bites. His parents talked of their concern for Sundi Lindgren, then began asking about Patrick's life in Chicago. He tried to talk while he ate.

Edie's eyebrows arched as she said, "Patrick! You know what I taught you about talking with food in your mouth."

"Oh, I'm sorry, Mom," Patrick said with a mock face of embarrassment. "I forgot. I was just trying to answer all these questions."

"Tell you what, boys," Edie said. "Let's eat our meal, then we can talk."

When the soup bowls had been replenished and emptied again, and the bread was gone, Edie poured fresh cups of coffee. Then she and Frank leaned back in their chairs, ready to hear all that their son had to tell them.

The subject finally came around to Patrick's return to the Lord, and his parents wept as they praised God for answered prayer and for working in Patrick's life.

Doc said, "Mom, I think it would be good if we had us a little praise meeting right here and now, and thank the Lord for bringing our son back to us."

"And while you're at it," Patrick said, "I want to praise the Lord for my parents, who never stopped loving this old backslider, and never gave up on him!"

All three bowed their heads, and each one prayed in turn.

As the O'Brien family said the final amen, Patrick covered a yawn, then stretched his arms, and said, "If you'll loan me a quilt again, Mom, I'll get back down to Miss Lindgren. I want both of you to get to bed early."

"You can use the quilt over there on the sofa. But I wish you didn't have to spend the night in that overstuffed chair down there. You won't get a good night's sleep until you can sleep in the spare bedroom."

Patrick smiled at his mother. "I wouldn't sleep good in the spare bedroom right now, anyway, Mom. I want to be close by in case there's any change in that young lady."

"Good night, Pat," Doc said.

"Night, Dad."

He hugged both parents, thanked them again for loving him, and carried the quilt out the door.

CHAPTER SEVENTEEN

Sundi Lindgren seemed less fitful when Patrick returned to her side. He tested her temperature again and found it an even 103 degrees—a slight drop from what it had been. After getting her to swallow more salicylic mix, he spent an hour applying snow packs.

Before retiring for the night, he loaded the potbellied stove with wood and lowered the wick on the lantern, then made himself as comfortable as possible in the overstuffed chair and pulled the quilt over him.

Just as he was settling down, he heard the rear door open and close. Soft footsteps followed, and Patrick made out the stooped figure of his father in the dim light.

"Pat, I'm sorry to bother you, but I just had to come down and see how Sundi's doing."

Patrick laid the quilt aside and rose to his feet. He smiled with obvious affection and said, "Always the doctor, aren't you, Dad?"

"Well, I—"

Patrick laid a hand on his shoulder, his voice full of admiration. "My dad...always putting his patients first. I love you for the dedication you've shown to your patients as far back as I can remember."

Doc sighed. "I guess I'm too old to change now, son. You'll

just have to bear with me." He stepped up beside Sundi and laid his hand on her brow.

"Her temperature is down slightly," Patrick said. "An even 103. You can see that she's resting easier now. I think we're about to see a turn for the better."

"Good. I knew my boy would make a difference."

"Back to your statement about being too old to change…I wouldn't change you for the world, Dad. My prayer is that someday I can be the kind of physician you are, and the kind of person you are."

"You'll do just fine, son. Just fine. You've got the personality for it. In a country practice, your patients also become your friends, and you form a close bond with them. You're perfect for this kind of life."

"I've seen some of that bond between you and your patients already. I'm looking forward to becoming a part of this community, more than I can tell you."

Doc smiled at his son and squeezed his shoulder.

"I want you to get to bed now," Patrick said. "If you don't get some rest, you're going to be down yourself."

"All right, son. I'll go. Just let me say how pleased your mother and I are to have you here."

"You've both shown me that, Dad, and I'm so glad to be here. Good night, now."

"Good night, Pat. Come and wake me if you need me."

"Only in a dire emergency will I do that."

Doc chuckled. "You're a case, Patrick Michael O'Brien, you know that?"

"Yeah. I had a good teacher."

Patrick was dozing in the chair when he became aware of movement in the room. He sat up and heard a low moan. He threw off the quilt and hurried over to Sundi, his heart pounding. The sheen of perspiration was on her face.

"Thank You, Lord," he said. "Her fever's broken."

Sundi was licking her dry lips and trying to open her eyes. Patrick reached over and raised the wick on the lantern.

Sundi finally opened her eyes and blinked a few times, trying to clear her vision. She focused on the face above her and tried to speak.

Patrick took hold of her hand and said, "Don't exert yourself too much, Miss Lindgren. You've been a very sick young lady."

Sundi's eyes widened a little. "Oh," she said, her voice barely above a whisper. "At first I thought you...were Doc. You're his son, aren't you?"

"Yes, I am. Hello, and welcome back to our world. You've been delirious for a few days."

"I'm trying to think...Patrick. That's it. You're Dr. Patrick O'Brien."

"That's right."

"Please excuse me. My...my mind is kind of...fuzzy."

"You've had a very high fever. It was high when I arrived here, and it just broke. In fact, I need to take your temperature now and see what it is."

"Doctor...what day is it?"

"Well, since it's past midnight, Miss Lindgren, it's Wednesday."

Sundi closed her eyes. "Wednesday?"

"Yes."

"I got sick on Friday. It's been five days?"

"Yes'm. I got here on Monday, and your sister took care of you from Friday till Monday...night and day, around the clock."

Sundi let a smile curve her lips. "Bless her heart."

"And Pastor Kelly has been in and out, checking on you."

She licked her dry lips once more. "I'm so thirsty. Could I

please have a drink of water?"

"Yes, but only small sips at first." Patrick poured water into a glass. "Here, let me support your head a little."

Sundi fought the desire to gulp the water down and sipped it slowly.

"That's all for now. You can have more later. Now let's take your temperature."

Patrick got a reading of 100 degrees and was elated. He took a soft cloth, dipped it in the nearby basin of water, and wiped away the traces of perspiration from her face.

"As I said, you've been a very sick young lady, Miss Lindgren, but barring any complications, you'll be as right as rain soon."

"That's good to hear. Do…do you happen to know about the school? My students?"

"I understand they closed the school, ma'am. So many of your students were down with influenza. I don't think they'll reopen school until you're able to teach again. They figure by that time you'll have most of your students back, if not all of them."

Sundi nodded.

"Miss Lindgren, we need to get some broth into you, but I think we'll wait till morning. Mom's been working awfully hard, and she'll have to be the one to make it."

"That's all right, Doctor. I can wait. I…I still feel a bit groggy."

"The best thing for you right now is sleep. But before you go to sleep, ma'am, I'd like to pray with you if you don't mind. Just to thank the Lord for answered prayer. Many people have been praying for you."

Sundi managed a smile. "I'm sure that's true. Please do, Doctor."

Patrick laid a steady hand on her arm and squeezed it lightly as he led them in prayer, thanking the great Physician for saving Miss Lindgren's life. When Patrick said amen, Sundi's eyes remained closed. He adjusted the pillow under her head, and she opened her eyes and tried to focus them again.

Patrick whispered, "Sleep, now, young lady. I'll be right here close by. You need all the rest you can get in order to recover."

Before the words were out of his mouth, her eyes closed and she fell into healing slumber.

At the burial ground next to the Crow village there was the sound of mourning. An icy wind whipped over the hills and through the surrounding trees. The people formed a circle around the scaffolds that held the most recent dead.

Already, six fresh graves held the bodies of those who had died as a result of the influenza. On the scaffolds at the moment were an elderly man who had died during the night, and a young warrior who had died just after sunrise.

Broken Wing stood in the crowd of mourners along with other boys his age. He shuddered as the wind whipped around them. He looked on with a sense of dread as Red Wolf—who was also running a high fever—lifted his trembling hands toward the sky. Red Wolf's voice cracked as he cried to the Great Spirit, pleading a safe journey for the two souls.

Broken Wing wiped tears. He had been close to both men whose bodies lay on the towering scaffolds. He wondered about them. Did Lame Horse and Three Fingers go to heaven? Broken Wing had learned enough from Chris Cooper to be concerned about his own soul and the sins he had committed before the Sky Father, whom Chris's Bible called God. What if Broken Wing came down with the white man's disease and died, as eight others had?

Broken Wing thought of what he had been taught all of his young life by the medicine men and his parents. When a Crow died, the body must be placed on a scaffold at least a full day before burial to give the soul opportunity to leave the body and go on the long journey to meet the Sky Father and the Sky People.

But Chris had told him that according to his Bible, at the instant of death the soul left the body and went to its eternal destiny. Broken Wing wrestled with the thought that if the white man's Bible was true, Red Wolf's prayers for the souls of Lame Horse and Three Fingers were useless. Their souls were already wherever they would be forever. These thoughts stayed with Broken Wing, even when the wailing ceremony was over and the people returned to the warmth of their tepees and their ailing loved ones.

Broken Wing joined his mother as she walked through the snow to their tepee.

His father, Chief Two Moons, had gone with Red Wolf to the tepee where the ailing Running Buck lay. Though Running Buck was much improved, he was still unable to get up. Inside the tepee, two middle-aged squaws knelt beside Running Buck, burning stalks of sage and fanning the smoke onto him. The squaws had also made sargigruag tea.

Red Wolf removed his headdress and laid it aside, then eased onto the pallet next to the other medicine man and pulled a heavy blanket over him. He was perspiring profusely. With just a look at Red Wolf, the squaws knew that the full responsibility for Running Buck's care was now theirs.

Two Moons sat down cross-legged at the feet of both medicine men and said, "Two Moons must discuss with Running Buck and Red Wolf this illness overtaking our people."

The squaws did not look up from their work.

"Two Moons thinks it best to send braves to Fort Bridger and ask for help from Dr. Robert Blayney or Dr. Frank O'Brien. We must also ask Colonel Ross Bateman to give us food."

Red Wolf mopped sweat from his face with the blanket and shook his head.

Running Buck shook his head, too, then said to Two Moons, "Running Buck and Red Wolf have discussed this. We fear that if this is done, the gods will be displeased and punish the Crow. We should not look to white men for help when the gods have given Running Buck and Red Wolf power to heal the Crow people."

The chief's features tightened. "Two Moons means no disrespect. He agrees that the gods have given healing power to medicine men, but it is not working well. Yes, some of our people are beginning to feel better. But we have also had six burials, and two more tomorrow. Since influenza is white man's disease, possibly white man's medicine could cure it. Certainly if this is so, the gods would not be angry."

Red Wolf closed his eyes, and one of the squaws mopped perspiration from his face. His breathing was becoming irregular and ragged.

Running Buck said, "Our chief has given us much to think about and discuss. Now Red Wolf cannot talk. He must allow the smudging and sargigruag tea time to work."

Two Moons nodded. "We will talk of this in the morning."

When Two Moons ducked into his tepee, he found Sweet Blossom and Broken Wing sitting by the fire. Sweet Blossom was stirring their day's meal in a steaming pot. The flickering flames cast eerie shadows on their gaunt faces, and their skin had a sallow look. Two Moons knew he had lost weight, but he didn't care for himself. But to see his wife and son undernourished brought him great pain.

Sweet Blossom looked up at her husband. "Did Running Buck and Red Wolf agree with Two Moons's plan?"

"This they did not do." Two Moons explained the attitude of the medicine men, adding that he would talk with them again in the morning.

"And if they refuse to go along with my husband's wishes?"

Two Moons sighed. "This is difficult."

"Sweet Blossom knows that Two Moons does not wish to anger the gods. But it seems the gods are not providing food for us, and the medicine men have little power against the white man's disease. Must we bury more of our people before we ask for help from Dr. Robert Blayney?"

Two Moons remained silent.

Sweet Blossom took a deep breath and said, "Two Moons's squaw does not wish to step beyond her bounds, but she must remind her husband that as chief, he has the power to go against the wishes of medicine men."

Two Moons felt the gaze of his son on him as he looked into Sweet Blossom's dark eyes and said, "This chief sees his people dying with white man's disease, and he sees his own family growing thin for lack of food. He also fears to infuriate the gods. If Running Buck and Red Wolf agree we must not ask white men for help, the gods will be watching."

"My husband, even medicine men can sometimes be wrong."

"This is true. Possibly they are wrong in this situation. Two Moons must pray to the Sky Father for guidance lest he anger the gods who have power on earth."

"Father," Broken Wing said, "may I ask a question?"

"Yes, my son."

"Broken Wing understands why Running Buck and Red Wolf do not want to ask for help from Dr. Robert Blayney. This offends their pride. But why do they object to asking Colonel Ross Bateman for food? Would that not be better than seeing our people starve? This will happen soon if we do not get food."

Two Moons nodded. "Your father will discuss this with Red Wolf and Running Buck in the morning."

That night, as Broken Wing lay on his pallet in the darkness, he thought of how weak his mother had become, and how sunken her cheeks were. He decided that if Broken Wing would ask the white men for food, the gods would only be angry with him…if they existed at all. Since talking with Chris Cooper, Broken Wing had been having many doubts about the tribe's gods and their rules.

Broken Wing listened to his parents' even breathing as they slept. He rubbed his head in an attempt to clear away the dizziness he had been experiencing since morning. He wiped a palm over his forehead and found it wet with perspiration. Would hunger cause this? He must quickly do what was in his heart.

Sweet Blossom awakened when dawn's light touched the walls of the tepee. She yawned and glanced toward her son's pallet on the other side of the tepee.

Broken Wing was not there.

She went to the flap and pulled it aside to look out into the village. No one was moving about yet, and there was no sign of Broken Wing. She awakened her husband. A few minutes later, Two Moons stood at the rope corral and ran his eyes over the herd of horses. Broken Wing's pinto was gone. The chief enlisted a half dozen warriors to ride with him after his son.

Broken Wing lay in the snow. He had reached the halfway point between the village and the fort when a strong wave of dizziness came over him. The next thing he knew, he had fallen off his horse and was lying in the snow.

He struggled to his knees. His throat was sore, and he coughed raggedly as he staggered to his feet. His horse stood close by and nickered as Broken Wing stumbled toward him. When he reached the animal's side, he tried to mount but was too weak and dizzy.

He leaned against the pinto's side, trying to clear his head.

Suddenly he heard a horse whinny, and his own horse whinnied in return. The boy looked over his shoulder and saw his father and a band of warriors riding toward him.

In Cincinnati on Friday, January 27, Adam Cooper came home after a hard day at the office and was met by Theresa and his six-year-old son, Seth.

"Is the princess napping?" Adam said after hugs and kisses.

"She was, but I think I heard some gurgling and cooing going on just as you were guiding the buggy into the driveway."

Adam picked Seth up and said, "C'mon, son. Let's go see if baby sister's awake."

Theresa followed her two men, and when they went into the bedroom, little Anna Cooper was indeed awake. Adam eased Seth to the floor and lifted the baby out of her bassinet.

"Isn't she beautiful?" he said, holding her so he could look into her tiny face.

Seth nodded. "Mrs. Jeffries thinks Anna looks like me!"

Both parents laughed. The baby gurgled, then made another cooing sound.

"Hey, did you hear that?" Adam said. "Only sixteen days old, and she said Dada!"

"No, what she said was Mama."

Seth said his little sister was really saying his name, and the family laughed together as they went back to the parlor with Adam carrying the baby.

They sat down near the crackling fireplace, and Adam said, "Okay, what is it?"

"What is what?" Theresa said.

"I know that gleam in your eye. What do you know that I don't?"

"I know plenty more than you do, darling. But now I know something really special."

"Out with it."

"Question. What one thing have we talked about and prayed about of late more than anything else?"

"Owning our own newspaper out west."

"And what one thing has stood in our way of realizing that dream?"

"The money to do it."

"Right. Well, that problem is now solved. The Lord is making the way for us to fulfill our dream."

"What? How?"

"We got a letter from Hannah today, and she has some very good news."

"Well, let me see it!"

Theresa took the letter from her apron pocket. "Give me Anna, and you read it."

Adam studied her eyes as he took the letter from her hand. "Really? The money problem is taken care of?"

"Read it, darling."

Adam Cooper looked at the envelope and noted the postmark. "December 28! It was mailed one day short of a month ago! I've never known a letter to take more than two weeks to get to us from Hannah."

"Honey, don't you remember that your own *Cincinnati Post* has been reporting about the hard winter out west? One blizzard after another?"

"Guess that would slow the mail some, wouldn't it?"

Theresa watched Adam's face as he read the letter.

December 28, 1870
Dear Adam, Theresa, and Seth,

Greetings from the North Pole! Well…almost. You probably know about the blizzards we've been having here. The old-timers tell us it's the worst winter in these parts in a generation.

I won't go into detail in this letter, but our little Patty Ruth was abducted several days before Christmas. We didn't know whether she was dead or alive until she was brought home on Christmas Eve. The Lord kept His hand on her. She was not harmed in any way. We've got a big birthday party planned for her, day after tomorrow.

Shortly before Patty Ruth was abducted, I got into a conversation with our town's mayor (and barber), Cade Samuels, and the owner and president of the Fort Bridger Bank, Lloyd Dawson. I told them about your dream to come west and establish your own newspaper. I explained that the lack of finances was what was hindering you.

Those two men got very excited. They want you to come to Fort Bridger with your dream. They say the town is ready for its own newspaper. Mr. Dawson told me that when I wrote to you, I should tell you the Fort Bridger Bank will seriously consider extending you a loan to help establish the paper.

Mr. Dawson says to please write him if you are interested. He will communicate with you, and the two of you can get down to details. He said to tell you that he realizes there will have to be a building erected, printing presses purchased and shipped to Fort Bridger, plus office furniture and equipment. He is willing to consider a loan that will cover it all.

Mayor Samuels says he will help find temporary quarters for the newspaper, if you wish. Please let him know.

The children and I are so excited at the prospect of you coming! Both Mr. Samuels and Mr. Dawson believe the newspaper will do exceedingly well because of the growth of the town and more ranchers and farmers steadily moving into the area. They are sure that people in smaller towns all around will want to read every edition of the paper.

I have hired a man from New York City to run the store for me. His name is Jacob Kates. He was in the mercantile business in New York for many years. Jacob said that as a former big city man, he can tell you that a newspaper would do well in Fort Bridger. He knows that small towns love to have their own newspaper.

Well, I guess this letter has become a lengthy one, but I wanted to give you the information about Mr. Dawson's generous offer and to let you know how both he and Mr. Samuels feel about your coming here to establish your newspaper.

I'm having a few minor complications with my unborn baby, but my doctor is watching me closely. Please let us hear from you soon. Misters Dawson and Samuels, too!

The children send their love. And so does their mother! God bless you!

Love, hugs, and kisses,

Hannah

There were tears in Adam's eyes as he folded the letter and looked at his wife. "God bless that sweet Hannah! She really wants us to come and live in Fort Bridger, doesn't she?"

Theresa laughed, blinking at her own tears. "What was your first clue? It looks like the Lord wants us there, too, wouldn't you say?"

"It does." Adam shook a fist in the air. "It sure does!"

That evening, after Seth and Anna were asleep, Theresa sat beside her husband as he composed three letters. The first was to Hannah to thank her for talking to Mr. Dawson. In addition, he told her of Anna's birth in case the letter announcing it hadn't gotten to her. He also told her that he was sending a letter to Lloyd Dawson and one to Cade Samuels.

When he was finished with the three letters, Adam and Theresa bowed their heads and prayed for the Lord's guidance.

Later that night, lying in bed in the darkness, Adam and Theresa clung to each other, talking excitedly of their dream and the possibility of living in the same town with Hannah and her children. It was quite a while before they were able to sleep.

CHAPTER EIGHTEEN

On Friday, February 3, Dr. Frank O'Brien and Edie stood over Hannah as she lay on the examining table.

"Hannah, dear," Doc said with a relieved sigh, "I can't find anything wrong with the baby. The heartbeat sounds strong, and even though this one is still not as active as you say your other children were at this stage in your pregnancies, I have no reason to believe that your bout with the influenza has done any harm."

Hannah blinked at the tears in her eyes. "Thank you, Doc. So you still feel that the baby will be born in mid-March?"

"I believe so."

"Oh, I'm so relieved. Doc, Edie, thank you for all you've done for me."

"You're like our own daughter, honey," said Edie, patting her cheek. "There's no limit to what we would do for you."

"That's right," Doc said. "And that goes for Patrick, too."

"Patrick," Hannah said in a tender tone. "If he hadn't hazarded his life to bring that salicylic acid, the baby and I might not have made it."

Doc nodded. "True. And others might not have made it, either. Especially Sundi."

"I'm glad Sundi has been able to go home."

"Yes, aren't we all," Edie said.

"How's the food supply at the store holding out?" Doc asked.

"The rationing has helped, but the food will be gone in about two weeks. Curly tried day before yesterday to wire the suppliers in Cheyenne City, but the lines were down somewhere along the line, and he couldn't get through. He still can't."

"Well, all we can do is keep praying," Edie said.

When Hannah was ready, the O'Briens walked her into the outer office. Pastor Andy Kelly and Rebecca rose to their feet.

"So what's the verdict?" Kelly asked.

"Everything's fine," Doc said. "No sign that Hannah's influenza did anything to harm the baby."

"Praise the Lord!" said Rebecca, going to Hannah and putting an arm around her.

"Thanks be to our wonderful heavenly Father for answered prayer!" Kelly said.

Mary Beth cooked supper that evening so her mother could rest, and Jacob Kates ate with the family. B.J. was almost back to normal and Patty Ruth, as usual, was slipping Biggie part of her supper under the table.

"I'm so glad Miss Lindgren is getting better," Mary Beth said. "We should be able to get back to school soon."

"Whoopee," B.J. said dryly.

Jacob chuckled. "Someday when you become a man, B.J., and have the responsibilities that go with adulthood, you'll look back to your school days and realize how good they were."

"That's what I've tried to tell him, Uncle Jacob," Chris said, "but he doesn't think so. Papa used to tell us the same thing."

"Well, your papa was right."

"Papa was right about everything," Mary Beth said. "Just like Mama."

Hannah smiled. "You just keep believing that, honey."

Silence fell over the table for a few minutes, then Jacob looked at Hannah and said, "I'm a bit concerned about the Crow people. It's been a long time since I've seen any of them in town."

"Really? I wasn't aware of that."

"Well, you've been out of circulation for a while. I'm wondering if they heard about the epidemic and have been staying away because of it."

Hannah thought on it for a moment, then said, "Either that, or they've been hit with an epidemic, too. They could have, since they had those infected soldiers in their village."

"I sure wouldn't want Broken Wing to get the influenza," Chris said.

"I hope nobody in the village has come down with it," Mary Beth said. "Since I started teaching out there last fall, I've really grown to love them."

Jacob set his coffee mug on the table. "Somebody ought to go to the village and see if those folks are all right."

"Good idea," Hannah said.

"Probably be best if Dr. Blayney would convince Colonel Bateman to send a cavalry unit up there," Jacob said. "And Dr. Blayney would probably be more apt to take the initiative if the suggestion came from Dr. O'Brien."

"Mm-hmm," said Hannah. "I agree."

"Tell you what. Right after supper I'll go over to the O'Brien apartment and talk to Doc about it."

"I'll go with you, Uncle Jacob," Chris said.

"We'll go just as soon as we eat some of Mary Beth's sugar cookies." He reached across the table where the cookies were piled on a plate near Patty Ruth, whose hand was under the table.

Hannah set her eyes on the little redhead and said, "Biggie likes Mary Beth's sugar cookies, too, doesn't he, Patty Ruth?"

Patty Ruth's face turned crimson.

The next morning, Dr. Robert Blayney was leaning over a soldier in the infirmary when he heard the door open. He glanced that direction and smiled. "Well, Dr. O'Brien! To what do I owe this pleasure?"

"I need a few minutes with you, if you have time."

"Sure. I'm just finishing here. Be right with you."

A minute later, Dr. Blayney ushered the older physician into his office at the rear of the building and gestured toward a chair. He poured them each a mug of hot black coffee from the ever-present pot on the small stove.

"Ah, just what I needed," said O'Brien, smacking his lips.

Both doctors were glad to have a few minutes to catch up with each other and share conditions in town and fort. They talked about the decrease in the number of people coming down with influenza in the past few days and rejoiced together that no one had died from it.

"Thanks to your gallant son, Doctor," Blayney said. "If he hadn't brought the salicylic to us, it would be a different story. So, what did you need to see me about?"

"It was brought to my attention last night by Jacob Kates that no Crow have been seen in town since Captain Fordham and his men were in the village."

Blayney's eyebrows arched. "Oh? I hadn't realized that."

"Me, either. I remember that you and I talked about the Crow after your men came back with the influenza. We were concerned that the disease might strike them, but I guess we've both been too busy to think about it. The reason I've come to you, Doctor, is that I figured it would be best if an army unit rode up to the village to see if they're all right."

"I can talk to Colonel Bateman. After what Two Moons and his people did for our men, he'll be glad to check on them."

Lieutenant Dobie Carlin led his six troopers past the burial ground at the Crow village. "Look at that, men," he said drawing rein. "Nine fresh graves."

"Lieutenant, I think the colonel's fears were well founded," one of the troopers said.

"Over there, Lieutenant," said another, pointing to two scaffolds, each bearing a corpse.

Carlin shook his head. "Let's hope one of those graves doesn't hold Two Moons."

As they neared the edge of the village, with its long rows of tepees, two Crow sentries came from a nearby tepee to meet them. Their faces were drawn, and there was a dullness in their eyes. Carlin raised his hand in a sign of peace.

"Yellow Bird, Sun Man, my greetings to you. We have come by order of Colonel Ross Bateman to learn if all is well here."

"I will take you to Chief Two Moons," Sun Man said.

"Wait here, men," Carlin said as he dismounted.

Sun Man was silent as he guided the lieutenant to the tepee where the medicine men were being cared for. He clapped his hands and called out, "Chief Two Moons. Lieutenant Dobie Carlin is here to see you."

The chief raised the flap and emerged from the tepee. "Lieutenant Dobie Carlin. Welcome."

"Thank you, Chief. I and my men are here at Colonel Bateman's command to find out if you and your people are all right."

"This is much appreciated." The cold morning breeze plucked at the feathers in Two Moons's headdress. His gaze traveled to the edge of the village, where he saw the other soldiers sitting their horses.

"Chief," Dobie said, "I counted nine fresh graves in your burial ground, and two bodies on scaffolds. Is it the influenza?"

Two Moons nodded. "Yes. These eleven have died with the white man's disease."

"You have others that are sick with the disease?"

"Yes. There are many, and Two Moons fears that more will die. Both medicine men are very sick and have not been able to tend others. Running Buck became sick first, then Red Wolf. Running Buck started to get better, but now has taken turn for the worse."

"Chief, would you allow either Dr. Robert Blayney or Dr. Frank O'Brien to come and treat your sick ones?"

"Lieutenant Dobie Carlin remain here. Two Moons return in a moment."

He moved inside the tepee and stood over the medicine men and the two squaws who were fanning smoke on them. Running Buck and Red Wolf looked up at him with glazed eyes.

"Lieutenant Dobie Carlin is here," the chief said. "Other soldier coats are with him. They have come to see if we are well. They saw the graves and bodies on the scaffolds. Lieutenant Dobie Carlin asks permission to bring one of the white doctors here."

Neither medicine man spoke.

"It is in my mind that we should have asked for the white doctor to come when the disease first struck our people. I believe Running Buck and Red Wolf are sick because the gods are angry at our foolishness. It is the white man's disease. Only white doctors have the power to heal those who have it."

Still, the medicine men did not speak.

"We must allow the white doctor to come, or we will further anger the gods. Very possibly Running Buck and Red Wolf will die…and others, including Broken Wing."

Red Wolf painfully cleared his throat and said, "Chief Two Moons speaks with wisdom. It appears we have angered the gods. Red Wolf says bring the white doctor."

Two Moons looked at Running Buck, who nodded his assent.

The chief returned to Carlin and said, "Two Moons would very much like Dr. Robert Blayney or Dr. Frank O'Brien to help us. Running Buck and Red Wolf wish this too."

A smile spread over the young lieutenant's face. "Good,

Chief. We'll ride back to the fort and tell Colonel Bateman."

Two Moons laid a hand on Carlin's shoulder. His voice broke slightly as he said, "Thank you for coming."

"We are your friends, Chief. We care about you."

Tears filmed Two Moons's eyes as he watched Carlin hurry through the snow to his waiting men and mount up.

Dr. Robert Blayney was giving salicylic acid to a soldier in the infirmary when the door opened and Colonel Bateman entered with Lieutenant Carlin.

"Could you spare us a couple of minutes, Doctor?" Bateman said.

"Certainly, sir. I'm almost through here. Please go into my office and sit down."

When Blayney joined them, he said, "So what did you find at the village?"

"That's what we're here to talk about. Tell him, Lieutenant."

Carlin explained that Chief Two Moons had conferred with his two sick medicine men, and they were in agreement to ask for a white doctor to come before more Crow died.

"I know you are very busy, Dr. Blayney," Bateman said. "And so is Dr. O'Brien. I think you and Lieutenant Carlin should go and talk to Dr. O'Brien, tell him the story, and between the two of you decide on a schedule to alternate who goes to the village and when."

Lieutenant Carlin and Dr. Blayney pushed open the examining room door at the O'Brien clinic.

"Mrs. O'Brien said we could talk to you, Doctor," Blayney said as he and Carlin stepped inside.

"Sure. Just let me take this boy out to his mother and then

we can talk. I'll have Patrick join us."

When Doc and Patrick returned, Carlin told them what he had discovered on his visit to the Crow village.

"So what we need to do, Doctor," Blayney said, "is to work out a schedule between us, so we can alternate going to the village."

"No need for that," Patrick said. "Both of you men are needed here. How about I go everyday until the epidemic is stopped?"

Doc rubbed his chin. "I like that idea, son. It'd be good if you got to know Chief Two Moons and his people."

"Sounds good to me," Blayney said. "And you're sure, Dr. O'Brien, that taking your son away from the clinic for a time will be all right?"

"Of course. He's been a real help to me here, but I think it works best for Pat to go. Will you be escorting him, Dobie?"

"Yes, Doc. Colonel Bateman said it was to be me and the six men who went with me today. We'll escort you every day, Dr. Patrick, till you don't need to go anymore. How soon do you want to leave?"

"Right away."

"Today?"

"The sooner the better. I'll finish up on my patient and be ready to go in half an hour."

"All right, Doctor." Carlin turned to Blayney and the senior O'Brien. "Something else. The Crow look like they're not getting nourishment. Even Chief Two Moons has lost weight. Everyone I saw looked gaunt and sort of hollow-eyed. I think they're low on food."

"You'd better look into it, son," Doc said.

"I will, Dad."

Two Moons knelt beside Broken Wing while Sweet Blossom gave him water to drink.

"Broken Wing is not as hot today," Sweet Blossom said, "but he is still hotter than he should be. He must drink plenty."

The boy swallowed and gave his mother a wan smile. Suddenly there was the sound of a hand clap outside, and Sun Man said, "Chief Two Moons. Soldier coats have come."

"Two Moons will be there shortly," said the chief. Then to Broken Wing he said, "You must not tell the white doctor or soldier coats that we have little to eat. And do not tell the white men that you attempted to go to the fort and ask for food."

Broken Wing nodded his assent.

Two Moons emerged from the tepee as the riders from the fort were drawing up to the edge of the village. Sun Man and Yellow Bird were there to greet them while others of the village looked on. Two Moons made his way toward them and noted the white man not in uniform who was carrying a black medical bag.

Lieutenant Carlin introduced Dr. Patrick O'Brien to the chief as Dr. Frank O'Brien's son, and Patrick explained that he had come to Fort Bridger to be his father's partner at the clinic. He had volunteered to come to the village because he wanted to meet the chief and his people and to help them.

Two Moons expressed his gratitude, saying that he would provide warm tepees for the soldier coats while Dr. Patrick O'Brien was tending the sick.

"Chief," Patrick said, "I have medicine that will make the sick ones cooler, and it will help make them well. I need you to take me first to the ones who are the most ill."

Two Moons nodded. "Crow medicine men are sickest. We go there first."

Patrick administered salicylic acid to Running Buck and Red Wolf and gave suggestions to the squaws on how to better care for them. Next he was taken to the elderly who were ill, and then they began working their way among those who were not as ill.

"Chief," Patrick said as they were walking from one tepee to another, "I can't help but notice that even your people who have not been affected by the influenza look very thin, and their color is not good. You and your people are not getting proper nourishment. I know this has been a hard winter, and game has been scarce. Are you low on food?"

Two Moons did not answer as he led Patrick into the next tepee.

When they came out and were heading to the next one, Patrick said, "Chief, you did not answer my question. I am very concerned that you and your people do not have enough food."

"Two Moons very much appreciates concern of Dr. Patrick O'Brien. Crow people will survive the winter." Two Moons glanced at the lowering sun and said, "You must return to fort soon, Dr. Patrick O'Brien. Many more sick ones to care for tomorrow and maybe next day. I have one more for you to see before you go today."

"Of course," Patrick said. "Lead on."

"This one is my son Broken Wing, Dr. Patrick O'Brien," Two Moons said as they neared the tepee. "He is some better than past few days, but he needs your medicine badly."

"Your son? Maybe you should have brought me to him earlier."

"Two Moons cannot choose his son over others who are sicker, though in his heart he wanted to." He led Patrick into his own tepee and introduced him to Sweet Blossom, then the two men knelt beside the boy, whose face was beaded with sweat.

"Broken Wing, this is Dr. Patrick O'Brien. He is son of Dr. Frank O'Brien."

The boy looked at Patrick, managed a faint smile, and said, "Broken Wing happy to meet you, Dr. Patrick O'Brien."

"He has good medicine to give Broken Wing," Two Moons said.

The sound of a hand clap was heard, and a warrior and his squaw asked if they could have a short talk with the chief and Sweet Blossom. The chief and his wife went outside the tepee, leaving doctor and patient alone.

Patrick gave Broken Wing small sips of the mix and found the boy friendly and talkative. When the cup was drained, Patrick said, "Broken Wing, as a doctor I know what people look like when they are not getting enough to eat. I see that in your village. I can see the Crow people have a food shortage. What can you tell me about it?"

Broken Wing avoided the doctor's gaze as he said, "Crow people find winter very hard, Dr. Patrick O'Brien. But we make it through the winter. We just have to eat smaller meals."

The parents returned at that moment, and Patrick told them that with the medicine he had given Broken Wing, and with continued care, he would get better soon. As with the others Patrick had treated today, he would repeat the treatment with Broken Wing tomorrow, and would have even more time to treat others.

Sweet Blossom expressed her deep gratitude to the doctor for coming, and Broken Wing added his words of thanks.

Snow was falling lightly when chief and physician stepped outside. Two Moons walked with the doctor to the edge of the village and waved as Patrick rode away with the soldier coats.

Patrick arrived back at Fort Bridger and made his report to Colonel Bateman and Dr. Blayney. Blayney then asked what he had learned about the food situation at the village.

"I talked with Chief Two Moons, but he stonewalled me. When I asked Broken Wing, he was reluctant to talk, and I think the situation is worse than he would admit. All he and the chief would say is they would make it through the winter."

Colonel Bateman nodded. "No doubt Two Moons is hesitant

to reveal the real state of their food supply because he doesn't want us to think he's hinting for us to meet their needs."

Dr. Blayney agreed, then told Patrick that his father had sent word for him to hurry to the office as soon as he could after returning to the fort.

Patrick headed for the door, telling Lieutenant Carlin that he would meet him and his men at the fort gate at six o'clock in the morning so they could get to the village early.

It was still snowing lightly as Patrick hurried to the clinic. When he arrived, his mother told him that Glenda Williams was preparing a meal at the Cooper apartment, and that he was invited, along with his parents and Pastor and Mrs. Kelly. Supper would be in half an hour.

Patrick said he would meet them at the Cooper apartment. He wanted to go by the Lindgren sisters' house and see how his patient was doing.

Heidi Lindgren opened the door and greeted the handsome, young doctor with a warm smile. "Won't you come in, Dr. O'Brien?"

Patrick removed his hat and stepped inside the toasty house. Marshal Lance Mangum was standing a few feet behind Heidi holding a steaming cup of coffee.

"Hello, Marshal," Patrick said, smiling.

"Good evening, Doctor."

"Lance is having supper with Sundi and me," Heidi said. "I can put another plate on the table."

"Thank you, ma'am, but I already have a supper engagement. I just wanted to look in on my favorite patient. How's she doing?"

"As well as can be expected. She's in the parlor. I'll take you in."

"Doctor, I heard you went up to the Crow village today,

that the influenza has hit them," Mangum said. "Is that so?"

"Yes, sir. They've had eleven people die with it. I hope, since I have the salicylic acid to give the sick ones, there won't be any more deaths."

Lance nodded. "We'll pray that the Lord will help you to save the rest of those who are down with it."

"We're all glad you're here, Doctor," Heidi said. "Without that medicine and the special care you gave Sundi, I doubt she would have lived."

"I'm just glad she's on the top side of it."

"Can I take your coat and hat, Doctor?" Lance asked.

"Thanks, but I can only stay a few minutes."

Heidi moved ahead of him toward the parlor door.

"I see it's still snowing," Lance said. "You think we're going to get another bad storm?"

"I don't think so. The moon is peeking through a break in the clouds."

"Good. We've had enough blizzards for one winter."

A fire was burning brightly in the fireplace in the parlor. The logs snapped and popped, adding a relaxed atmosphere to the room. Sundi was sitting in an overstuffed chair, close by the fire. She had a warm afghan draped over her lap and a book in her thin white hands.

"Look who's here to see you, honey," Heidi said.

Sundi gave Patrick a welcoming smile, her pale features reflected in the fire's glow. "Hello, Doctor. I recognized your voice when you came into the house."

Patrick laid his hat on a table and knelt before her. "And hello to you, Miss Lindgren." He placed a palm on Sundi's forehead. "Feels normal. I'm glad for that. How have you been feeling?"

"My energy level is still quite low, and I feel pretty weak when I walk. And I feel cold most of the time."

Patrick nodded. "Those are the usual effects of a bout with

influenza. Especially the one you had. Those things will improve day by day." His crooked grin appeared. "You sure look better than you did the first time I saw you."

Sundi closed her eyes and shook her head, putting a hand to her forehead.

"What's the matter?"

She opened her eyes and looked at him. "I've thought about the first time you saw me, over and over again. My hair was stringy and matted. I must have been a sight."

Patrick laughed. "I didn't mean that! I was talking about how pale you were and the dull look in your eyes."

Sundi smiled again. "Thank you, but my hair was still a mess."

"Miss Lindgren, I'm a doctor. I understand about a lady's hair and all that, but it's pretty hard to keep it looking good when you're delirious and running an extremely high fever. I must say that your hair looks nice now, however."

A slight tint surfaced on Sundi's cheeks. "Thank you. Heidi washed and brushed it for me. Dr. O'Brien, would you do me a favor?"

"Name it."

"I think we've gotten to know each other well enough that you can call me by my first name. You don't have to call me Miss Lindgren any longer."

"Well, all right. Then I can call you Miss Sundi?"

"Yes, that would be fine."

Patrick gave her that lopsided grin again. "All right, Miss Sundi," he said rising to his feet. "I'll drop in and check on you tomorrow evening."

"I'll look forward to it, Doctor," she said, her smile lighting up her eyes.

CHAPTER NINETEEN

Patrick O'Brien hurried along Main Street, his thoughts with Sundi and the magnetic pull of her personality. He arrived at the Cooper apartment just in time for supper. He greeted the Cooper family and guests then joined them at the table where Pastor Kelly gave thanks for the food.

"Son, I've told everyone here what you said about the apparent food shortage at the Crow village," Doc said. "How about filling us in on how serious the influenza epidemic is?"

"Well, I'm afraid the epidemic is a bad one. So far eleven people have died, and there's a chance the two medicine men could die as well. But the salicylic acid should make a big difference, and I'll be going back every day until every sick person is better. From what I can put together, it was the extreme sickness of Red Wolf and Running Buck that got Chief Two Moons to call on us for help."

"I'm glad he did," Kelly said. "There's a lot of fear among the Indians toward their gods. They're very careful about offending the medicine men."

"Another element that I'm sure played a part in Two Moons calling on us for help is that his son is quite sick."

A sharp gasp came from Chris. "Broken Wing has the disease, Dr. Patrick?"

"Yes."

"Is he real bad?"

"Well, from what I know, he was worse before I got there today, but he's still pretty sick. His fever is over a hundred. I gave him a big dose of salicylic mix, so he should be better by morning. Either way, I'll give him another dose tomorrow."

"Dr. Patrick," Chris said, "would you take me with you tomorrow? I want to see Broken Wing. He's my best friend."

"Honey, it's best that you not go," Hannah said. "You'll be exposed to Broken Wing's influenza."

"But, Mama, he's my best friend. I want him to know I care about him. Besides, he's showing real interest in what I told him about Jesus dying for his sins on the cross. He's close to getting saved, Mama. Please let me go. You will let me go with you, won't you, Dr. Patrick?"

"Chris," Hannah said, "I very much care about Broken Wing being saved, but I don't want you in the close quarters of that tepee, breathing the infected air."

Patrick cleared his throat gently. "A lot of people have a natural immunity to the disease, Miss Hannah. This is why most of the people in this town and the fort never came down with it, though they were exposed. Chris, Mary Beth, and Patty Ruth no doubt have that natural immunity, or they would've gotten it by now, especially with mother and little brother having been so sick with it right here in the house."

Hannah frowned and glanced at the older doctor.

"I feel certain, Miss Hannah," Patrick said, "that it would be all right for Chris to pay a visit to his best friend. As far as I'm concerned, he's quite welcome to go along. I'm sure Lieutenant Carlin would let him go. He talked a lot about Chris while we were riding today. From what he said, Chris had a lot to do with him coming to the Lord."

"He did, Doctor, but—"

"Please, Mama," Chris said.

Patrick smiled. "Please, Mama."

"All right, Doctor. If you say there's no danger…"

"There really isn't, Hannah," the senior Dr. O'Brien said. "Like Patrick said, the way Chris has been exposed, if he was going to get influenza, he would've done it by now. We haven't had anybody come down with it in town or fort for more than a week. Chris should be fine."

"Thanks, Mama," Chris said, leaving his chair to give her a hug.

Hannah patted his cheek. "You really love Broken Wing, don't you?"

"I do, and I want him to be saved. Maybe this will be the time, since he's been so sick and others in the village have died."

"Bless you for caring like that, Chris," Pastor Kelly said. "It's not easy to reach the Indians, they're so steeped in their superstition and age-old religion. I've carried a real burden for the Crow ever since Rebecca and I came here and I first met them. I've talked to Chief Two Moons on several occasions about Jesus and salvation, and though he was polite about it, each time he made it clear that he and his people have their own religion and their own gods."

"I've gotten the same polite reaction when I've talked to Two Moons and Sweet Blossom," Hannah said. "My heart is heavy for them. They are such sweet people."

"All of us at this table should agree to pray everyday for Two Moons's salvation," Kelly said. "If he gets saved, he could be the instrument to bring the other Crow to the Lord…and the first ones would be Sweet Blossom and Broken Wing."

"Broken Wing seems to hold back for fear of what his parents would do if he became a Christian," Chris said.

"That's understandable," Gary Williams said. "The Indian children are taught to revere their parents. The thought of turning from the tribe's religion and the possible consequences it could bring has to put a great deal of fear in the boy's heart."

"We have to pray that Broken Wing will come to the place where he fears God more than he fears his parents," Patrick said.

"In essence," Kelly said, "it's the same way with any lost sinner who fears what other people will think, say, or do if they become a child of God. It's just harder for someone like Broken Wing, whose people have been steeped in their superstitions for so long. It's ingrained in them from very early in life. And like Gary said, the Indian children have been taught from the time they can remember to revere their parents—which is good. But in cases like this it makes it harder for the children to turn to the Lord. That's why it would be so much easier if Two Moons came to Christ first."

"Well, one thing about it," Rebecca said, "the Lord Jesus loves those precious Crow people more than we ever could. If we do our part to see that they get the gospel because our hearts are full of love for them, and pray earnestly while we do it, we can see them saved."

Chris nodded. "Yes, ma'am. And I plan to give Broken Wing some more gospel tomorrow."

"How about some more details about the food shortage at the village, Patrick?" Hannah said.

Patrick told everyone he had seen telltale signs in the faces of the Crow people of the lack of food. When he explained how Chief Two Moons had avoided talking about it, Hannah said, "Well, Dr. Patrick, while you're visiting the village you keep an eye on those people. No matter what it takes, we can't let them starve to death."

At six o'clock the next morning, an excited Chris Cooper mounted his horse, Buster, and rode to the Crow village with Dr. Patrick and his army escort. When they rode up to the village, they could see Chief Two Moons standing in front of his tepee, talking to a couple of braves. Two Crow sentries greeted the doctor and the lieutenant in a friendly manner, and led them toward the chief.

Two Moons's eyes lit up and a smile broke across his drawn features when he saw his son's best friend.

"Looks like he's spotted you, Chris," Dobie Carlin said.

"Yes, sir," Chris said, his heart pounding.

Two Moons greeted the doctor and the lieutenant, then moved to the fourteen-year-old boy and said, "Chris Cooper, welcome! You have come to visit Broken Wing, I know."

"Yes, sir."

"Broken Wing will be very happy to see you." The chief looked at Dobie and said, "Lieutenant Dobie Carlin, you and your men are welcome to tepee over there. Please enter and warm yourselves. The fire is burning inside."

Dobie thanked him and hurried back to his men, boots crunching in the frozen snow.

"Chief," Patrick said, "if it meets with your approval, I will look at Broken Wing first, and give him more medicine. I will leave Chris with him while you and I go to the other sick ones."

Two Moons agreed and led them to his tepee. He stepped in first and looked down at his son on the pallet. "Broken Wing has a special guest today."

Sweet Blossom, who was adding wood to the fire, smiled when she saw Chris come in.

When Broken Wing saw his friend, his eyes brightened. "Chris Cooper!" he said, showing his teeth in the widest smile he'd had since coming down with the influenza.

Chris knelt down, took hold of Broken Wing's hand, and said, "I get to stay all day."

Since Sundi Lindgren had planned to start school again on Monday, February 13, Chris Cooper took advantage of the time in between to go to the Crow village every day with Dr. Patrick O'Brien. On the seventh day since his first visit to Broken Wing, Chris was glad to see his friend sitting up.

Since Dr. O'Brien had begun the salicylic treatments, no one else in the village had died. Those affected by the disease were all doing better, including the medicine men. Both Red Wolf and Running Buck were friendly toward the white doctor.

Chris had not yet been alone with Broken Wing. He had prayed each day that the Lord would give him the opportunity to talk to his friend in private about being saved. Today he sat on the grass floor of the tepee with Broken Wing and talked about summer and the chance once again to ride their horses together.

Sweet Blossom was happily putting venison stew over the fire to simmer. She found a moment of silence in the boys' conversation and said, "Chris Cooper, have Patty Ruth Cooper and Mary Beth Cooper become ill with white man's disease?"

"No, ma'am. The doctors say they probably won't get it now."

"This is good. I am very happy that Chris Cooper did not get it, either. And Hannah Cooper and B.J Cooper are all right now?"

"Yes, ma'am. They're still a little weak, but they're doing better everyday."

"That is good, Chris Cooper," said Sweet Blossom, and went back to her work. Moments later, she left the tepee.

"Broken Wing," Chris said, "there's something I've wondered about for a long time and have never gotten around to asking you."

"What is it, Chris Cooper?"

"Why do Indians always call people by their full name? I mean, you always call me Chris Cooper. You don't call me Chris. Your mother just asked about my family, and called each one by their full name. When your father talks about the colonel, he always calls him Colonel Ross Bateman. Never just Colonel or Colonel Bateman. Dr. Patrick is always Dr. Patrick O'Brien. I've never heard your mother address my mother as

Hannah. It is always Hannah Cooper. How come?"

Broken Wing grinned. "Why do you not call me Broken? Why does your mother not call my mother Sweet? Why do the white men always refer to my father as Two Moons? They never call him Two. We do not call Red Wolf, Red…nor Running Buck, Running. So I do not call you Chris. I call you Chris Cooper."

"Oh, sure. I get it," said Chris, nodding.

Chris sniffed the aroma of the venison stew and said, "I'm glad your braves were able to find some deer, Broken Wing. I've been concerned that your people have such a hungry look, even you and your parents. Is most of the village's food gone?"

Broken Wing cast a glance toward the tepee's opening. "Our food is very scarce, Chris Cooper," he said licking his lips. "For many moons we have been eating only one time a day. And even those meals have been small. Sometimes almost nothing. Our grain supply is nearly gone, and we have had to rely on what meat the hunters can bring home. So many of our men have been sick with the white man's disease, only a few have been able to go out and hunt."

Sweet Blossom returned and said, "Broken Wing, your father wants me with him and Dr. Patrick O'Brien in some of the tepees. It will be some time before I come back. Chris Cooper, will you put more wood on the fire when it grows small?"

"Yes, ma'am."

"Thank you," she said with a smile. "You boys have a nice visit."

"Broken Wing, I want to do something about your lack of food. I'm not sure what just yet, but I can't just sit by and do nothing while you and your people go hungry. But there's something else, something more important even than food, that I'd like for us to talk about, if it's all right with you."

"What is that, Chris Cooper?"

"Have you thought about where you would have gone if you…if you had died with the influenza?"

"Yes. Broken Wing thought about it much. I have become very afraid of dying. I remembered many things you told me about Jesus Christ, and feel something in my heart that says it is true. I am having many doubts about the Crow religion. I have watched people of our village dying around me, and I have wondered if instead of going to meet the Sky Father and the Sky People, as the medicine men say, they may have gone to hell."

"My good friend," Chris said, "Jesus wants to save you and forgive you of your sins. I can help you to know how to call on Him for salvation if you will let me. You don't have to be afraid to die."

Broken Wing licked his dry lips. "Chris Cooper, I am afraid to die and to go to hell. I want to go to heaven. But…I also fear what my parents and the medicine men would do if I became a Christian."

Chris leaned close to his friend. "Broken Wing, I understand the fear you have about your parents and the medicine men. But the Bible says, 'The fear of the LORD is the beginning of knowledge: but fools despise wisdom and instruction.' More than anything, you need the fear of God. If you let the fear of your parents or the medicine men keep you from being saved, God says you are a fool who is despising His wisdom and instruction."

Broken Wing's lips trembled. "Chris Cooper, would you tell me the story again about Jesus Christ and the cross?"

By the time Chris had gone over the gospel, the Indian boy was weeping.

"I fear God more than anyone," Broken Wing said, wiping tears. "I want to be saved."

Chris had the joy of leading his best friend to Jesus. When Broken Wing finished calling on the Lord, Chris prayed for him, asking the Lord to give him peace about his salvation and confidence that he would go to heaven when it came his time to leave this world.

"This peace I have, Chris Cooper. Jesus is in my heart, and I know I am going to heaven."

"What are you going to do now, Broken Wing?"

"You mean about my parents?"

"Yes."

Broken Wing drew in a deep breath. "I must be honest and tell my parents that I have become a follower of Jesus Christ, and no longer believe in the gods of the Crow. I will wait to do that after you and Dr. Patrick O'Brien have gone."

At sundown, Chris rode toward Fort Bridger between Dr. Patrick O'Brien and Lieutenant Dobie Carlin. The six troopers followed, riding two by two.

When the Crow village was out of sight behind them, Chris glanced at his riding companions and said, "I've got something wonderful to tell you! You both know I've been witnessing to Broken Wing for many months."

Both men nodded.

"Well, today he got saved!"

"Praise the Lord!" Dobie said.

"Your family is going to be happy when they hear about this!" Patrick said.

"We've been praying for the Crow for a long time, and especially for Chief Two Moons and his family. Mama and my brother and sisters know how much I've wanted to lead Broken Wing to the Lord. Oh, I'm so happy!"

Dobie said, "I'd sure like to see their faces when you tell them, but I've got to do some things with Travis as soon as I get home."

"I'd like to see their faces, too," Patrick said. "Do you suppose it'd be all right if I come to the apartment with you, Chris?"

"Of course. We'll plan on it." Chris was quiet a moment, then said, "We need to be praying for Broken Wing. He's going to tell his parents right away about becoming a Christian. He feels he should be honest with them."

"Let's pray for him right now while we ride," Dobie said.

The sun's upper rim was still in view on the western horizon and was painting the wall of the tepee a bright orange as Chief Two Moons sat cross-legged across the fire from his son. Broken Wing's mouth watered at the sight of the stew as his mother dipped it from the pot into his plate. The portions would be small, for the stew would have to last them several days.

Broken Wing knew he had to learn more about praying to his new heavenly Father, but in his heart he talked to God the same as he would talk to his earthly father aloud, asking for help when he told his parents about becoming a Christian.

A plate of stew was placed before Two Moons, and he smiled at his squaw and sniffed its aroma. Sweet Blossom sat down with her own steaming plate and looked to her husband.

Broken Wing trembled inside as his father raised his hands toward the heavens, lifted his eyes upward, and gave thanks to the Sky Father for what little food they had. Two Moons had tears streaming down his cheeks as he implored the Great Spirit to supply food for his family and his people.

Broken Wing was so nervous he could hardly eat, in spite of his hunger. He prayed again in his heart, asking the Lord to calm him, and when the calm came, he was able to devour his food in the manner his parents were used to seeing.

When the meal was finished, and his parents were drinking a hot brew Sweet Blossom had made from the powder of berries she had prepared in the summer, Broken Wing offered another silent prayer for help, then said, "Father, Mother, something happened to me today that I want to tell you about." His heart was banging his ribs.

"Of course, son," Two Moons said. Sweet Blossom set her dark eyes on him, smiling.

"You both know that Chris Cooper is a Christian. Today, with Chris Cooper's help, I became a Christian. I am now a follower of Jesus Christ, the Son of God."

Sweet Blossom's smile faded as she looked at her husband, who suddenly jumped to his feet. Slowly she rose to a standing position too.

There was a flare of anger in Two Moons's eyes. "My son has forsaken the gods of the Crow?"

"Yes, Father. Jesus Christ is the true God. He has forgiven my sins. When I die, I will go to be with Him in heaven."

The Chief's breathing was erratic. "How can this be? Broken Wing has brought shame to his father and mother! What will I tell the medicine men? What will I tell our people?"

Sweet Blossom moved to her husband, laid a hand on his arm, and said, "Sweet Blossom asks Broken Wing's father to consider something seriously."

"Speak on," he said, his fiery eyes on the boy.

"Sweet Blossom reminds her husband that Jesus Christ is the God of Hannah Cooper, as well as of her children. Hannah Cooper has proven herself to be a friend of Two Moons and Sweet Blossom and of the Crow people. She also has talked to us about her Jesus Christ. Are we to be angry with our son for turning to Hannah Cooper's Jesus Christ?"

"Hannah Cooper is a good woman," Two Moons said. "She is a friend indeed. But—"

"Does the father of Broken Wing not appreciate his son's honest heart?"

Two Moons turned his gaze on Sweet Blossom, a question in his eyes.

"Our son has been honest with us, my husband. He could

have kept his new faith from us. We must be glad for his honest heart."

Two Moons stood motionless for a moment, then leaned down and laid a hand on his son's shoulder. Broken Wing brought his gaze up to meet his father's.

"Broken Wing," Two Moons said, "your father very much appreciates his son's honest heart. He was wrong in saying that Broken Wing has shamed his father and mother. Since your faith in Jesus Christ is the faith of Hannah Cooper and Chris Cooper it is acceptable."

"My father, what will Red Wolf and Running Buck do when they learn that Broken Wing has turned from the Crow gods to white man's Jesus Christ?"

"Your father will talk to them about it. Since Dr. Patrick O'Brien saved the lives of many Crow, including Red Wolf and Running Buck—and is still coming to care for all the sick of the village—Red Wolf and Running Buck would appear very unwise to show anger toward Broken Wing for turning to white man's Jesus Christ. They will not do that. And for the same reason, the Crow people will not be angry with Broken Wing."

The boy saw a look of relief wash over his mother's face. Silently, he talked to his Jesus Christ, thanking Him for answering his prayers.

CHAPTER TWENTY

With Patty Ruth's help, Mary Beth Cooper had supper almost ready. Hannah sat at the kitchen table, watching her daughters at the cupboard and stove while the color of the sunset stained the sky outside the window.

B.J. sat in the parlor by the fireplace with Jacob Kates. From his comfortable chair, B.J. was taunting his sisters. When he had them saying they wished he hadn't gotten well so quickly and was still in bed, Hannah spoke some stern words to him, and the taunting ceased.

Jacob and Hannah were discussing the shortage of food and supplies in the store when they heard rapid footsteps pounding the outside staircase.

The door burst open, and Chris bounded in with Dr. Patrick on his heels. Patrick closed the door as Chris removed his hat and said, "Hear ye! Hear ye! Christopher Cooper, noted herald of Fort Bridger, has a huge, gigantic announcement of great magnitude!"

Biggie got up from under the kitchen table and stared at Chris.

Hannah smiled. "All right, noted herald, what's this big announcement?"

"Broken Wing opened his heart to Jesus today! He got saved!"

"Honey, that's wonderful!" Hannah hurried to Chris and

gave him a hug. "We want to hear all about it. Mary Beth, do we have time to hear it before supper's ready?"

"I believe so, Mama."

"Then tell us, son," Hannah said, hugging him again.

Chris removed his coat, and carried it and his hat to the pegs by the door. "You sit down again, Mama," he said.

Hannah smiled at Patrick O'Brien. "Do you want to sit down too, Dr. Patrick?"

"Thank you, ma'am, but I'll stand. I'm here because I wanted to be in on it when Chris made his huge, gigantic announcement of great magnitude."

Hannah returned to one of the chairs around the kitchen table, and Chris eased onto the chair next to her. The Cooper family shed many tears as Chris described how the Lord had allowed him to lead his best friend to salvation. Patrick had a lump in his throat as he saw the impact the story had on Hannah and her other children.

Jacob Kates observed it all in silence. In his Jewish religion, there was no such joy in the hearts of the people when they saw someone come into their faith.

Patty Ruth moved close to her mother and proclaimed to all, "Pretty soon I'm gonna ask Jesus to come into my heart."

"It won't be very long, sweetheart," Hannah said. "You just need to understand a little better about sin."

B.J. chuckled. "She does? Well, she sure knows how to do it!"

Little sister stuck out her tongue and made a face.

"Brett Jonathan…" said Hannah, giving him a frown.

B.J. looked at the floor and sighed.

"Supper's ready," Mary Beth announced. "You boys get your hands washed."

"How about Patty Ruth?" B.J. asked.

"She washed her hands before she started helping me with supper."

Hannah left her chair and went up to Dr. Patrick. She

didn't see B.J. glance at his little sister and get another dirty look accompanied by a protruding tongue.

"Doctor, could you stay and eat with us?" Hannah said. "It'll be no problem to set another plate on the table. With the food shortage on us, it isn't much more than meager, but I don't think you'll go away hungry."

Patrick gave her his crooked grin. "You sure it'll be no trouble?"

"Of course. But I wonder if your mother is expecting you for supper."

"She won't hold it for me, ma'am. Since I've been going up to the village these days, I've told her that if I'm not home by suppertime, she and Dad should go ahead and eat without me. So it'll be all right. I'm really honored that you would ask me to stay and eat with you."

"We're honored to have you." Hannah saw Jacob standing next to her and patted his cheek. "We're honored to have this fine young man, too."

Jacob laughed. "Young man? Thank you, Miss Hannah!"

When everyone was at the table, Hannah asked Dr. Patrick to lead them as they thanked the Lord for the food.

As they began to eat, Mary Beth looked across the table at her older brother and said, "Chris, is Broken Wing going to tell his parents that he has become a Christian?"

"He said he was going to tell them after Dr. Patrick and I left for home."

"It's going to come as a blow to Two Moons and Sweet Blossom," Hannah said. "We need to pray that the Lord will keep His hand on Broken Wing."

Mary Beth nodded. "I believe that if we pray hard, the Lord can use Broken Wing's salvation to save others in the village."

"That's right, Mary Beth," Patrick said. "Broken Wing is now a beacon in the Lord's hand to shine His light into the darkness of the Crows' superstition."

"If Chief Two Moons lets Miss Lindgren and me come back and teach on Saturdays this spring," Mary Beth said, "I'll weave some Bible stories into the lessons."

B.J. chuckled to himself, and every eye turned to him.

"What's so funny, son?" Hannah said.

The boy chuckled again. "It's really good that the Lord planted His truth in the Crow village by putting the first Christian right in Chief Two Moons's tepee!"

Patrick laughed. "You're right, B.J. God knows what He's doing!"

Soon the meal was over, and as Jacob pushed his empty plate away, he said, "As tight as things are around here these days, I'm sure thankful we still have food on the table."

Others voiced their agreement.

Hannah saw Chris's face pinch. "Chris, what's wrong?"

"When I was alone with Broken Wing, I asked him about the food supply in the village. They're about to starve, Mama. They did have a little venison brought in by some of the hunters recently, but Broken Wing told me that the Crow are eating only one meal a day, and even that meal is very small."

"I knew by the looks of the people that they were under-nourished," Patrick said. "I asked Two Moons about it, and all he said was that they would make it through the winter. I think he just didn't want to appear to be a beggar by telling me the facts."

"That sounds like Two Moons," Hannah said. "He doesn't expect white men to come to his aid. He'd have to be in dire straits before he'd ask us for help. I mean, the situation would have to be really desperate."

Patty Ruth looked at her mother with furrowed brow. "Mama…"

"Yes, honey?"

"Would Mr. Two Moons get mad if we took some food to

the village for him and the other In'ians to eat?"

"Well, I don't think he'd get mad, Patty Ruth. It might hurt his pride. We all have some of that in us. What do you have in mind, honey?"

"I'll go without eatin' some days so the In'ians can have my food."

Hannah smiled. "That's very nice of you, sweetie, but I think we'll have to do something different than that if we're going to help Chief Two Moons and his people."

Mary Beth smiled at her little sister. "I'm proud of you, Patty Ruth. That's very unselfish of you."

Later that night, after prayer and Bible reading time with her children, Hannah lay in the darkness, unable to sleep. The wind was howling around the eaves, and she was sure the temperature had dipped well below zero when the sun went down. She turned her head on the pillow and could see frost covering the glass, obscuring the glow of the cold winter moon.

"Oh, Sol," she said in a whisper, "I can't stand the thought of those dear Crow people existing on one insufficient meal a day. I know the supply of food on the shelves and in the storeroom is very low, but I can't simply stand by and let Two Moons and his people go hungry. Yes, I've rationed sales to my customers, but they're still eating three meals a day, even if some of them are meager. I have to help my Indian friends, Sol. I have to."

Hannah rolled onto her side, and after a while she rolled onto her other side. Sleep would not come. All she could think of was the hungry Crow.

"Dear Lord, I've got to do something. Those dear people are on the verge of starvation. What should I do, Lord?"

Suddenly a verse of Scripture came to her mind. She couldn't remember the exact words, but it was about a person who saw someone else in need and had the means to supply it but lacked the compassion to do so. It was in 1 John, she knew that. She tried to bring the words to mind, but they simply wouldn't come.

She found her robe in the dark, wrapped it tightly around her, and slid into her slippers. She lit the lantern on the bedstand, picked up her Bible, and turned to 1 John, scanning the pages of chapter 3. She found it.

"But whoso hath this world's good, and seeth his brother have need, and shutteth up his bowels of compassion from him, how dwelleth the love of God in him?"

Hannah read it over twice more, then said, "Lord, the only Indian in the village who is my brother in Christ is Broken Wing. But all of the Crow are my brothers and sisters in the human family. Two Moons and his people have a need, and I have food yet on the shelves. You know I have compassion in my heart toward them, and I must do something."

A sweet peace stole over her and tears warmed her eyes as she closed her Bible and laid it on the bedstand, then doused the light. She removed her robe and slippers and once again nestled down into her bed.

"Lord, there will no doubt be customers who will object, but because Your love dwells in me, I must share what food we have with the Crow."

She dabbed at her tears with the sheet, and a still small voice seemed to say within her heart, "You do right by my Word, Hannah, and I will take care of the rest."

Hannah let God's peace settle over her, and as her heavenly Father had promised in His Word, He gave His beloved sleep.

At the breakfast table the next morning, Hannah told her children how the Lord had spoken to her last night, then read them 1 John 3:17. She looked up from her Bible and said, "As long as there is food on the shelves of the store, I have to share some of it with the Crow. It tears my heart out, especially to think of those little Indian children going hungry. Do you understand?"

"Of course we do, Mama," Mary Beth said. "You've taught us we should pray daily that God will help us to be more like His Son. And just think of the compassion the Lord Jesus has shown to this whole world, including us."

"I wish the rest of you could see how thin the Crow people have become," Chris said. "I'm glad you're going to give them food, Mama."

Hannah set her eyes on B.J. "Do you understand, son?"

"Yes, Mama. I want you to give them food."

Hannah smiled at her youngest. "You've already made it known that you would even give up your own food to help feed the Indians, honey."

Patty Ruth nodded. "I'm glad Jesus talked to you and told you to give them food, Mama."

"Now there's one thing I should tell you, children. You know there are people who live around here who hate all Indians, no matter what tribe they are. When those people learn that I've given food to the Crow, they're going to be very unhappy about it. We might even face some trouble over it."

"But we have the Lord on our side, Mama," Mary Beth said. "You're doing what He told us to do in His Word. We can trust Him to handle any troublemakers in His own way."

"Papa would want you to give food to the Indians, Mama," B.J. said.

Hannah smiled. "Yes, he would. I assume you're going to the village again today, Chris?"

"Unless you have something you need me to do."

"No. It'll be good for you to be with Broken Wing. What I wanted to say was, I don't want you to tell anyone what we've discussed here this morning. I want to do it in my own way, and I want to surprise Chief Two Moons and his people when I do it."

After Chris had ridden away with Dr. Patrick and the army escort, Hannah said to Mary Beth, "I'm going down to the store and talk to Jacob about the food I want to give to the Crow. You watch over B.J. and Patty Ruth. I'll be a while, so don't worry about me. If I'm not back by lunchtime, you go ahead and fix something."

"But Mama, it's not even opening time for the store. What's going to take you so long?"

"After I have my talk with Jacob, I have somewhere else to go in order to fulfill my plan."

"You shouldn't be going anywhere in the snow by your-self. You'll—"

"I'll find someone to walk me through the snow. You and the other two clean the house good, okay?"

"All right, Mama. I'll take care of things here."

Hannah bundled up warmly and made her way down the stairs. She hadn't been in the store since the influenza epidemic hit full force. When she stepped inside, she took a deep breath, inhaling the familiar scents, and realized how much she had missed it. She glanced over the shelves as she moved toward the counter and noted some empty spots. She wondered if they were completely out of the items that were usually there.

"Well, good morning, Miss Hannah," Jacob said as he emerged from the storeroom carrying items from the dwindling supply. "It's good to see the boss lady in the store again."

"Thank you, Jacob. I was just thinking how much I've missed it. I noticed several empty places on the shelves. I assume we're totally out of some things?"

"Mm-hmm. I'm putting the last of several items on the shelves now. The storeroom is starting to look a bit barren."

"But you still think we can go another couple of weeks on

the most important items?"

"Well-l-l, maybe. Give or take a day or two."

A shadow of doubt crossed Hannah's mind. Should she go ahead as planned? She thought again of the assurance she had received from the Lord the night before. She knew where the doubt was coming from and said in her mind, *Get thee behind me, Satan. My God shall supply all your need according to His riches in glory by Christ Jesus.*

"Jacob, I want to talk to you about something."

"Yes, ma'am?"

"You're probably going to think I've lost my mind, but I must send some of this food to Chief Two Moons and his people."

Jacob's eyes widened. "Pardon me, Miss Hannah, but did I hear you right? You're going to take from what little we have left for our customers and give it to the Crow?"

"I've been concerned about them, Jacob. And...well, last night, I couldn't sleep. The Lord spoke to me from His Word, and I couldn't get any peace or rest until I made up my mind to do this."

Jacob scratched his head. "Well, ma'am, I do have to say that since Chris told us last night about the Crow having only one meager meal a day, it's really been bothering me, too. But..."

"But what?"

"I'm worried about how our customers will take it. I've seen starvation in New York City. Hungry people can become quite unreasonable. We could have some trouble."

"I'm sure that's true, but I must do this because the Bible says to."

"It does?"

Hannah went to the shelf where books and Bibles were stocked. She took a Bible in hand and turned to 1 John.

"I realize you don't accept the New Testament in the

Jewish religion, Jacob, but you'll see the truth of this verse, I guarantee you." She placed the Bible in his hand and ran her finger to the place. "Right here. Verse 17. Read it."

Jacob read the verse silently, nodded, and said, "It couldn't be said more beautifully, Miss Hannah."

Colonel Ross Bateman was both surprised and pleased to see Hannah ushered into his office by one of his aides. He rounded the desk to greet her, then thanked the corporal, who stepped into the hall and closed the door.

Hannah was out of breath and panting slightly from her trek through the snow. Her cheeks were rosy from the cold, and even though she was still a little pale from her illness, her eyes were alive with determination.

"I can see by the look in your eyes that you have a specific purpose for asking to see me, Hannah," Bateman said. "I'm concerned, though, that you walked from the store to the fort alone."

"I didn't walk alone, Colonel. Jack Bower escorted me and is waiting in the outer office to take me back."

"Well, good for him." Bateman guided her to a chair in front of his desk, then eased into his own chair and leaned forward on his elbows. "Now, what can I do for you?"

Hannah explained what she intended to do and said she would need an army wagon to load the food in and a cavalry escort to the Crow village.

Bateman seemed a bit surprised. "I agree that it's the right thing to do, especially because of what the Crow did for my men when they needed shelter and care. But I must warn you, Hannah, when people find out what you've done, many of them are going to object angrily."

"I'm fully aware of this, Colonel, but I must do it anyway.

I have to look Hannah Cooper in the eye everyday in the mirror, and what I'm doing is the right thing, no matter who doesn't like it."

Bateman smiled. "Hannah, you would've made a good soldier if you'd have been a man."

"I was married to a good soldier, sir."

Bateman nodded. "Captain Solomon Cooper was one of the very best officers who ever fought under my command."

The mention of her husband brought tears to Hannah's eyes. She wiped them away and said, "Will the wagon and escort be provided, Colonel?"

"They most certainly will. When do you want this wagon and escort?"

"Tomorrow morning. No later than eight o'clock."

"Consider it done."

"Thank you, sir. And...I want to go along and give the food to Chief Two Moons and his people. And please don't lecture me as to why I shouldn't."

Bateman chuckled. "Oh, I wouldn't think of it. You dress warm, all right? And we'll provide heavy blankets."

"Thank you, Colonel."

CHAPTER TWENTY-ONE

Hannah entered the store and headed toward the counter and Mandy Carver, who had volunteered to help out for the day. Jacob's back was toward Hannah as he arranged some items on a shelf.

"Hello, Miz Hannah," Mandy said, releasing a brilliant smile. "You all right after your walk in the snow?"

Hannah removed her scarf and started unbuttoning her coat. "I'm fine, Mandy. Deputy Bower took good care of me."

Jacob turned around. "Everything go okay?"

"Yes, everything's set. Did you tell Mandy what I'm doing?"

"No. I'll let you tell her."

"Tell me what?"

"The Lord has put something on my heart to do, honey."

"Well, if the Lord tol' you to do it, it's gotta be good."

Hannah had just finished explaining her plan to Mandy when a few customers entered the store.

"Well, Miz Hannah," Mandy said, "there's no question it's the right thing to do, even if some folks don't like it. The Lord will bless you for it."

Jacob glanced at the customers, who were spreading out to walk the rows of shelves. To Hannah, he said, "When is this going to happen?"

"Tomorrow morning at eight. Colonel Bateman will provide the wagon, the driver, and the army escort. The soldiers will load the wagon for us."

"I'm glad the colonel is cooperating. Was there any hesitation?"

"None. He warned me of the trouble it could bring, but he's with me all the way. I'll leave you two to your work," Hannah said. "Right now, I'm going to the storeroom and mark the items to be loaded on the wagon."

Hannah had just started to look over the items in the storeroom when she heard a customer say she had overheard part of Hannah's comments and wanted to know what she was taking to the Crow. When Hannah didn't hear either Jacob or Mandy reply, she stepped outside the storeroom and said, "It's all right to tell folks what I'm doing. There's nothing to hide."

She went back to her task, and when she finally returned to the counter, she said to Mandy, "Did I hear Curly Wesson's voice?"

"Yes'm. When I tol' him that you were in the storeroom, he said to tell you that the telegraph wires are still down. He thinks maybe some of the hostile Indians cut the wires in several places."

"Oh. Well, I appreciate him letting me know. Thank you, Mandy." She turned to Jacob. "I need you to help me take some items off the shelves. I'll point them out if you'll carry them to the storeroom for me."

"Anything else, Miss Hannah?" Jacob asked as he carried the last of the items into the storeroom.

"That'll do it, Jacob. Thank you."

Suddenly a harsh male voice blared, "Where's Hannah? We wanna talk to her!"

"She's busy in the storeroom right now, Mr. Killian," Mandy said.

"Well, we don't care how busy she is!" another voice boomed. "We want to talk to her! What she's plannin' to do for those savage Crows is dead wrong. You go get her, woman!"

"Word is spreading fast," Jacob said in a low voice. "I think the other one is Roe Dahmer."

Hannah took a deep breath. "Well, we might as well go out there and face them."

Other customers looked on as Hannah approached the two ranchers with Jacob at her side.

"You gentlemen wanted to talk to me?" Hannah said.

"Yeah!" Killian said. "Me and Roe come into town today to stock up as usual, and folks outside told us you've been rationin' your sales 'cause the supply wagons haven't been able to get here from Cheyenne City."

"That's right. Sorry I can't let you stock up as usual, but our inventory is getting low."

Roe Dahmer took a step closer, his face flushed with anger. "We understand that, woman, but what we don't understand is this business about the stinkin' Indians."

The door opened and Glenda Williams came in. Several others filed in behind her.

"How can you be givin' food to those low-down Crows when everybody around here is runnin' low on food!" Killian said.

Jacob started to speak, but Hannah touched his arm and said, "I justify it, sir, because Chief Two Moons and his people are beyond running low on food. They're on the verge of starvation. I can't just stand by and let it happen as long as it's in my power to help them. And they are not low-down…and they are not stinking Indians! They are flesh and blood human beings with needs and feelings just like you!"

Dahmer's jaw jutted out. "Hannah, you ought to care about white people who are on the verge of starvation! What's the matter with you?"

"You don't talk to Miss Hannah like that, mister!" Jacob said. "She's a lady! You treat her like a lady!"

Hannah moved up beside the little man and fixed Dahmer with eyes like flint. "What's the matter with me, you ask? The matter with me is that I don't know of any white people who are only eating one next-to-nothing meal a day to survive!"

"Well, there'll be plenty of white people around here coming to that if those supply wagons don't start showin' up! You oughtta keep the food in this store for white people and let the stinkin', no-good Indians fend for themselves!"

"That's enough, mister!" Jacob said. "If you two can't keep a civil tongue in your mouth, and treat Miss Hannah with respect, you can leave!"

Killian laughed, looking Jacob up and down. "And you're gonna throw us out, are you, little fella?"

"He won't have to," Jason Drumm said.

"That's right," another man said huskily. Hannah's eyes darted to the owner of the voice. It was Lieutenant Greg Sullivan, whose wife, Melissa, stood beside him.

Dahmer cleared his throat and said, "We're customers of yours, Hannah. You should be concerned about our needs."

"I am, sir. I'm concerned about all of my customers. And you are welcome to purchase your share of goods in this store, as are all these other customers."

"Mrs. Cooper," another rancher said, "I don't agree with the way Roe and Max have been speaking to you, but I do agree with what they're saying. Shouldn't you be more concerned about us than the Crow?"

"George, you heard what Hannah said about that," a townsman said. "Ain't any of us havin' to stretch our food out like Miss Hannah said the Crows are."

"Hannah, I mean no disrespect to you," farmer Chester Pittman said. "You're a fine lady. But are you going to enjoy seeing white people going hungry sooner than if you'd kept the food for them?"

"Chester, I wouldn't enjoy seeing anybody go hungry, but what I'm doing is based on Scripture. I'm depending on God to bless my faithfulness to His Word in supplying food to the starving Indians. He will also take care of the people in and around Fort Bridger—including my own family and unborn child—because of it."

Glenda Williams moved closer to Hannah and Jacob. "Hannah, you're doing the right thing," she said. "Gary and I will donate food from the café's supply. When are you planning to go to the village?"

Hannah smiled at her friend. "Tomorrow morning. Eight o'clock."

"All right. Gary and I will be here with our donation at eight."

People continued to come into the store, and it was becoming difficult to find standing room.

"You said that what you're doing for the Indians is based on Scripture, Hannah," a woman said. "Would you mind telling us what passage you're referring to?"

"First John 3:17, Frieda. 'But whoso hath this world's good, and seeth his brother have need, and shutteth up his bowels of compassion from him, how dwelleth the love of God in him?' As a Christian, I certainly want to have compassion on those in need, and I want the love of God to be able to dwell in me."

Just then loud voices were heard outside. Above them was the voice of Andy Kelly, trying to get the crowd's attention. Hannah moved toward the door, and the people cleared a path for her. She stepped out on the porch in time to hear Kelly defending her.

Hannah inched up closer to the pastor's side, and when he saw her, he smiled and said, "Hannah, I want to commend you before all of these people for your plan to give food to the hungry Crow. You're doing the right thing. Certainly the love of God dwells in you."

Many shouted agreement, while others loudly declared their opposition. One man shouted, "Pastor Kelly, why should white people starve to keep the Indians from starving?"

"Nobody's going to starve," Kelly said, looking him square in the eye. "Hannah is demonstrating what 1 John 3:17 is all about. She sees the need, and she has the means to at least partially meet that need. She's fulfilling what Jesus called the second great commandment: 'Thou shalt love thy neighbor as thyself.' The Lord will bless her deed, and in His own way He will take care that no one starves."

A man shouted, "Chief Two Moons and his people have shown themselves to be friends of the white people! We should help them!"

Some cheered while others booed.

"But what about us, Hannah?" called out a woman who was a member of the church. "I'm not against helping the Crows, but are you keeping enough food in store to care for us until the supply wagons can get through?"

Hannah was beginning to shiver in the cold for lack of a wrap. "I'm doing my best, Tillie. I'm praying every day that the Lord will resolve the Indian problem so the supply wagons can get through."

Roe Dahmer and Max Killian had joined the crowd in the street. Dahmer said, "While you're prayin', Hannah, you'd better remember it's just that...the Indian problem! And the Crows are Indians!"

Men and women began to rail at each other, and the sound of angry voices grew.

"Hey!" shouted Deputy Marshal Jack Bower, raising his hands to get their attention. "Listen to me!" Jack tried again to shout above the noise, but he couldn't be heard. He whipped out his gun and fired it twice into the air.

Instantly the crowd quieted.

"Listen to me…everybody!" Jack said. "I want this thing broken up right now before it gets ugly. Hannah is owner of the general store, and she has a right to do what she pleases with her food supply. In my opinion, she's trying to do right by everybody, including the Crow."

"That's right, Jack!" Marshal Lance Mangum said.

People quickly made room for him to get through the crowd. He moved up between his deputy and a shivering Hannah Cooper and ran his gaze over the crowd. "This dispute is over. Now go on about your business, or I'll start arresting different ones of you for causing a disturbance."

The people slowly began to disperse.

Suddenly Hannah's knees buckled, and she broke down and wept. Jack Bower took hold of her and Glenda rushed up and threw her coat over Hannah's shoulders. "I'll take her up to the apartment, Jack. Thank you. Come on, honey, let's get you inside. You're freezing."

"Hannah," Pastor Kelly said, "I know this is upsetting, but don't give up. You're doing what's right before the Lord."

Hannah looked at him through her tears. "Thank you for standing by me, Pastor."

"Thank you for standing by the Word and doing what's right. The Lord will bless you for it."

Hannah was still shivering when she and Glenda entered the apartment. Glenda guided her toward the warm kitchen.

"Before you take off your coat, Hannah, come over here by the stove and soak up some heat. I'll put in some more logs."

Soon Glenda had built a roaring fire. She then removed Hannah's coat, placed a chair close to the stove, and sat Hannah down on it. Glenda filled the teakettle and set it on top of the stove.

Hannah stared vacantly into space and shook her head.

"Honey," Glenda said, taking her hand, "don't let them get to you. You know what God wants you to do, and He has promised to supply. Most of those people are speaking out of fear. They don't know the Lord or the grace He provides."

Hannah blinked and focused on her friend's face. "You're right, Glenda. I feel sorry for them. I understand their fear, but the anger they displayed was disturbing. When they were shouting so angrily, I felt some fear myself. Fear of them. And I had to claim Psalm 56:3 while I was standing there: 'What time I am afraid, I will trust in thee.' God's Word is perfect, isn't it, Glenda? It meets our every need."

"It sure is, and it sure does."

"You know, I knew that some people would object when they found out what I was doing to help the Crow, but when it actually happened, it hurt."

"Of course it hurt. All of those people are your customers, and you know most of them well. It has to hurt."

Hannah shook her head. "But as bad as this incident has made me feel, I'd feel worse if I let the Crow go hungry."

Just then the teakettle started whistling, and Glenda set about making tea.

Hannah turned her chair around and sat down at the table. Glenda set a steaming cup in front of her and said, "I want you to drink this, then you're going to lie down and take a nap."

Hannah smiled. "Yes, Mother."

"And don't you forget it."

"You're a bit young to be my mother, aren't you?"

"Yes, and don't you forget that either."

They laughed together, then Glenda said, "Now, what can I do to help you get the items ready that you want to send to the village?"

"Jacob already did it for me. It's all ready for the soldiers to load in the morning. Thank you, though, for the offer. You're such a good friend. The Lord knew exactly who I needed when we came here and He had our paths cross. I love you, Glenda."

"I love you too, Hannah. You are exactly what I needed in a friend, too."

"Then I guess we're both happy, aren't we?"

"We sure are, and our relationship grows sweeter all the time, just the way it should."

By the time Hannah finished her tea, her nerves were calmed and her spirit renewed. She sighed as she looked across the table at Glenda and said, "I'm still a little washed out from the influenza, and a nap sounds very inviting. I'll let God fight my battles. He can do a far better job than I. Thank you, my dear friend, for being here for me."

Glenda stood up, gave Hannah a hand to help her up, and said, "You are more than welcome." She gave Hannah a gentle nudge in the right direction. "Now, off with you. Get a good nap, and I'll see you later."

That evening, Chris Cooper arrived home just as the family and Jacob Kates were sitting down to supper. They prayed first, then Chris hurriedly washed his hands.

"Mama, the sentries told us what happened here today," Chris said as he dried his hands. "Do you think there'll be more trouble over giving food to the Crow?"

"There could be, but we're going ahead as planned."

"Your mother has the majority of people on her side," Jacob said. "They know she's doing the right thing. And wasn't it good to see Jason Drumm take our side, Hannah?"

"The little talk Doc had with him the other day had some effect," Hannah said, smiling. "Tell us, Chris, how did Broken Wing's parents take the news that he had become a Christian?"

A smile broke over Chris's face. "Mama, the Lord answered our prayers. Broken Wing told me that at first his father was very angry. He felt that Broken Wing had shamed him, his mother, and the tribe. But his mother reminded him that the Jesus that now belonged to their son was also Hannah Cooper's Jesus. This calmed Chief Two Moons, Broken Wing said, and they have accepted it quite well."

"The Lord is so good," Hannah said, wiping tears from her eyes. "He definitely is working in the hearts of Two Moons and Sweet Blossom or they wouldn't have had such a good attitude. This encourages me to believe that they, too, will be saved one day soon."

Jacob ate in silence, taking it all in.

"Oh, Mama," Mary Beth said, "wouldn't it be wonderful if everybody in the village would come to the Lord?"

"That would be wonderful, sweetie."

"That's what I'm praying for," Chris said. "The greatest thing in this world is seeing people get saved." Chris looked at Jacob as he said it. Jacob met his gaze, then turned his attention back to his food.

Patty Ruth looked down at the little rat terrier and said, "Biggie, I'm gonna get saved as soon as I understand more about sin. Maybe you'll get saved when you understand about sin, too."

B.J. laughed. "Patty Ruth, that's silly."

"What's silly?"

"What you just said about Biggie gettin' saved. Dogs can't get saved."

"Why not?"

"'Cause Jesus didn't die for animals."

"He did, too!"

"No, He didn't."

"How come?"

"'Cause animals don't sin."

"Oh yes, they do! How 'bout the time Mama tol' Biggie

not to get up on the table when he smelled roast beef, but when nobody was lookin', he did it anyway? Huh? How 'bout that? The Bible says it's a sin to disobey your parents."

B.J. sighed and laid his fork down. "Little sister, what Biggie did wasn't sin. He's a dog and doesn't understand about that. Besides, Mama isn't his parent. She's just his boss."

Patty Ruth frowned and squinted at him. "So it wasn't sin for him to disobey?"

"No. He's a dog."

Her lips curved in an impish manner. "Do you understand about sin?"

"Sure."

"How come you do it?"

"I…well, I don't—" B.J.'s face turned red. "I mean—"

"You don't sin?" Patty Ruth said. "How 'bout a couple weeks ago when Mama tol' you not to eat any of the cookies she'd tooken out of the oven? And you snuck one an' she caught you when you was chewin' it. That was sin, wasn't it?"

B.J.'s features tinted deeper. He glanced at his mother, then looked his little sister in the eye and said, "I was just testin' that cookie so if somebody had slipped poison into 'em, nobody else in the family would die."

Patty Ruth looked down at the little dog and said, "Did you hear that, Biggie?"

Hannah looked at B.J. "Whether Biggie heard it or not isn't important, but God did. You know that's a lie, Brett Jonathan."

B.J. forced a hollow laugh. "I was only foolin', Mama!"

"Okay, but we must make sure we keep things straight about sin. It was sin when you took that cookie, wasn't it?"

"Yes, Mama, it was sin when I took that cookie." B.J. set piercing eyes on his little sister. "If Patty Ruth doesn't know enough about sin to be saved, how come she can spot the sin in me and Chris, like she does so often?"

"'Cause I'm a woman!" Patty Ruth said.

CHAPTER TWENTY-TWO

A s the laughter at the table subsided, footsteps were heard on the landing, followed by a knock at the door. Chris pushed his chair back. "I'll get it." He opened the door to find Pastor and Mrs. Kelly standing there, and he invited them in.

Pastor Kelly looked toward the kitchen and said, "We need your mother to come to the door."

Chris hurried back into the kitchen. "Mama, Pastor and Mrs. Kelly need you to come to the door."

"Did they say what they want?" Hannah asked as she rose from her chair.

"No, they didn't, but it has to be something good the way they're smiling."

Hannah smiled when she saw her visitors. "Pastor, Rebecca, please come in out of the cold."

"We need you to come out here," Rebecca said. "Is your coat close by?"

"Yes. I'll get it."

Hannah slipped into her coat and stepped outside, closing the door behind her. Suddenly from the alley below came loud cheers and whistles. Hannah moved to the railing to see a crowd of people smiling up at her. The Cooper children and Jacob Kates went to the windows.

Rebecca put an arm around Hannah as the pastor said,

"Every member of the church who isn't still at home recuperating from influenza is down there, Hannah. All of us want you to know that we are behind your plan to give food to the Crow."

One by one, people began calling out encouragement, saying she was doing the right thing. Many told her they would be at the store in the morning with food from their own cupboards for Chief Two Moons and his people.

Hannah wiped tears from her cheeks and called down, "Thank you for your support! You will never know what an encouragement this is to me. The love of God most certainly dwells in each of you!"

Later, when her children were asleep, Hannah lay awake, talking to Solomon as she so often did. She told him of the opposition that had cropped up at the store that day, and of the church people coming in the evening to speak their words of encouragement.

She closed her eyes and said, "Dear Lord, thank You for the peace You've given me. I know You will not fail me. You will provide food for my customers and my family in Your own way and Your own time. Good night, Lord. I love You."

Hannah slept like a baby and was awake long before sunrise. She was eager to get the day under way and had awakened the children early, hurrying them along with their breakfast. While they were eating, she told them she wanted to go down to the storeroom and make sure all was ready before the army wagon arrived.

The children caught her excitement, and breakfast was over more quickly than usual. Cleanup was accomplished in record time, and the family hurried down the stairs.

Jacob was already in the store, adding what he could to the shelves, when the Cooper family came in. The fire in the potbellied stove was beginning to warm the store. The children ran to Jacob and hugged him.

"Good morning, Jacob," Hannah said as she joined the children around him.

"Good morning, Miss Hannah. Aren't you down a little early? The wagon and the escort won't be here for another half hour."

"I want to go over one more time the items I'm sending. Just to be sure everything is exactly like I want it."

"All right. I'll help you."

"No need. You're busy getting ready to open up. The children can help me take inventory."

"All right. But if you should need me, you holler."

Hannah led her troops to the storeroom and gave each child a section to check, except for Patty Ruth, who stayed at her side as her mother's self-appointed helper.

Once the inventory was done to Hannah's satisfaction— with a few more items added—she had Chris unlock the double doors leading to the alley. The family then went into the store, and Hannah made her way to the stove where she sat down to warm herself. She had no more than eased onto the chair and caught her breath when the rumble of a wagon was heard, along with the pounding of hooves.

Jacob unlocked the front door and saw a large crowd in the street. When those who had gathered saw the army wagon and the mounted escort turn into the alley, they followed them around the building.

Hannah stood at the double doors as Chris opened them. It was a brittle cold day with a crystal-clear blue sky. Not a cloud was in sight, but a brisk breeze was blowing out of the west.

Wearing her warmest shawl, Hannah stepped outside to

greet the soldiers. Her eyes were alive and shining with excitement, and she felt as if she could tackle the whole world. She had such peace and joy in what she was about to do that her heart was near to bursting with happiness.

Let the opposition come, she thought. *I'm doing the right thing, and I know God will bless this effort.*

"Good morning, gentlemen!" Hannah said.

The soldiers returned her greeting, and Lieutenant Dobie Carlin dismounted. "If you'll show us what goes on the wagon, Mrs. Cooper, we'll get it loaded."

The crowd came into the alley as the soldiers were loading the wagon. Chris tapped his mother's arm and pointed at Marshal Lance Mangum and Deputy Jack Bower as they came around the corner of the building. Both lawmen nodded at Hannah and smiled. She smiled back, glad they were there.

Andy Kelly and Rebecca appeared, having come through the store and into the storeroom. Andy began helping the soldiers load the wagon, and Rebecca moved up where Hannah stood with her children just outside the door, and put an arm around her.

The church people came with their dried fruit and canned goods, which were also placed in the wagon. Gary and Glenda Williams drove up in their wagon, which bore several boxes of food, along with flour and potato sacks.

Hannah saw Roe Dahmer and Max Killian push their way through the crowd, along with some of their rancher friends. She noted that the two lawmen were watching them.

Max said loudly, "Mrs. Cooper, me and Roe and some of the other ranchers wish to protest what you're doing. You should care more about your own kind than about those savage Indians!"

"What do you mean, my own kind?" Hannah said. "I'm human; the Indians are human. So we're two of a kind."

"But you're not a savage, Hannah," one of the ranchers

said. "Those savages need to shift for themselves! The white people have a right to purchase food in your store...and here you are givin' it away to those Indians!"

"Colonel Bateman," an older townsman shouted, "as commandant of the fort, you should be defending the rights of the white people! You represent the government of the United States, and you should stop Hannah Cooper from taking food to the Indians!"

Colonel Bateman stepped forward and said, "Ralph, the American Indians—including the Crow—have the same rights under the United States government as anyone else in this country. This is especially true of the Crow, because they are friendly toward the government."

"That's right, Colonel!" Sergeant Bo Maxwell said.

"You all know that the Crow often serve as scouts for the army. They've proven themselves absolutely loyal. They deserve our utmost gratitude. And just as white people and those of all other skin colors in this country have a right to live without starving, so do the Crow."

The majority of the crowd cheered Bateman's words, and several men shouted out that the colonel was right. There was a burst of applause.

A warm feeling washed over Hannah. It grew warmer when Chris leaned over and said, "I wish Papa was here to see what you're doing, Mama!"

Mary Beth inched closer. "Papa's watching from heaven, Chris. And he's cheering for Mama, too!"

When the applause and cheers began to die down, Mitchell Ward, a silver-haired farmer and retired army sergeant, spoke up loudly. "Colonel Bateman, I had to fight Indians in this part of the country for years. I respect your opinion, sir, but you haven't been here a year yet. When you've battled those red savages for a while, you'll find out they ain't worth savin'. The whole country would be better off if they all starved to death…includin' the Crows! I don't care how friendly they seem, they'll turn on you one of these days!"

"You're wrong, Mitch!" Hannah said. "The Crow are our true friends. May I remind you of what Chief Two Moons and his warriors did to save the lives of Captain Fordham and his men when they were under attack by the Blackfoot war party? They were badly outnumbered, and Captain Fordham himself told me that he and his men would not have survived if the Crow had not come to their rescue."

Captain Fordham stepped out of the crowd and stood near Hannah. "She's telling you the truth, Mitch. My men and I would be dead if Chief Two Moons hadn't come to our aid, even though they were hazarding their own lives to do so."

Many of the military people who had been opposing Hannah grew quiet. A corporal among them said, "Mrs. Cooper, I'm sorry for standing against you in this. I was wrong."

"You indeed were wrong, Corporal, but I accept your apology." Then Hannah looked over the crowd and said so all could hear, "Let me remind all of you how the Crow took the patrol to their village after they saved them from annihilation. They took them into their tepees to protect them from the blizzard, and gave care to the wounded troopers and to the troopers coming down with influenza. As a result, the Crow had their own epidemic that took eleven lives. If it weren't for Dr. Patrick O'Brien risking his life to bring salicylic acid on horseback from Cheyenne City, more Crow—and more of us—would be dead by now."

A few more faces in the crowd took on a look of shame.

"I have faith that the Lord will supply food for my store shelves because I am obeying His command to have compassion on those in need."

"I thank God for Hannah Cooper!" Andy Kelly said. "We all need the kind of compassion she's demonstrating here today!"

"God bless you, Hannah!" someone shouted from near the back of the crowd.

Hannah found the owner of the voice and a smile curved her lips. It was Jason Drumm.

Lieutenant Carlin said, "Hannah, there's so much stuff here, we can't get it all in the wagon. The Williamses have offered to drive their wagon along with us."

Hannah looked at the wagons and laughed. "Well, hallelujah! Let's get on the road!"

"I'll help you into the wagon, ma'am," Sergeant Maxwell said.

Jacob Kates dashed from the storeroom and said, "Everybody go out on the street! Hurry!"

"What is it, Jacob?" Hannah said.

"Come and see!"

The crowd quickly headed up the alley between the general store and the clothing store.

By the time Hannah and her family reached the front of the store, people were standing in the street waving their arms and pointing at the long train of supply wagons coming into town. An army escort rode alongside the wagons. The shouting grew louder, and people were weeping for joy.

Pastor Kelly stood up on the porch and waved for silence. When he had the people's attention, he said, "I remind you, folks, that only moments ago, Hannah told us she had faith that God would supply food for her shelves because she was obeying His Word! Here are wagonloads of it! That train has at least twice as many wagons as usual. Anybody need further proof that God honors those who honor His Word?"

Curly Wesson stood on the boardwalk, holding his wife's hand. "Only a fool would deny that, Pastor!"

"That's right, Curly!" Doc O'Brien shouted. "Only fools doubt God's Book!"

Wide eyes watched as the wagons entered the town in a

long, single line. The officer in charge of the military escort saw Colonel Bateman and headed toward him. Hannah stepped off the porch and into the street. When the lead wagon ground to a halt, she smiled broadly at the wagon master and said, "Charlie Wiggins, you are a sight for sore eyes! I didn't know you were coming, but I'm sure glad you're here!"

The wagon master scanned the crowd, then grinned at her and said, "Sorry for the long delay, Miss Hannah, but you know the army's been tied up fighting the hostiles. Well, the hostiles finally got tired and went back to their villages and camps. The distributors in Cheyenne City tried to get through to you on the telegraph to let you know the wagons would be leaving there twelve days ago. The lines have been down. They must still be."

"Yes, they are," she said. "We've been trying to get through to the distributors too!"

"Well, they doubled your last order, knowin' you had to be runnin' low." Wiggins looked at the crowd again. "Some kind of meetin' goin' on, Miss Hannah?"

"I guess you could call it that. I'm about to leave for the Crow village up north of here and take them some food. They're on the verge of starvation. There's been some opposition to this from some of these people. Others are here to show me their support."

"Oh. I see."

Pastor Kelly stood on the porch and said in a loud voice, "Folks, we need to thank God for getting these wagons through. The rationing is over, and we can all fill our cupboards and pantries!"

There were cheers and applause.

"Let's bow our heads right now and give our thanks."

Many tears were shed as the preacher led them in a prayer of gratitude to the Lord.

Hannah motioned for Jacob to come to her, and when he

drew up, she said to the wagon master, "Charlie, Jacob will direct you in unloading the goods."

"Good to see you again, my friend," Wiggins said.

"It's better to see you," said Jacob, chuckling.

"Jacob," Hannah said, "would you go tell Colonel Bateman I need to see him for a moment, please?"

Jacob quickly threaded his way through the crowd and returned with Bateman.

"Yes, Hannah?" the colonel said.

"My storeroom won't hold all the goods on these wagons. May we put some of it in the old sutler's building inside the fort?"

"Of course."

"Thank you. Charlie, Jacob will show you where to unload what, okay?"

"Yes, ma'am."

"It's nice to see you, Charlie. Don't make it so long next time!"

Wiggins laughed. "I'll try to do better next time!"

"Charlie, if you'll let your drivers know what's going on," Jacob said, "I'll make an announcement to this crowd, and we can get the unloading started."

"Will do," Wiggins said, leaving the seat to climb down.

Jacob stepped up on the porch and said, "Folks, I know you'll all want to come into the store and buy food and supplies. Give me about two hours, and I'll be ready for business!"

Hannah's children rushed up to her. "Can we go along, Mama?" Mary Beth said. "We want to be there when you present the food to the Indians."

"Can we, Mama?" Patty Ruth said.

"Excuse me, Miss Hannah," Jacob said, "but I just thought I'd let you know that six of the ladies who've been helping me at the store have volunteered to stock the shelves and wait on customers for the rest of the day."

"Bless their hearts," Hannah said. "You thank them for me until I can do it myself."

"I will. See you when you get back."

"Can we go with you, Mama?" Patty Ruth said. "Please?"

Gary and Glenda Williams were standing near. Gary said, "If you want them to go along, Hannah, they can ride with us in our wagon."

"All right. Thank you, Gary."

"Oh, boy!" B.J. said. "Come on, let's get in the wagon!"

"I think Patty Ruth should ride in the army wagon with Sergeant Maxwell and me," Hannah said.

"Oh, goody!" said the little redhead, jumping up and down.

Some of the people crowded close to Hannah, complimenting her on the stand she had taken to feed the Indians. While they were speaking to her, Hannah noticed Roe Dahmer and his rancher friends walking away from the crowd, angry looks on their faces. Max Killian shook his head as they tried to get him to leave with them. When they were gone, he moved up to the crowd that encircled Hannah and stood, listening. When the group had dwindled to just a few, Hannah glanced at Max and smiled at him.

Finally, when the last person had stepped away, Max stood before Hannah and said, "I want to apologize for the way I acted, ma'am. I'm sorry. I ask your forgiveness. I was a blind fool. This whole thing has helped me to see how wrong I was about Chief Two Moons and his people, and about the way I treated you. I'm really sorry."

"Max, we've all been wrong about things in life. I appreciate your good attitude, and I forgive you."

"Thank you, Miss Hannah. I'll be back with Clara tomorrow, and we'll load our wagon."

Chris trotted up on Buster at the same time Dr. Patrick appeared on his horse. Sergeant Maxwell helped Patty Ruth and her mother into the army wagon while Mary Beth and B.J. settled into the Williamses' wagon. B.J. was in the back with the goods, and Mary Beth sat on the seat between Gary and Glenda. Most of the crowd was still there to cheer and applaud as the wagons and army escort pulled out of town and headed north toward the Crow village.

Hannah's heart was light as the procession made its way over the rough, snow-laden terrain. The sun was shining brilliantly under a canopy of blue.

When they were about halfway there, everyone's attention was drawn to a jackrabbit being chased by a fox. Soldiers and civilians alike shouted encouragement to the rabbit, and they cheered when it dived safely into its hole. The frustrated fox stood over the hole and yapped.

Soon the village came into view, and Hannah's heart pounded in anticipation of what was about to happen.

Lieutenant Carlin, Dr. O'Brien, and Chris rode point. When they reached the edge of the village ahead of the others, the hollow-eyed sentries welcomed them.

"Good morning, Sun Man, Yellow Bird," Dobie said. "Mrs. Hannah Cooper has enlisted us to help her bring food for the Crow people. Would you tell Chief Two Moons we are here, please?"

"Yes, Lieutenant Dobie Carlin," Yellow Bird said. "I will find him while Sun Man leads you into the village."

The soldiers dismounted, ground reined their horses, and followed the wagons on foot. Chris and Dr. Patrick left their horses and walked with them.

Yellow Bird spread the word as he hurried through the village to find Two Moons. By the time the wagons rolled to a halt in the center of the village, a crowd was building. Hannah spotted Chief Two Moons, Sweet Blossom, and Broken Wing threading their way through the crowd. Chris ran up to Broken Wing, and they greeted each other warmly.

Hannah, with her other three children at her side, stepped forward to meet the chief and his squaw.

"Good morning, Chief Two Moons. And good morning, Sweet Blossom. We have brought food for you and your people."

Sweet Blossom put a hand to her mouth. Two Moons blinked in confusion.

"Hannah Cooper, it is understanding of Two Moons that you very low on food. What you are doing is very much appreciated, but we cannot take food that is needed by people of town and fort."

Hannah took a step closer and said, "Chief, we are friends, are we not?"

"Yes, Hannah Cooper, we are friends."

"May I speak to you as a friend?"

"Of course."

"As human beings, we all have some pride. But sometimes we have to put our pride aside and let our friends help us. It has been on my heart for a few days to bring food to you and your people, although our own supplies were running low. This is because I love you, your family, and all of your people."

Sweet Blossom's eyes filled with tears.

Two Moons smiled. "We are aware of this love, Hannah Cooper. And we love you the same."

"Then as friends who love each other, we can speak frankly, right?"

"Yes."

"Chief, please do not let your pride keep you from accepting this food. You and your people are looking very thin. My heart is hurting for you, and so are the hearts of my children, Dr. Patrick, Lieutenant Carlin, and these other soldiers…as well as your friends back at the fort and town. We want you to accept this food."

"But we cannot take food when our white brothers and sisters are going hungry."

"We are not going hungry, Chief. Just this morning, my wonderful God in heaven brought many wagons from Cheyenne City, loaded with food. We now have plenty. Please let us give this food to you."

Two Moons looked at Sweet Blossom, who was wiping tears from her cheeks. He ran his gaze over the thin, pinched faces of his people. When he turned back to Hannah, there were tears in his own eyes.

"We are very much honored that you would do this good deed, Hannah Cooper, and Chief Two Moons is very glad to accept your kind gift of food."

The Crow raised their hands toward the sky and shouted for joy.

Mary Beth wiped tears from her cheeks and turned to B.J. "Look at Chief Two Moons. He's crying."

"I know, isn't that amazing."

The Crow helped the soldiers and the Williamses unload the wagons while Dr. Patrick checked on his patients.

When it was time to go, Hannah spoke again to Two Moons and Sweet Blossom, who were trying to express their gratitude.

"We will never be able to repay you for what you have done, Hannah Cooper," Two Moons said.

"No repayment is necessary, Chief. This is a gift of love and friendship. My wonderful Jesus Christ has made it possible."

Sweet Blossom stepped to Hannah, wrapped her arms around her, and said, "Hannah Cooper is true friend. Sweet Blossom loves her."

Hannah hugged her and said, "And Hannah Cooper loves Sweet Blossom."

Many of the Indians were still weeping as they stood at

the edge of the village and watched the procession move away
on the snow-covered land.

CHAPTER TWENTY-THREE

annah Cooper sighed as Sergeant Maxwell stopped the wagon in front of the store and helped her down.

"Tired?" Maxwell said as he led her to the boardwalk.

"A wee bit."

The sergeant went back and lifted Patty Ruth from the wagon seat, carried her to the boardwalk, and stood her beside her mother. Tweaking her nose, he said, "Someday I'm going to get married, Patty Ruth, and when I do, I hope I can have a little girl just like you."

B.J. climbed down from the Williamses' wagon as Gary helped Mary Beth down. Hannah thanked the Williamses and Bo Maxwell, then turned to enter the store. Curly Wesson's shrill voice was heard from down the street. He was running along the boardwalk.

"Miss Hannah! Miss Hannah!"

He hurried to her side and handed her two envelopes, saying breathlessly, "Stagecoach came in just a few minutes after you left this mornin', Miss Hannah. These here letters come for you...both from your brother-in-law in Cincinnati."

"Oh, wonderful! Thank you, Curly."

Patty Ruth clapped her hands. "Oh, boy! Read 'em to us, Mama!"

"Tell you what," Hannah said, "let's go up to the apartment, and we'll read them there. Chris should be putting Buster away about now."

Hannah looked inside the store and saw that the place was packed with customers. She decided to check with Jacob later and took the children around the side of the building toward the alley. Chris was just coming from the barn.

They entered the apartment and removed their wraps, then Chris and B.J. built fires in the fireplace and kitchen stove. The family sat down in the parlor by the fire, and Hannah looked at the postmarks on the envelopes. The first one was January 13, and the second one January 27.

Hannah read the first letter to her children, which was the announcement of the birth of six-pound-three-ounce Anna Marie Cooper, born on January 12. They all laughed when Adam wrote that they named her Anna Marie because it rhymed with "Hannah Marie."

In the second letter, Adam wrote that it was looking like they would be coming to Fort Bridger soon to establish the newspaper. They would know for sure when they heard back from Lloyd Dawson about the loan. Adam told them he was sending a letter to Dawson in this same mailing, answering questions Dawson had asked in previous communication. He was also sending a letter to Mayor Cade Samuels about finding a temporary building for the paper.

"Well, children," Hannah said, "I imagine Mr. Dawson has probably read Uncle Adam's letter by now. I'm going over to the bank and see what he can tell me."

"I'll walk you over there, Mama," Chris said.

Lloyd Dawson was occupied with a customer when Hannah and Chris entered the bank, but he saw them approach the railing that surrounded the officers' desks, and waved. Dawson's secretary, Lorna Camp, came from a room at the back of the bank. She smiled and said, "Hello, Hannah, Chris. Did you want to see Mr. Dawson?"

"Yes, please. Whenever he's finished there."

"Shouldn't be too long. Just have a seat over here by the railing."

Chris took his mother's arm to usher her to a seat.

"Oh, Hannah," Lorna said. "I heard about what went on in front of the store this morning. If I'd been there, I would've cheered for you. It was wonderful what you did for the Crow."

"Thank you."

Moments later, the man at Dawson's desk left, and Lorna called for Hannah to come through the small gate. Chris accompanied her. Dawson stood to welcome mother and son, then bid them sit down.

A wide grin curved the banker's lips. "I got a letter from Adam. I suppose you know we finally had a stage come through from Cheyenne City."

"Yes, we heard from Adam too. Curly gave us the letters as soon as we returned from the village."

"Ah, yes…the village. I want to commend you for what you did, Hannah. I can imagine how happy the Crow were to get all that food."

"Very happy, Lloyd."

"Wonderful! Now, what can I do for you?"

"Actually, I came to see if you had read Adam's letter yet, because in one of his letters to me he said he was writing back to you."

"As a matter of fact, I did read the letter. Have a big stack to go through yet, but when I saw Adam's name on one of the envelopes, I read the letter right away."

"What do you think? Can you grant him the loan?"

"I most certainly can. He's quite the young man, Hannah. I have no doubt he'll succeed in establishing a newspaper in this town. We're going to loan him the full amount he needs to construct the newspaper building, furnish it with presses, and everything else he needs. If the telegraph lines weren't down, I'd wire him today and tell him to pack. But I'm sending a letter out of here on tomorrow's stage with the same message."

"Wonderful!" Hannah exclaimed.

"I know you've made a lot of dear and close friends here in Fort Bridger since last September, Hannah, but I'm sure it will be a real blessing to have family living here, too."

"You're right about that. And thank you for helping to make it possible."

On the following Sunday, Pastor Kelly stood in the vestibule with Rebecca at his side, welcoming people as they came to church. When the Coopers came in, Jacob Kates was with them.

Kelly greeted Hannah and the children, then shook Jacob's hand. "My friend, I'm so glad to see you! Thank you for coming."

Hannah turned after greeting Rebecca and said, "And Pastor, it was his own idea. Nobody in this family pushed him."

"It's so good to have you, Jacob," said Rebecca, shaking his hand.

Jacob cleared his throat and said, "Pastor, Mrs. Kelly, my coming today is my way of thanking God for the arrival of the supply wagons just in time."

"We're all filled with gratitude to the Lord for that," Kelly said.

When Sunday school was over and people were gathering in the sanctuary for the morning service, many came by the pew where Jacob sat with the Cooper family and welcomed him. Soon the song leader had the people on their feet to open the service with a rousing hymn. Organist Lila Sparrow played a few opening bars, and the singing began.

Pastor Kelly stood next to his chair on the platform and looked the congregation over as they sang. He was surprised to see three people entering the sanctuary, and when the crowd noticed the look on his face, many turned to see what had caught his attention.

Chris touched Hannah's arm. "Mama, it's Broken Wing and his parents!"

One of the ushers guided the Crow family down the aisle and placed them in the pew just in front of the Coopers. Chris left his mother's side and sat next to Broken Wing.

Two Moons smiled at Hannah, then noting that the men wore no hats, he removed his headdress.

Hannah gripped Mary Beth's hand and moved her lips to say "Praise the Lord" as she looked at the Indians in front of her.

The service went on, and after Julianna LeCroix sang a heart-touching solo, Pastor Kelly walked to the pulpit and opened his Bible.

"Please turn in your Bibles to the epistle of 1 John, chapter 3. My sermon title this morning is 'Touch of Compassion,' and I think it is most appropriate in light of what has happened in Fort Bridger this past week."

Many tears were shed as Kelly told the story of Hannah Cooper and the Crow Indians, tying it all to the truths of his text. He applied the truths to every Christian's life and weaved in the gospel for those who sat before him without Christ. Then following the invitation, Pastor Kelly baptized two young people who had been saved during their bouts with influenza.

Kelly returned to the pulpit and talked about how the Lord had used the influenza epidemic to touch many, bringing families closer together and drawing people to Himself. He then called on one of the men to come to the platform and close the service in prayer.

Before the man reached the platform, Chief Two Moons walked to the front and said, "Pastor Andy Kelly, would you allow Chief Two Moons to speak briefly to you and your people?"

"Why, of course. Come on up here with me."

Two Moons mounted the platform, still carrying his head-dress, and the congregation looked on in amazement. Kelly said something in a low tone to the man who had come to pray, and the man sat down in the pastor's chair.

"Folks," Kelly said, "most of you know our friend, Chief Two Moons of the Crow tribe. He and his family have graced our service today by their presence. Chief Two Moons has asked if he could speak briefly to you."

Two Moons did not try to cover his emotions as he publicly thanked Hannah Cooper for spearheading the gift of food to his people. He also thanked those in the audience who had sent food to them, and Dr. Patrick O'Brien for coming to the village and saving many lives.

Two Moons blinked at the tears filling his eyes. The tears came faster as he said, "Chris Cooper has become my son—Broken Wing's best friend. Broken Wing was very, very sick with influenza disease, and day upon day, Chris Cooper came to see him. Two Moons has learned that often when the boys have been together, Chris Cooper has talked to my son about faith in Jesus Christ.

"On a recent day, Chris Cooper was with my sick son in tepee. He talked to him again about faith in Jesus Christ. This time, Broken Wing told Chris Cooper he wanted to pray to Jesus Christ to save his soul and forgive his wrongdoing. Chris Cooper helped him to pray this.

"Chris Cooper taught my son that after a person begins following Jesus Christ, he is supposed to be dipped in water as others did a few minutes ago. Broken Wing has been given my permission to do this."

Pastor Kelly laid a hand on the chief's shoulder and looked around at the crowd. "Anybody who wants to leave may do so, but we are going to baptize Broken Wing right now!"

Not a person left his seat. Tears were freely shed all over the congregation as they watched the Indian boy go into the baptismal waters.

Jacob Kates observed all this with a strange look on his face. Hannah noticed it and prayed that the Lord would soon convince him that Jesus was the true Messiah.

After the service was over, Broken Wing came out of the back room, his eyes shining with joy. The Coopers were still at their pew, talking to Two Moons and Sweet Blossom. Chris was sharing his elation with some of the Christian young people who had come to congratulate him on winning the first Crow from the village to the Lord.

His hair still damp, Broken Wing stepped up to Chris, threw his arms around him, and said, "Thank you, Chris Cooper, for loving me enough to tell me about Jesus Christ! Just like the pastor said about your mother...you have the touch of compassion!"

Printed in the United States
by Baker & Taylor Publisher Services